S0-ASK-029

ACKNOWLEDGMENTS

I will forever be grateful to my extraordinary
agent, Helen Breitwieser, for being a tireless
champion of this book. For her enthusiasm
and smart direction, I thank my editor,
Joan Marlow Golan. Thanks, too,
to Innocentia Mhlambi and Mphutlane Ntsane
of the University of Witwatersrand for sharing
with me their expertise in African languages.
I thank Wayne Greenhaw, a brilliant writer
and true Southern gentleman, for his time and
guidance. And, on a more personal note,
I thank my husband, Egidio, for his unending
support, my mother, Pam Kissane, for crying
when she read my manuscript, and my daughter,
Emma, for being the sweetest little piglet I ever
could have wished for.

Vanessa Del Fabbro

The Road to Home

Steeple
Hill®

Published by Steeple Hill Books™

For Egidio and Emma, with love

STEEPLE HILL BOOKS

Steeple
Hill®

ISBN-13: 978-0-373-78601-5
ISBN-10:   0-373-78601-8

THE ROAD TO HOME

Copyright © 2005 by Vanessa Del Fabbro

www.SteepleHill.com

Printed in U.S.A.

A NOTE FROM THE AUTHOR

The Road to Home takes place in 1998, four years after the first democratic elections in South Africa, which swept the African National Congress (ANC) into power. The euphoria has since subsided and people are working hard to build an equitable society.

In the early 1990s, following a long period of resistance by various antiapartheid movements, most notably the ANC, the white National Party government began to negotiate itself out of power, lifting the ban on the ANC and releasing its leader, Nelson Mandela, after twenty-seven years in prison. Most South Africans credit Nelson Mandela's commitment to reconciliation for the country's peaceful transition to democracy. When South Africans of all races went to the polls in April 1994, apartheid was finally laid to rest after an infamous forty-six-year rule.

In the new South Africa, all people are free to live where they want, work in any field, marry whomever they want, say what they want and vote for any party. The majority of the country's people were not granted any of these basic rights under white rule.

At this particular time in South Africa's history, with political conflict largely resolved, other issues have become more prominent, most notably crime and the AIDS pandemic.

Every day there are 1,500 new HIV infections in the country. Every day 600 people lose their lives from complications due to AIDS. Many of them are parents of young children. Sadly, in 1998, the government is still five years away from agreeing to make antiretroviral drugs publicly available.

Also, the high level of violent crime is causing outrage among the citizens of the new democracy, but it will be years before the government acknowledges the severity of the problem.

This book is my tribute to the bonds that women share, no matter their skin color, and the amazing healing power of love.

Chapter One

Monica

Through the bars on the tall, uncurtained windows the garden looked invitingly cool, syringa trees providing a shifting shade that the women and children chased with their blankets on the kikuyu grass. Inside, the room smelled of sour milk, butternut squash and diapers. Tattered posters of zebra, wildebeest, lions and springbok littered the whitewashed walls; cardboard boxes overflowed with building blocks, dolls with no clothes or hair, chewed rubber rings, and toy telephones with broken dials or missing receivers.

The baby girl turned her head away from the approaching teaspoon of pap and got an earful of it instead.

"She's one of our sicker little angels," explained Big Jane, who had agreed to my interviewing her for South Africa's National Broadcasting Corporation radio news. She wiped away the porridge with a damp cloth. "If you come next month, she might not be here."

Shrieks of laughter floated in from the garden, where the other angels of the Soweto Home for Orphans had piled onto one of the helpers. I wondered how many of them would be gone, too. Most of them were three years old or younger, but there was one little boy of five who, said Big Jane, had surprised everybody by surviving that long. Although the name on the wooden plaque outside didn't indicate it, this was a place of refuge for children with AIDS, a place where they lived out the rest of their lives—often only a few months, because, as Big Jane explained to me, the disease moved quicker through tiny bodies than adult ones.

She lifted the baby girl out of her high chair and slid the infant over one broad shoulder and onto her back. Then, hunching forward, she wrapped a plaid blanket around them both, tucked the end in over her enormous bosom and secured it with a large safety pin.

"*Thula baba.* Be quiet, baby," she cooed, as the baby started to whimper.

As I followed Big Jane outside, I noticed that she wore her penny loafers as though they were backless, flattening the brown leather under her broad feet. The calluses on her heels had split open, and I could tell from the raw pink patches that she'd been peeling them like onions.

"*Sies.*" Yuck, she told a little boy of about three, taking away the garden snail he was about to put into his mouth.

His bottom lip began to quiver, but then she hauled him up under his arms and his face brightened, as though he knew what was coming.

"Fly, my little one," she said, spinning around slowly.

The baby on her back stopped whimpering, and after about four turns she deposited the little boy onto his feet. He staggered like a drunkard, giggling and begging for more.

The top half of his left ear was a crimped ripple of pinched skin, a pink seashell against his dark brown complexion.

"His mother abandoned him in the veld when he was

two days old, and the rats got to him," explained Big Jane, noticing that I was staring.

"Why would she do that?"

"Probably because she knew she didn't have long to live herself. And if her family had shunned *her,* why would they take in a child with AIDS?"

I could not answer, could not make any comment on something I understood so little. Yes, I'd seen the glossy news magazines with their maps and percentages, Sub–Saharan Africa colored deep red to indicate its status as the disease's hot spot, with seventy percent of the world's cases. I'd studied the specifics for South Africa: 250,000 people died each year from AIDS, and 420,000 children had been orphaned. I knew the dire projections for the impact AIDS was going to have on the underfunded health system, as well as the entire economy of the country. But I'd never seen the disease up close, seen its too bright eyes, its feverish brow, its thin wrists and overfull diapers.

Being with Big Jane and her group of five women volunteers made me feel selfish, as if I were breathing oxygen I didn't deserve.

"Why do you do it?" I asked her.

She untied and then retied the floral scarf she wore on her head, all the while looking at me as though this were a strange question, one she'd never thought of before.

"I don't want God's little angels to be frightened and get lost on their way to heaven," she said finally. Seeing the confusion on my face, she continued, "So I hold their hands and love them, and they fly right up with no trouble."

She picked up the little boy and kissed his ragged ear. Grinning broadly, he nuzzled his head against her shoulder.

I began to feel an unnerving envy of this woman and her quiet conviction. She allowed herself to love these children even though they would be taken from her. I never allowed myself to be vulnerable, which was clearly why I felt such an affinity for my profession as a journalist. Wrapped up in my cocoon of objectivity, I lived a perfectly insular life, one that made me fairly content—or so I'd thought.

The love Big Jane talked about could be seen in her eyes, in her fingers as she stroked the children's hair while she talked, in the turn of her head every time a child cried. I loved my boyfriend, Anton, but the depth of my feelings for him didn't come close to this. I loved that he made me laugh with his droll observations of life, that he knew when to back away and allow me to let off steam, that he always called to check that I'd made it home safely. Like secret agents we always reported our movements to each other. "Yes, Mr. X, I've reached the site." I couldn't go to sleep at night if he didn't call to let me know he was home and hadn't been attacked getting out to open his garage door in the dark. But I never looked at him the way Big Jane looked at this little boy.

"How do you endure the heartbreak?" I asked her. "And the physical demands of caring for such ill children?" Surely the ebb and flow of life in this home would tax even the strongest love.

Big Jane did not hesitate. "This is what the Lord wants me to do, and so He gives me the strength to do it."

I hadn't thought of the Lord for a long time, not since my brother died and my father "withdrew" our faith. That's how he'd put it: withdrew our faith, as though we were entered in a team triathlon and had to retire due to injury.

He'd never been happy with me attending my mother's Afrikaans church, even though he'd agreed they would raise any children they might have in her faith. A devout Catholic he was not, but it was the way in which his father-in-law had decreed that he marry my mother in their church or not at all that had rankled him.

My mother didn't argue with my father. We just kept going to church, albeit under the pretense of visiting Luca's grave. But then the pills started to make Mom act strangely, and after a while we really did end up at Luca's grave on Sunday mornings. Instead of being in our usual pew at the *Kerk van die Goeie Herder,* the Church of the Good Shepherd, we'd lie on the grass next to Luca, sipping diet cola, eating licorice, "keeping him company," as my mother called it.

In the years since, I hadn't become an atheist, but I hadn't given any thought to spiritual matters, either. Life had become a journey, yet there was no map, no route markers, merely a meandering road and a number of stops along the way that served as pleasant distractions from a horizon with no destination in sight. This was not Big Jane's life. Hers had purpose. I believed that my radio reports were useful to the public, yet if I fell off the face of the earth that very afternoon, Taryn or Mike or Frik or any one of my colleagues could take up where I'd left off without any trouble. But if the same were to happen to Big Jane, who would step in to take her place? Who would care for her little sick angels without worrying about the personal risk?

Despite the cloud of gloom that had settled over me, I had to continue the interview. "And how do you afford to keep this place going?" I asked.

"We get a small stipend from the government, and the rest just appears."

"From where?"

"People give me cash, people I've never seen before in my life. Brown people, black people, white people, yellow people. They just appear at the door with an envelope or plastic bag."

"Does anybody ever want to adopt…?"

She shook her head before I'd even finished the question. "Never. People are too afraid."

The butternut squash was ready, and the other women had moved the children inside. Those children who could sat on the floor, feeding themselves the orange puree sprinkled with brown sugar; the babies sat in high chairs, and the women moved between them, filling the little mouths from the same plate with the same teaspoon.

Big Jane unwrapped the little girl from her back and returned her to the high chair, but still she would not eat. Her eyes were wet, but there were no tears on her cheeks. All of a sudden, without any change of expression, she vomited a pink pool of blood and milk onto the tray before her.

"It's okay, baby, it's okay," murmured Big Jane, stroking her head. Then she began wiping up the mess.

I watched the cloth become squelchy in her ungloved hands and stepped back, afraid for myself, afraid for her and ashamed of my fear.

I had enough of Big Jane on tape as well as an interview with one of the other women, and I'd recorded the sounds of the children at play as well as the song they'd sung for me when I'd arrived.

"Maybe you'll get more donations after people hear my report on the radio," I told Big Jane, as she was seeing me off.

It sounded patronizing, and I wondered if it was because I felt guilty about having climbed into my car without shaking her hand.

She shrugged. "The Lord provides. Drive carefully now and watch out for the *ditsotsi*. The bad men."

I locked the doors and pushed my tape recorder and handbag under the passenger seat. No need to place temptation in full view, although it took less than that for criminals to stop you nowadays.

This was only the second time I'd been to Soweto. A white photographer had been killed in an ambush there just before the first democratic elections in the country in 1994, and for a couple of years after that editors had sent only black journalists into the townships. White journalists were grateful. Our fear of being in the wrong place at the wrong time with the wrong skin color was stronger than our desire to get to the news.

I had only gone to Soweto that first time because my black colleagues were out of the country covering an Organization of African Unity summit. A strip mall was being opened in the township, and the paucity of existing business in the area had made it big news. What had made my four-minute piece so powerful was the uninhibited, infectious joy expressed by women who no longer had to catch two buses into downtown Johannesburg to buy a bolt of fabric or a new pap pot.

To whites, Soweto had always been the wrong turn you didn't want to take. When television arrived in the country in 1975, the images beamed into our homes from this hotbed of dissent shook the orderly existence of the sheltered white suburbs. Who could forget the infamous *necklace*—a petrol-filled tire placed over the head of an alleged police spy and then ignited by the baying mob?

Soweto is a sprawling dormitory town, built to house Johannesburg's black workers, who until 1991 were forbidden by law from living in white areas. Every morning, trains and minibus taxis—packed way beyond legal capacity—transport its residents to their places of work. The ones who remain are the unemployed and those who scratch out a living for themselves, selling fruit, cigarettes and liquor, repairing radios and bicycles, straightening hair.

White journalists have started going back in; still, some opt not to. In the past it was because of political unrest; now it's because criminals have a stranglehold on the township. Carjackers are so brazen in Soweto, they knock on the front doors of their victims' houses to demand the car keys. It's like the rest of the country now, only seen through a magnifying glass with the full glare of the sun behind you.

At a red light, I took the cassette out of the recorder and inserted it into the car's tape player. There was no news angle, so I didn't have to hurry to get it ready for the evening news and actuality program. I could take my time, maybe make the report a bit longer than usual.

The roads were busier than when I'd arrived midmorning, and I had difficulty locating signs to tell me I was retracing my exact route. Nothing looked familiar. I felt a flutter of panic. All I needed was to get lost. But then the truck blocking my view in front pulled off the road, and I was relieved to see the gas station I'd used as a landmark this morning.

The light at the entrance to the highway stayed red for so long I considered flooring the accelerator. I didn't though, because it was still daylight, and a cop wouldn't be as lenient as he might if it were late at night, when this was common practice. The bridge shuddered as cars flashed by down below, skipping in and out of lanes, racing each other to the next exit, a thick, shimmering tapeworm of crowded steel that had left Johannesburg empty, like a great big shin bone sucked dry of marrow.

I drummed my fingers on the steering wheel; the children on the tape gurgled and chattered. The doors were all locked, the car was in gear, my foot revved the accelerator. There was not a soul around. Suddenly, a head popped up next to my window. I heard myself scream and felt a short, sharp pain in my chest, as though I'd been stabbed with a knitting needle. I went hot, then cold. My scalp prickled with sweat.

"Get out of the car, white scum!" he said, aiming a silver gun right between my eyes.

Guns had always been present in my life, stashed in glove compartments, locked in safes, under the cushions of the sofa, tan leather holsters peeping out the bottom of trouser legs. I knew they were there, but, like edge trimmers, I'd never had a call for them. They were objects on the periphery of my life: necessary, convenient, just not something I ever used.

"I said, get out!"

As he motioned for me to open the door, the spine of his gun caught the glare of the late afternoon sun, blinding me with its flash, making him disappear from before my eyes. Could this be a dream? No. The milky haze shifted and he was still there, blue black, beads of sweat trickling down the shiny dome of his shaved head and disappearing in rivulets behind the mirrored sunglasses.

"Now, not tomorrow!" He looked about thirtyish, but his voice was high-pitched, unsteady, adolescent.

Why couldn't I move? My brain sent signals telling my legs to swing out of the car and plant themselves on the road, but my hands were locked so tightly on the steering wheel I felt a spasm in my shoulders. A woolly numbness began to fill my head, and I realized I was holding my breath.

He took off his sunglasses and wiped his sleeve across his forehead, leaving a slick dark stain on the turquoise silk. The whites of his coal-black eyes were tinged with yellow.

A strange, frantic whining grew loud in my ears, the sound of an impala caught in the metal teeth of a poacher's trap.

"Shut up!" screamed the man.

Then I realized it was me making the hideous noise. I slouched farther into the driver's seat, trying to put as much distance between the gun and myself as possible, and burrowed my chin into my chest so I didn't have to look at my reflection anymore. The pinkness of his nails turned chalky as he tightened his grip on the pearly handle of the gun.

Crack! The only gunfire I'd heard before had been in the distance. I felt my mouth snap shut, and the whining stopped. I tensed, anticipating pain. *Crack!*

He's shot me again, I thought.

I patted my chest and stomach, frantically searching for the stickiness, the damp patch on my crisp white linen blouse.

Crack, crack, crack!

He wasn't stopping. He really wanted to kill me. I looked up into his face, hoping he would stop when he saw the fear in my eyes.

"Not yet, baby," he said, smirking. "I haven't shot you, *yet.*"

Crack, crack, crack! He rapped the snub nose of the gun against the window, then threw back his head and almost choked on loud, guttural laughter. Quickly, I put my hand on the keys to restart my stalled car, wincing as they clinked against each other. But he didn't seem to hear; his head was still thrown back, his whole body shaking with laughter. I turned the key. The car strained to life, jolted forward and died again.

Suddenly, there was a crash and a shower of glass onto my lap. Cool metal jabbed my cheek.

He screamed a curse at me, his index finger shaking on the trigger. Then he leaned closer, stroking my cheek with the spine of the gun, his voice becoming a reedy purr. "If the car's in gear, you have to keep your foot on the clutch." He pressed his lips to my ear and shouted, "Now, get out or I will shoot you!"

Still I sat staring danger stupidly in the face. His eyes darted left, right, right, left. Little rodent eyes. He opened the door, grabbed my forearm and pulled me from my seat. With a dull, crunching thud, I fell face first onto the road.

His shoes were brown wing tips, polished to a dazzling shine, the shoes of a player, a debonair man-about-town.

A gust of wind blew my dress up, and I felt the sting of the summer sun on the backs of my thighs. The traffic growled on the highway below. I gave a dry heave.

"Give me the keys, white pig!"

I don't know why I'd yanked them from the ignition. One of his wing tips crushed the back of my hand as he ripped the keys from my fingers.

"Think you're clever?" He ground his shoe as though extinguishing a cigarette. I wondered why I didn't feel any pain. "You all think that."

There was another crack, and everything went black.

A dark, blurry circle hovered above me. I tried to focus. Were they clouds? Birds? Gradually, the circle became individual faces, black faces, staring at me wide eyed, lips puckered. What did they want? My arms wouldn't move to shield my face; it was as though I were covered by a thick blanket of sunbaked sand.

"She's awake! Call the doctor!" said a female voice, and the group scattered noisily in a blizzard of dazzling white uniforms and matching stockings, leaving me in the company of an orchestra of machines.

Standing guard over me and beeping every five seconds was a gray box with a screen of green peaks and valleys that I presumed showed my heartbeat, because I was linked to it with three patches stuck to my chest. Another screen, spattered with red numbers, made no noise but was attached to a black fabric cuff on my arm that inflated after every third beep of the other machine. A plastic sheath and tube perforated the skin near my collarbone, and led to a bottle on a stand. Fastened to the side of my bed was a translucent bag filled with a dark yellow liquid. There was a brace around my neck.

Rubber soles squeaked on the tiled floor.

"Welcome back," said a stout, middle-aged woman. She had a little white triangular cap clipped with bobby pins to her tight black curls. "You've been sleeping for a week."

I tried to ask what I was doing here, but the words sounded like bubbles underwater.

"Shh, now. Here's your doctor."

"I see you've finally decided to join us," said a young man in faded jeans and a once-white coat. "In case you don't know, you're in the Soweto Regional Hospital. I'm Dr. Novak." His accent sounded East European.

He picked up a clipboard at the foot of my bed and flipped through the pages, while a beeper he wore on his belt added a syncopated beat to the electronic symphony of the room.

"You're lucky you're here. Both our last two carjack victims didn't make it."

The surviving child had survived again. So many times I'd wished that it was me they'd brought home from the airport in that pathetic forty-pound bag, not the only parts of my brother the army managed to find in the scorched Namibian veld. I used to lie in bed imagining how different things might have been if it had been me. My father would not have become a bitter shell of a man, my mother would not have craved sleeping pills as though she needed them for life itself, and I would not have had to live with the constant pressure of trying to be *two* children when I was barely capable of being a dutiful *one*.

Why had I been spared now, when the last two carjack victims in this hospital had not? When my own brother had not? How ironic that the very same afternoon I'd pondered how little impact my own disappearance from this earth would have. Could the doctor be correct? Was it just chance that I was lying here instead of in the city morgue? Or might there be a reason that the bullet had not done its worst? I hesitated even to put shape to the idea forming in my head. Was there a divine purpose that required my life be spared?

Chapter Two

Ella

My son is older than his years. Sometimes I think he was sent to teach me about life, not the other way around. There's not much in my life I can hold up as an example to him, unless it's how not to do things. Maybe this is punishment for wishing my life away: years and years spent wishing for the balance to tip in our favor, wishing we could get out, wishing we could come back, wishing for life to begin. Little did I know that my life happened while I was wishing. Now I wish for the past, for my mother to be here again, for those simple days sewing wedding dresses in our two-bedroom house in Lusaka, Zambia. *Going South* said the little label we sewed into the linings, for we were to do just that when the call came. I think of all those girls wearing dresses sewn with the dreams of a long-lost homeland and hope that we didn't jinx their marriages.

I was an overqualified seamstress then, just as I'm an overqualified secretary now—officially, my position is Public Relations Officer, but those are just words. A bachelor's degree from the University of Havana, Cuba, a master's from the University of Toronto, and what am I doing?—organizing visits to a paint factory for troops of journalists. Why we don't just send them a check for a meal at a restaurant of their choice, I don't know—the only reason they come is for the food. At the interview they told me I'd have to use my language skills, that they'd never had an applicant who could speak French, Spanish, English and Sotho. But there are only two things I need to say: "Yes, there are more sausage rolls, and no, there's no more wine." And words are never really necessary; a simple nod or shake of my head always suffices.

Spanish is my favorite language—it fizzles on my tongue like sherbet. But now my student days in Cuba seem like another life, another world.

The Spanish weren't as greedy as the English, French, Belgians and Portuguese when they came to Africa. The land they called Spanish Sahara is not much more than a bandage on the bulge of the African continent, and Equatorial Guinea is just plain tiny. For this reason I'll never have to say, "No, there's no more cheese and crackers" in Spanish. French is always a possibility, as sometimes we get a journalist from the Gabon, Senegal, or Sierra Leone tagging along with a South African journalist friend before the opening of the summit or conference they've really come to the country to attend. Nobody gives a hoot about paint manufacturing.

"Ven aquí." Come here, I call to my son.

He's standing next to the swings, watching a boy soar higher and higher into the air. The empty swings jerk with the vibrations. He looks at me with those big eyes of his father's before slouching over.

"English, not Spanish, Mommy," he says for about the twentieth time today.

"Sorry, I forgot." Today has been one of those days of wishing we were somewhere else.

Sipho peers into the stroller. "He sleeps while we're at the park, but tonight he'll want to play." He shakes his head like a weary first-time father.

Mandla stirs and sticks his thumb in his mouth. He's my little whirlwind, full of energy, always laughing as though the world is one big cartoon produced solely for his enjoyment. He laughs when he's tired, hungry, stuffed up with a cold—there's always a reason to laugh. I used to be like that, but I've lost my energy. Some days are better than others, but today I feel like an old flannel shirt that's been pressed through my mother's wringer.

"We should go home now, Mommy. It's getting dark."

It is barely five o'clock and the summer sun is still high above the horizon, but I know what Sipho means; as the afternoon shadows grow long and skinny, we feel a lot safer behind our iron security gate and our triple locks. It is no coincidence that lockdown at prisons is also at five; bad things happen as darkness approaches. These streets are no place for anyone to be at night. The saddest thing for me is that eight-year-old Sipho knows it.

I lift my face to the cloudless sky and whisper, "You were right, Ma, our faith got us what we wanted. But what now?"

What sort of freedom have we won when we cannot let our children play in the park alone, when we have to look over our shoulders as we walk to the store in broad daylight, when we cannot answer a knock on the door after the sun has gone down?

My husband says it would be different if we'd had the war like we were supposed to. How that man cursed when the election date was set. His greatest disappointment in life is that the olive-green uniform he wore for training in Zambia as a member of *Umkhonto weSizwe,* the armed wing of the African National Congress, never saw real battle. I hear it's getting him a lot of action now, though. Does he think I'm stupid, that I don't have any friends?

I smell it on him, the cheap perfume of women who forgo their customary fee to sleep with the hero, the returning freedom fighter. Yes, this is some freedom we've won.

"Mommy, let's go," says Sipho.

He's right; it's time to leave this park. Its leafy green conjures up too many memories anyway of our little house in Lusaka, its vegetable garden in front, the fruit trees out back, the lawn, and the neighbors, our fellow exiles, roasting a lamb at our monthly community parties under a wide-open, star-filled sky.

My flat in Berea is gorgeous compared to the one in Hillbrow that the ANC put us up in when we came back to South Africa. What a pathetic homecoming that was: not a band or Welcome Home Comrades banner in sight, just two bored-looking ANC officials who turned out to be merely bus drivers sent to take us from the airport to our lodgings.

I could not stand the noise and dirt of Hillbrow. What was once a melting pot of races, even during the time of apartheid, is now a melted mess of junkies and gangsters. Berea is only a few miles east, but it is not yet afflicted by the inner city's malaise. There's a sprinkling of small parks, and the municipality has planted trees in large concrete barrels on the sidewalks. My building is a neat, four-story block with balconies displaying potted geraniums, miniature palms and cacti if the residents are elderly, tricycles and rocking horses if they are young parents like me. I knew this was the place for us when I stood on the balcony and could see the trees in the park two blocks up. My dream is to move my family to a house in the suburbs, but there I go with more useless wishing.

"I have one for you," says Sipho, holding on to the stroller with one hand as I have taught him to.

"Okay, let me hear it."

"I hunt in a pack at night, my favorite prey is zebra or wildebeest, and I make a very strange noise."

"You're a leopard."

"No."

"A lion."

"No." He chuckles. "Do you want another clue?"

"Okay."

"I'm brown-gray with black spots."

"I give up."

"I'm a laughing hyena," he says, his face glowing with the thrill of having taught his mother something.

"But hyenas are scavengers."

He shakes his head. "That's what people used to think, but they're really vicious hunters. I saw it on TV."

"Well, that makes it eleven-four."

"Twelve-four."

"Really? You're wiping the floor with me."

Instantly, his smile disappears. "What does that mean, Mommy?" he asks in a small voice.

"Relax, Sipho, it just means you're winning."

He looks so relieved I want to stop right here on the corner of our street and smother him with kisses, but I restrain myself to spare him the embarrassment.

After laying Mandla on a pillow on the floor so he can toddle around when he wakes up, I slide the two dead bolts across the front door and fasten the chain. If someone really wants to get in they'll find a way, but they'll probably have to saw through the metal security gate first, and I'll hear that for sure. This door is as strong as doors can be. My father forgets a lot of things, like his name and the country in which he lives, but he never forgets to check the locks on his way to bed. It's as though the memories are not stored in his atrophying brain, but in the marrow of his bones.

The door on our three-roomed cement block house in Soweto only had one lock: a padlock on the inside. When the knock came in the quiet hours of the dead night, we knew our routine. It was simple—what more could we do than huddle under the kitchen table, holding each other and praying that the padlock and heavy dresser my mother and father had pushed against the door before going to bed would hold up? My mother would rock me and sing songs about a time long ago when Africans were proud tribesmen with acres of land and large herds of livestock, a time when a girl longed to be spotted by the chief's handsome son. My father would tell her to stop filling my head with romantic nonsense, and her reply was always the same: "This land was once ours. If we have faith, the Lord will deliver it back to us. Faith is all we'll ever need in this life."

The knocking on the door would end, and then stones and broken bricks would rain down on our tin roof like artillery fire. Sometimes a brick would fly through the window and shower the kitchen floor with gleaming shards that cut our feet when we eventually came out of hiding.

"Maak oop, terroris. Dis die polisie." Open up, terrorist. This is the police, barked throaty male voices in Afrikaans.

My father did as he was told the first time, only to be shoved to the floor by two meaty white policemen who reeked of rum. As they kicked him repeatedly in the ribs, three more policemen used batons to upturn mattresses, clear the shelves in the kitchen and pull clothes from the closet. My mother and I cowered white-eyed in the corner, with two snarling German shepherds straining at their leashes to get at us.

Never again, said my father, would he open the door and invite those gangsters in. In the future they'd have to break down his door. They did so on a regular basis after this, and old Elias at the end of the road grew accustomed to coming round in the mornings to help patch the holes in the door that steel-tipped boots had made.

When routine checks failed to unearth documents to link my father to the banned African National Congress, the police became more ingenious in their desperation.

They emptied my mother's tin canisters of flour and mealie meal onto the floor, poured the milk down the drain, slit open tea bags with pocketknives, and were not averse to frisking me for hidden documents when I began to show signs of budding womanhood at the age of twelve. But there was one place even the most ardent policeman would not investigate: the outhouse. Although my mother was a meticulous housekeeper, there was only so much she could do to keep the latrine sweet-smelling, and in a plastic grocery bag taped just under the rough wooden slats of the seat were the latest writings from the party's exiled leaders.

Sipho turns on the television to watch a wildlife documentary. A shaggy-maned male lion fights a young contender, while a female lion lies licking her cubs in the shade of a *marula* tree. My father shuffles in in his dressing gown and sits down in his favorite chair, his eyes glued to the screen, his face unshaven.

"Do you think Daddy will come back tonight?" asks Sipho.

He'll come back when he's finished with his woman, when he's had his fill of free vodka, when he's smoked until his eyes are red. When he's tired and needs a bath, he'll come back and expect us to tiptoe around him while he rests. I cannot tell from my son's voice if this is what he really wants. He sees things other children his age do not, but I don't know of any child who wouldn't choose this over absence.

"He has business to attend to," I tell him. "You know the *Umkhonto weSizwe* soldiers have joined with the South African Defense Force to form a new military. These things take a lot of organization."

Sipho looks up from the image of the bloody-faced lion returning to his mate, the challenger lying twitching in the dust. He nods, but I can see in his eyes he knows I'm conning him.

Chapter Three

Monica

"Aheee!"

The sound scooped me out of my cocooned warmth. It was early morning; I could tell by the honeyed smog through the window. A window! I'd been moved while I slept.

The female voices outside in the corridor grew louder. I couldn't understand the words, but their tone was angry, hysterical. A male voice joined the fray; there were sounds of blows, a woman's scream, and then a bone-chilling wail. It all came flooding back to me: the pathetic animal-like whining, my hand under a shiny brown wing tip, the mirrored sunglasses, rings of sweat, the growling traffic, the final loud crack. I lifted my right hand. It was bandaged.

A breeze puffed out the bleached cotton curtain on the window, bringing with it dust and smoke from the township's breakfast fires to mingle with the smell of hospital odors and undiluted antiseptic. I couldn't turn my neck because of the neck brace, yet a rhythmic rattle on my left and the wrinkle of pages being turned somewhere across the room told me that I was surrounded by other patients. There was a hot, dull ache in my lower back. Every part of my body felt heavy, waterlogged. I flexed my feet and thanked God they responded. I closed my eyes and saw the silver gun with the pearly handle.

Please come back inside, someone. Talk to me. Someone. Anyone.

The noise outside stopped, and the nurses drifted back in to congregate at the nurses' station, a solitary dark wood desk in the corner of the ward closest to the double doors. One of them came up to me, clucking and shaking her head like a demented chicken, and tapped the tube of my IV drip.

"What's going on?" I asked. At last I sounded intelligible. Maybe talking would clear away the dark images layering themselves in my mind.

"Huh! Oh, you gave me a fright. You haven't said a word since you came here from the ICU."

"What's the noise about, Sister?"

She hadn't introduced herself, but I thought it safer to err on the side of seniority.

"Agh, Johanna's husband came in here, like the big man he thinks he is, and hit her. He says she's been running around. Hmph, like my husband didn't see him at the shebeen with a woman last weekend. Anyway, she's been busy with NEHAWU work, not running around."

I knew what NEHAWU was—the huge union for nurses and other health workers. My brain, it seemed, was functioning.

"Did anyone call security?"

She snorted. "Did anyone call security? I'll have to remember that one. If we waited for them to get their fat, lazy bodies up here, Johanna would be dead. No, Jacob and Thabo, the porters, threw him out."

I wanted to ask who'd brought me to the hospital, but she appeared to be enjoying the story so much I thought it better to wait for the ending.

"Jacob and Thabo said they'd take him behind the doctors' carport and teach him a lesson. Now he'll probably accuse Johanna of sleeping with them, too. Men!" She shook her head. "Yours has been here every day…."

"Anton? Where is he?"

"He'll be here soon. I guarantee it. He's always getting under our feet, questioning our every move. If you didn't have such a nice face, I would have had him thrown out, too."

She moved on to another bed, and from the clicks on every fourth or fifth word, I recognized the language the patient spoke as Xhosa. Besides the doctor, I seemed to be the only white person in the hospital.

A familiar, earnest, deep voice woke me. "Are you sure, Sister?"

"Are you calling me a liar? Go and see for yourself and let me do my work."

He came hurrying over.

"Monica, you're awake. Thank God."

Typical of Anton—he managed to frown and smile at the same time.

Three centuries after his forefathers settled at the very southern tip of the great continent of Africa, the features of their lineage remained unaltered. With his brilliant blue eyes, sandy blond hair, and six-foot frame, Anton could have been any young man in Amsterdam, Rotterdam or Utrecht.

He wore the navy suit I'd helped him pick out less than a month back for a friend's wedding—with the middle button of his jacket fastened, as usual—and his burgundy alma mater tie, which meant it was Wednesday. Sometimes it took him three attempts in the mornings to get the knot right. His normally golden skin looked sallow and blotchy—proof of a daily vigil at my bedside, when he would normally have been at the lake windsurfing after work.

Facts were what I needed now, and, being an accountant, Anton was a good one for those. But he was also warm and witty in his own quiet way. At school he was the boy who whispered out the one-liners, which the big mouths picked up and passed off as their own.

He'd always been a good and obedient son—except for that brief period in his midteens when his parents caught him smoking marijuana in the tractor shed with the boys in his reggae band. His mother screamed at him that only weak-minded *Rooinekke,* English South Africans, took drugs, and his father beat him with a belt before commanding him to reveal the site of his crop. Hendrik felt the leaves, stuck his fingers in the ground at the plants' roots, and told his son that deeper furrows would have yielded healthier plants. Then he made Anton destroy the entire lot. In those days Hendrik still had a healthy respect for the South African Police Force.

My father compared Anton to Luca constantly. Anton was solid and hardworking, while Luca had shone with flashes of brilliance and charm. To my father, Anton was a dull sparrow next to Luca's radiant peacock. My father also had an idiosyncratic dislike of men who weren't as tall as he himself, even if the difference was a mere four inches. Somehow he equated it with a shortfall in honesty.

"You look good, Monica." Anton's fingers brushed my cheek.

"Why am I *here?*" I asked.

The nurses looked up from their work, and I realized my voice had come out louder and harsher than I'd intended.

"You were shot. Don't you remember?" His was soft and crooning.

The ward had grown still.

"But why am I *here,* in *this* hospital?" I knew I should lower the volume, but I couldn't help it. Soon Anton was going to leave me here, all alone. "Look around. Do you see any other *white* faces?"

The nurses congregated around the medicine trolley nudged each other and giggled behind their hands, enjoying the show.

"Tell me about it." His top lip twitched in a way I'd never seen before. "Your mother's tried to have you transferred to a hospital in her neighborhood, but your doctor says it's too dangerous to move you."

"I don't want to be here," I said, gritting my teeth as though that would stop the hysteria I felt coming. "I bet there's not another white patient in the whole hospital!"

"Absolutely right." It was warm in the ward, but he didn't take off his jacket or loosen his tie.

"Get me out of here. I want to go to a *white* hospital."

The giggling stopped and the nurses stared, eyes narrowed, jaws set, lips stretched tight. .

"We tried, Monica, we—"

"This is a *black* hospital."

He glanced dismissively at the patient in the next bed. "You know the law says there's no such thing as a black or white hospital anymore, and if an accident happens in some arbitrary circumference of a hospital, then that's where you go." He exhaled slowly, and I felt his warm breath on my face. "If this had happened before the laws changed, you'd have been taken straight to a *decent* hospital."

"Don't leave me here," I said in a small voice.

"I'm sorry," he said, stroking my cheek once more, "but your doctor said it would be on our heads if anything happened to you." His eyes swept the room. "You're packed in here like sardines."

"Who brought me here?"

"Shh," he said, putting a finger on my lips. "We don't have to discuss that now."

"I'm not a child." I closed my eyes and saw my terrified face in the mirrored sunglasses again. "I have a right to know."

"A taxi driver. Your father tried to give him money to have his minibus cleaned, but he wouldn't take it. He said his wife would get the blood out of the sheepskin seat cover he wrapped you in."

Apparently I was in a coma in the Intensive Care Unit for seven days. Anton believed that in the same way hibernation protected a bear from hunger pangs, oblivion took over when pain became too intense for the human body. It was a sweet, naive theory, and so typical of Anton.

He told me that the bullet had entered my lower back, nicked my spleen, ricocheted through my chest cavity, then lodged in my abdomen. On the day I was admitted, I underwent emergency surgery to remove the bullet and repair my spleen. My parents were told I had a fifty-fifty chance.

"Where do they get numbers like those?" I asked.

He wiped his eyes and muttered something about dust.

"I'm okay, Anton. Really, I am." It was an effort to talk. I wanted to escape back under the thick blanket of sand, but little by little it had been blown away, leaving me exposed to the stark, dry Highveld air.

"I almost lost you, Monica." His voice broke and he squeezed his eyes shut.

I'd never seen him cry. It frightened me.

The first time I'd ever felt real fear, the type that constricts your heart and makes you forget to breathe, was when I heard screams coming from the maid's room in the back garden. I must have been about seven years old.

"Help me, Master! He's killing me," shrieked Agnes.

My father grabbed a hammer and ran out the back door, while my mother trailed behind, crying, "No, Paolo, please, don't go."

In the end the hammer wasn't used, and my father told the wife beater to leave and never set foot on his property again. He wasn't supposed to be there anyway, he told me, and could get us into a lot of trouble with the police if they caught him without his passbook. The Group Areas' Act was still strictly enforced, and only blacks who were employed as maids, nannies, cooks and gardeners were allowed to live in the white neighborhood. Husbands could visit if they had their passbooks, but weren't permitted to stay over.

The next morning Agnes was at the sink washing our breakfast dishes, a huge bruise and an even bigger scowl on her face. I knew there was more to this than my daddy rescuing her. She sneered at me when I tried to help clear the porridge plates. She seemed angry at me, at my father, at all of us, and I didn't know why.

Four days later her husband came back.

"Blasted blacks," said my father. "Next time I'll let him beat her up. It's obviously what she wants."

She left us a year later to give birth to her third child at home in Hoedspruit, but promised to return soon after New Year. By the end of January, we were still waiting.

"The ironing's piling up," said my mother, "and if Agnes doesn't want this job, there are hundreds of others who do. Every other day someone knocks on the door looking for work and a room."

While my mother was busy in the garden one day, I sneaked into the maid's quarters to see why so many people wanted to live there. It was dark inside. The rest of the house had large windows overlooking the clipped lawn and swirling flower beds, but this room's single window was small and set high up in the wall. I couldn't imagine where I'd put my bed, desk and antique doll-house; the room was nothing more than a cubicle. It had a strange smell, too. Our house smelled of polish and baking—this smelled medicinal. The bed was high off the ground, each leg resting on a pile of three bricks so the *utokoloshe* couldn't reach up with his gnarled, evil fingers and put a spell on Agnes. She'd wrapped the bricks in old pieces of Christmas paper, as though they were something precious. Coffee cans, jam jars and cordial bottles were lined up in descending order of size on the dresser, all rinsed out, their labels soaked off, ready for her replacement to use.

The entrance to the bathroom was outside so the gardener could use it, too. There was a toilet and minuscule basin, but no bath, just a showerhead. There was a cold water faucet for the shower on the wall and a drain in the middle of the sloping, concrete floor. I picked up the little piece of red soap she'd left on the basin and put it to my nose. This was what the bedroom smelled of.

Then my mother called me and I ran out into the bright sunshine, none the wiser as to why so many people were eager to live in that dark little space.

After Anton left, I tried to sleep, but even with the sharp antiseptic vapors in the air, the stench of unwashed bodies mingled with other unpleasant odors was clearly discernible. I tried imagining a pleasant smell like freshly mowed lawn. I could almost hear the drone of the lawn mower and, if I kept my eyes shut, could see myself and Luca as children, lying in our school-issue swimsuits next to the pool, keeping watch for our mother because she said we'd get cancer from the hot bricks.

This was the smell of my childhood, the smell that evoked everything: school concerts, Scout meetings, soccer matches and Sunday barbecues in a country of sunshine, leafy suburbs and lurking threats, which Luca and I never quite got a handle on because we were shooed off to bed each night as the eight o'clock news began.

How far away that childhood seemed now.

Chapter Four

Ella

It's been four days. The longest he's ever been gone is three. One of his women must have a house with a nice, clean bathroom where he can shower and shave. Themba hates stubble. I wonder what he would have done if there had been a war.

I'd like to say I'm past caring, but what I am is too exhausted to summon any emotion. Somewhere deep down in the core of me is a terrible pain, but at the moment all I can think of is how difficult it is to breathe. My parents named me Ella after the late, great Ms. Fitzgerald. Breathing the way I am now, I don't think I could sing "Happy Birthday."

I have used up nearly all my sick leave at work, and today I caught my boss staring at me as though I were a cobra that might rear up and spit at him. He should remember that our office used to be a dance studio. Sometimes those reflections in the ceiling-to-floor mirrors tell a person all they need to know.

You wouldn't think I was ill just by looking at me. I'm still what Themba calls womanly—rounded and smooth, like a newly upholstered sofa. I am tall, too; we stand shoulder to shoulder, Themba and I. It never bothered him in the past, but who knows if that's changed? I try to stand up straight so that people won't see the worries weighing me down.

I've bathed Mandla, washed the gravy out of his hair, and tucked both children in bed. The television flickers soundlessly in the corner, some program about the future of the ballet in the new South Africa. Everything has to be a fight, a discussion, a vote, a committee. I suppose that's democracy. I used to think I'd play a role in the planning, the implementation, the fine-tuning…but now the only things I care about are paying my mortgage and bills on time and figuring out how I'm going to take care of my father when he can't do it himself. Right now I rely on him; he looks after Mandla all day and supervises Sipho after school. Every time the phone rings at work, I think it's someone calling to tell me he left a pot boiling and the building's burned down. I don't know what else to do. If Themba would stop spending all our money, I might be able to afford someone to come in once a day to check on them, maybe make lunch for them so my father didn't feel the need to use the stove.

There is a sound of scraping metal outside. Through the peephole I see Themba fumbling with his keys, cursing when he cannot find the keyhole. Then he finds it, but with the wrong key. He rattles the gate in frustration.

Quickly, I unlock the door and gate.

"You're going to wake the children," I say, hating the coldness in my voice.

"*Ho nepahetse.*" That's good, he says, thick-tongued. There is a pungent smell of marijuana on his clothes, a bottle of rum in his hand. "I have something important to tell them."

"Sssh. You're drunk and high."

"I've got to warn them about white women."

"Themba, shut up. Sipho's got school tomorrow."

"White women are evil."

"Is that where you've been? With a white woman?"

He spits on the floor, and I feel like kicking him. This beautiful flat I work so hard to keep is not one of the filthy bars he haunts.

"I will never touch a white woman as long as I live."

"But you have no qualms about touching other black women."

"Not that again. They're just being friendly. They want to hear about—"

"Your sons want to hear your voice, too. When will you get around to spending time with them?"

"They've got clothes on their backs, haven't they? Food in their mouths?"

"No thanks to you." I shouldn't have said that. I knew what would happen. But it doesn't hurt so much this time, and luckily it's on my ear; I can wear my braids down tomorrow and nobody will see it. Suddenly, I'm disgusted at myself for thinking such pathetic thoughts, the thoughts of a victim. I may be sick, life may be hard right now, but I will not allow Themba to treat me like this.

"Get out," I say.

He laughs and waves the bottle of rum in my face. "I need to mix this with something. *Tswa.* Out of my way."

My voice is soft. "I said get out."

As he reaches into the refrigerator for the plastic two-liter bottle of soda, he knocks over an open can of soup. "I hope the soda's not flat," he says, kicking the refrigerator door shut on the mess.

"This isn't a bar, Themba, and it's also not your home anymore."

I open the door. He swaggers over to me with a lecherous look on his face.

"I know what you need," he says, grabbing me.

Gathering all my strength, I put my shoulder to his chest and shove him out the door. He thinks I'm playing a game with him and stands smiling at me, his eyes raking my body from the fluffy yellow slippers on my feet to the braids I've tied up in a ponytail on the top of my head. But then he sees me turning the key in the security gate.

"Don't do this, Ella," he shouts, rattling the gate like a prisoner trying to get the attention of his warden. For once I do not care if the neighbors see my drunken husband.

I go to our bedroom and start taking his clothes from the closet.

"Here are your things," I say, stuffing shirts, pants, underwear through the bars. I make three more trips, and then it is done. His MK boots don't fit through the bars, so I go out onto the balcony and toss them over. They land with beautiful, consecutive thuds on the sidewalk below.

"You can't do this!" he yells. "This is *my* flat."

"Yes, I can, and no, it's not. It's in my name because I'm the one with a job, remember?"

"I can't work with those *Boere*. As soon as the new defense force gets rid of them, I'll go back."

"Nobody's going to get rid of the Afrikaner old boys, and it could be fifteen years before they retire. When they call it the integration of two armies, it's exactly that, Themba—integration."

"I will not take orders from our old enemies. How can you forget so easily, Ella?"

"Grow up, Themba." I go back to our bedroom and slide a suitcase out from under the bed. Then I throw it over the balcony, too. When I go back, Themba tries to grab me through the bars, but he manages only to catch the sleeve of my nightgown. It rips like old newspaper.

Themba laughs as I try to cover myself with my hands. "You won't get away with this," he says.

I kick the door closed, lock it, slide the two dead bolts across and put the chain on. He does not move, just stands there laughing, like one of Sipho's hyenas. Shivering, I sink to the floor and begin to cry. After a while, the laughing stops, and he kicks at the gate before thumping down the stairs, cursing loudly.

My father shuffles into the kitchen and turns on the light.

"What is it, Daddy?" I ask, trying to sound as normal as possible.

"Your mother wants a drink of water."

I bite on my ripped nightgown so he won't hear me sobbing.

It's a typical summer afternoon: crackling dry air, dark clouds massing on the horizon like troops, another quick electric storm on its way to squelch the heat. I love thunderstorms and the rich smell of soil and damp grass they leave behind—not that I'll experience it here, with the concrete sidewalks and melting asphalt, but still, the change of temperature will be comforting.

I'm later coming home than usual because I had a doctor's appointment after work. Dr. Ishmael has a low, mellifluous voice that makes me want to go to sleep right there in his examining room. I envy his children being tucked into bed at night by him, feeling as though nothing can ever harm them. He says I should stop working, that my white cell count is dropping and my immune system does not need added stress in its weakened state. "Help your body," he told me. But who will help Ella, the parent and breadwinner? I have no choice but to keep going.

One more road to cross. I step off the sidewalk and a truck careens around the corner, just missing me and a parked car. In shock, I stand in the middle of the road, not knowing whether to walk back or continue on. Is this a sign of the dementia they talk about? Did I step in front of that truck, or did it fail to stop at the intersection? Am I becoming like my father?

The truck is similar to the one we once hid in: a white four-tonner with faded green lettering on the sides. My father knew the driver from his secret party meetings, and the kind man cleared a space for us among the garden utensils he was transporting to Lusaka and tried not to take corners too sharply or drive too fast over rough roads. With bags of seed as pillows, we lay back against the hollow curves of the wheelbarrows and listened to my mother sing and tell jokes as though we were on a trip to the seaside. She stopped trying to entertain us when a box of spades came cascading off the top of a pile, missing her head by inches, and settled into the same sort of glazed lifelessness that had overcome my father and me as soon as the driver had swung the door shut with a loud clank.

We were delivered to the United Nations High Commissioner for Refugees office in Lusaka and, since we didn't have passports, they issued us identity documents that we later referred to as the *New York Times* on account of their length. ANC officials found us a house and set us up with a bit of cash; party coffers were full at that time because international donations had poured in after the Soweto riots.

I was thirteen years old and furious with my parents for having kept me at home that day in June of 1976 when ten thousand Soweto schoolchildren spilled out onto the streets to protest against the enforced use of Afrikaans—the language of the oppressors—in our schools. Looking back, I now understand my parents' caution. When the armored vehicles rolled in, three students were killed and twelve injured, and what followed was a scene no movie director could have imagined. The students went on a rampage, burning down government buildings to express their grief and rage. Police reinforcements were sent in, and within a few days several hundred protesters had lost their lives.

The grocery bags I'm carrying contain nothing more than milk and bananas, but feel as if they're packed with bricks. An old woman shuffles past, clutching her bag. We do not make eye contact. Nobody does on the street—to do so is to invite trouble. We drop our heads and walk right by the people who live around us, lest they see the fear in our eyes.

Today I wonder if it was wise buying a flat on the fourth floor in a building with no elevator. I'd wanted it because the sound of footsteps above my head would have driven me crazy, but now I think that these one hundred and ten stairs are more of a burden.

I put the bags down on my ladybug doormat and grab hold of the security gate while I catch my breath. When I'm sure I've reached a state that won't scare Sipho, I unlock the security gate and put my key in the front door. It turns in the lock, but the door does not open. My father has forgotten to slide back the dead bolts.

"Dad," I call. I can hear the sound of the television.

I knock and hear the shuffle of my father's slippers on the tiles in the entrance hall.

"Dad, it's me. Open up."

"Tsamaya!" Go away, he barks.

"Dad, it's me. Let me in."

"I'll call the police."

Tears spring to my eyes, but they are of anger, not pity. What gives him the right to make my life more difficult than it is already?

"Open the door," I shout, and immediately I'm ashamed of myself. "Daddy, it's Ella," I say in a gentle voice. "Please unlock the door."

"I don't know anyone by that name," he says.

I lean my head against the front door. My chest feels tight. I should not cry—it's hard enough to breathe as it is—but I've never felt so alone in my life.

I hear whispering at the door. "It's a crazy woman," says my father.

"No, Grandpa," I hear Sipho say, "it's Mommy. You go back and watch TV, and I'll let her in."

I am not alone. I have this wise little boy to help me. I have to hang on as long as possible for my sons.

I had a terrible night, and my boss didn't make things any easier this morning when I called in sick. He could barely disguise the tightness in his voice when he reminded me that I have only one sick day left.

I try to be cheerful walking Sipho to school.

"Give me one," I tell him, but he doesn't want to play our game.

When we reach the gate, he asks if he can come home with me. He hates to miss school; maybe he knows more than I realize. I force him to go because I don't want him to see me on a bad day. Tomorrow will be different, I tell myself.

My father is not yet up when I get back and does not appear in the half hour Mandla and I enjoy a sticky breakfast of white bread and apricot jam together.

Once I've wiped Mandla's hands and face and the kitchen wall, I take my father a cup of tea. The curtains in his room are still drawn.

"Time to get up, sleepyhead," I say, yanking them open.

He's lying on his back with his mouth open.

"Come on, lazy bones." I can't remember when exactly it was that I started speaking to him as I do my sons.

I put my hand on his brow. His skin is cold and dry.

"Mama, Mama," says Mandla, toddling in with a colored block in each hand. He drops them onto the floor and goes over to his grandfather to tickle his neck.

"Ntatemoholo." Grandpa, he says, giggling. When he gets no response, he looks at me with confusion in his eyes.

"Say bye-bye to *Ntatemoholo,*" I say.

Obediently, he kisses his grandfather on the lips.

"Now go and build Mommy a tower."

He picks up his blocks and toddles out. I pull up a chair and sit down next to my father. The man I knew left long ago, but I loved the shuffling, forgetful one who took his place just as much. In his weakened state he still did his absolute best for me, just as he had his entire life. I will miss them both.

Passengers in the center aisle sway like thick seaweed as the bus lurches through the traffic. Three young men on the steps near the driver duck and shift their weight like surfers catching a wave. The noise is incredible; we Africans do not speak quietly to one another unless we have something to hide. Unlike white people, our conversation is not a transaction; it's something we do for pure pleasure. But right this minute I take no pleasure in it, for it seems to be steaming up the already warm bus, fogging the glass, and forcing the nausea into my throat.

"We need some rain to cool things down a bit," says the girl next to me. She is dressed in a navy banker's suit and matching high heels.

"*Eya.* Yes." It's all I can say because I'm concentrating hard on not throwing up.

She is insulted by my taciturn manner and turns away to speak to an elderly woman behind her.

This is my second bus ride since six this morning, and now I'm wondering if I should have gone to the Johannesburg Regional instead of making this long trek to Soweto. "You have to go to the hospital immediately," my doctor told me. Then he promised to let them know I'd be coming. The Johannesburg Regional is only a short taxi ride from my home, but that's the problem. I consider myself a well-traveled, fairly sophisticated woman, but I don't want anybody from work, or any of my friends, to come and see me in the hospital. I am ashamed of my disease. I shouldn't be—nobody should—but the sad truth is that here in South Africa, with one in nine adults

HIV positive, we're still hiding out like lepers, as though a glance or a handshake might inflict our misery on others. Families say it was malaria, TB, pneumonia, that killed their son, daughter, father, and they ask the doctor not to put the word AIDS on the death certificate. Why is it this way? Because people presume you have done something wrong, have lived an immoral life, have brought the wrath of God or your ancestors upon yourself. I do not want to see their censorious eyes, their tight mouths, their hands covering malicious whispering.

I didn't do anything wrong, only something stupid: I trusted my husband. How many others trust him now, when they should be running for their lives? When I was diagnosed, he was off on one of his forays into the seedy undergrowth of Johannesburg—AWOL from home. I tried to find him, but in bars and clubs all across town, half-naked girls with bored faces said they didn't know where he was. One gave me a telephone number, but the woman who answered said she hadn't seen him for days. I told her she was better off kicking him out because he was most likely off carousing with someone else. She slammed the phone down on me. When he finally came home, I told him, and he gave me a right upper cut to the jaw and accused *me* of sleeping around.

So I will take the shameful disease my husband's vanity has inflicted on me to the Soweto Hospital, where I will give a friend's address so I can be admitted. Lying does not come easily to me, having been raised a Christian, but I am angry at God for not sparing me this dreaded disease. Then I will lie there worrying about my two children, now in the care of a neighbor's teenage daughter who wouldn't set foot in the house if she knew what I had. Come to think of it, if Thandeka's mother knew, she wouldn't have approached me at my father's funeral to offer her daughter's services—secretarial college fund or not. Yes, it's better for me to be in Soweto.

The bus stops under a footbridge on a wide-open space that looks like a park with no grass, or a parking lot with no asphalt. Vendors hawk oranges, American cigarettes and cold drinks in the shade of faded umbrellas, and men sit on upturned paint cans while barbers cut their hair with battery-operated clippers. Atop a high wall, barbed wire flutters with scraps of newspaper, chip packets and gold cigarette foil. I find myself thinking of Canada, of festive bunting at small-town fetes, of peanut brittle and cherry pop.

The bus empties out and pulls away in a cloud of red dust and diesel fumes. I follow the crowd through a gate in the wall, past the bored eyes of two security guards who sit smoking and listening to the radio in their portable cubicle. The buildings are all single story, except for one which looks as though it could be the administrative offices, and they're all linked by walkways with tin roofs. The crowd fractures, some heading off with purpose, others, like myself, looking for signs to the admissions area. I see a group of men standing outside a building with double glass doors, and my heart sinks. My 6:00 a.m. start was not early enough.

They do not move aside for us to pass.

"Etloka hosane." Come back tomorrow, one tells me.

"Hobaneng?" Why?

"Have a look inside." He stands back to allow me to thread my way through the layers of people into the waiting room.

Every inch of space is taken. Some sit on chairs, heads in their hands, or on the floor cradling fussing babies; others prop themselves up against the walls. Three Indian men sit behind a desk with piles of dog-eared cardboard folders lined up in front of them. Their faces show defeat.

"I'm sorry," one of them says to a tearful young girl holding a screaming baby, "we have to see to the emergencies first."

"But my baby's in pain." She chokes on the words.

"Gunshot wounds and stabbings take priority."

The girl returns to her seat, crying quietly.

He asks for my name, and I give him the letter my doctor has written.

"This says Johannesburg Regional."

"He made a mistake. I live in Soweto." I give him a friend's address.

"Fine. Take a seat. A nurse will call you."

There are no seats, but I find a place where I can lean against a wall. Feeling faint, I take out the sandwich and banana I brought with me from home. Sipho was upset this morning about me coming to the hospital, so I skipped breakfast to lie next to him in bed and sing one of the songs my mother used to sing to me when we were hiding under the kitchen table.

Two hours later a woman near me is called, and I slip into her seat. The young man I beat to it scowls at me, steps on my toe, and doesn't apologize. I've brought a book to kill time, but it's difficult to concentrate with the noise and heat. The back of my good caftan is soaked with sweat, and I have to keep dabbing my neck and face to keep the front dry.

Four hours later the room is almost empty, not because of the speed of the system, but because some have given up in disgust and gone home. Only six elderly women remain. One has brought a pillow and lies stretched out across the chairs, a collection of plastic carrier bags arranged next to her. I am dozing off myself when a nurse enters the waiting room and calls my name.

Shaking myself awake, I hurry to catch up with the nurse, who's already halfway down a dimly lit corridor, the clip-clop of her thick heels on the tiled floor telling me she hasn't got all day to dawdle. The corridor opens out onto a maze of curtained-off cubicles overflowing with family members bearing blankets and plastic carrier bags of food. I've been to markets that are more peaceful.

"In here," says my nurse, ripping back a curtain. "Wait your turn." And then she disappears into the crush.

I haul myself up onto the gurney and sit with my legs hanging over the edge. Minutes tick by. The noise around me swells and recedes like the waves of the ocean. I feel sleepy again. Maybe I'll lie down, just for a while. The plastic sheeting is cold against my hot skin.

Before long I am back in Havana. My head feels dizzy from the loud music and sultry night air, yet I feel a strange peace, as well.

Chapter Five

Monica

It's a typical Highveld day: fierce sun and air so dry your skin feels one size too small. Loeries jostle for perching space in the sketchy shade of thorn trees. It's hot work collecting pebbles in the dry riverbed. I stop to wipe the sweat off my face, and that's when I hear the roaring sound in the distance. There's a frantic flapping as the birds take to the air. The strange sound grows rapidly louder. The loeries wheel overhead, trilling in fright. I start to run. Over my left shoulder I see it coming closer, a giant wall of water, a tidal wave throwing up rocks and old branches in a powerful frenzy. I trip and feel a fine spray of cold water on my face. I scramble to get up, but someone steps on my hand and grinds it into the ground. I have to get up. It's going to hit me….

I woke up and stared at the pimpled beige ceiling and the buzzing fluorescent strip lights. It was a full minute before I remembered where I was. The doctor had to change my drugs; I couldn't take these nightmares any longer.

Something was different. I put my hand to my throat and felt scales of sweat and grime. The neck brace was off. For the first time I could see what I was wearing: a mint-green cotton hospital gown with ridiculous cap sleeves that stuck straight out like fairy wings. I moved my head to the side, and a pain shot down my back in a fiery bolt. I did it again and again, grunting in pain, soaking my sheets with perspiration, reveling in the absence of the frightening numbness.

"Keep still or you'll do yourself more damage," said a nurse, waving a finger. "Isn't it enough you may never walk again? Do you want to be a quadriplegic, too? Go back to sleep." She left, muttering under her breath.

Sleep! Is she deranged? I wondered. What did she mean never walk again? What's happening? Why haven't I been told?

I bellowed an ugly, primeval sound that reverberated off the institution-green walls.

"It's okay, I'm here now, sweetie," said a voice.

My mother. Thank goodness. As she smoothed my hair with her soft hands, I smelled apricots.

"Mom, what…?"

"Shh, sweetie. Don't talk. I'm so happy to see you awake. When Anton phoned to tell us, I burst into tears. Almost gave your poor father a heart attack."

"Mom, she said I—"

"We have to get you out of this horrible place. Do you know what we have to go through to see you every day? The sole intention of those guards at the gate is to harass visitors. Can you believe they want proof we're visiting a patient in the hospital?"

I knew my mother was nervous, because the flat vowels and harsh *r*'s of her childhood accent had reappeared. She grew up speaking Afrikaans in the small Karoo desert town of Laingsburg, but switched to English when she moved to Johannesburg to become a model at the age of twenty-one. Since then she'd worked hard to erase the Karoo from her speech.

At twilight the Karoo has an eerie sort of beauty, yet motorists traveling from Johannesburg to the coastal city of Cape Town race through it as fast as they can. My mother didn't feel as though she'd *left* the Karoo as much as *escaped* it.

At fifty-three, she's still told that she looks like a Scandinavian princess. Her admirers never see that serene smile slide, those radiant gray-blue eyes spark with irritation. That is a privilege reserved for her family. I've nagged her for years to cut her hair, but she insists on pinning it up, just like royalty. Every spring she follows the latest diet from America, and sometime near the middle of every summer she tries on her wedding dress. If it fits, the family is treated to a special dinner with candles and flowers; if it doesn't, it's like being around a monster. I wish she *had* become a model, but her career was over before it had even begun the day she saw the tall boy—who could have been a movie star if not for his big ears—in the lobby of the movie theater on Pretoria Street, Hillbrow. They were married three months later. Pregnant with Luca, then me, her ankles swelled, her face grew florid, and she sat at home eating ice cream straight out of the carton and big bags of cheese curls that turned her fingers orange. Not even maternity catalogues wanted her.

I once caught sight of her examining herself in the bathroom mirror, sucking in the flabby, stretch-marked folds of her belly. Even though I was just a child, I knew that she blamed us for the end of her dream.

"I had to get a note signed by your doctor for those guards at the gate. You'd think they'd remember us. You are the only—" she lowered her voice "—*white* patient here at the moment." She was trying to be cavalier, but I could see the fear in her eyes.

The newspapers were full of double-page spreads on the hopeless financial situation of South African state hospitals, but there were also small reports—often near the back with the municipal news—of something else, something sinister; hospitals were the scene of frequent crimes. At the Soweto Hospital, surgeons had been mugged while putting on their scrubs in the changing room; a doctor had been carjacked and killed a few blocks from the hospital; a nurse had been raped in a quiet corridor outside the psychiatric lockup ward; hospital property was being pilfered at such a rate patients were asked to bring in their own sheets and blankets; and at least five cars were stolen from the hospital parking lot every week—a whispering campaign claimed the security guards were in on it.

My mother stood up and tried to flatten the creases in her oatmeal linen skirt. I admired her taste in clothing, but she spent too much on it. I was not like my mother at all; my clothes could be made by the pixies at the bottom of the garden for all I cared. She could leave fashion magazines in strategic places around the house; she could drag me along on one shopping expedition after the other—I still refused to spend a month's salary on last season's leftovers from overseas. Overseas! It had such a provincial ring. The land at the end of the yellow brick road was filled with everything chic, tasteful and high quality. My mother didn't think you could buy clothes overseas that fell apart in the first wash, or leather shoes that were as hard as boards, or appliances that broke one day after the warranty expired. That only happened in South Africa.

"…What do *you* think, sweetie?"

I hadn't heard a word she'd said.

"Mom, what does she mean I'll never walk again?"

The color drained from my mother's face. "Who told you that?"

"The nurse."

"I'll have her fired. I'll…" Her gold watch jiggled up and down as she shook her fist.

"Stop it! Is it true?"

"Oh, sweetie, I know you're angry," she said, stroking my arm.

"Is it true?"

"The doctor didn't…umm…he didn't say that, exactly. He said you were lucky because the bullet passed close to your spinal cord but missed it. That's good news." She would not look me straight in the eye.

"So she just sucked the story out of her thumb?"

"Well, yes. I mean, no."

"Please, Mom."

She looked down at her woven leather sandals from Brazil. "They're a bit worried because the movement in your legs is diminishing, not increasing like it's supposed to."

"So what are they going to do?"

She looked up. "More tests, I think."

"You think? You don't *know?*"

"Shh, sweetie. Don't talk." She squeezed my hand. "You'll just get yourself worked up again. Do you want me to wash your face? I brought a cloth."

"Are they going to do more surgery?" I forced myself to speak in a calm, even voice, but what I really wanted was to punch something.

"I don't know. Try not to think about it." She pulled the cloth out of her bag, and all eyes in the room followed her as she glided across the speckled tan-and-black tiles to the single sink next to the window.

I needed a wash, but she was doing it to avoid discussion. I heard the water running. Then she came gliding back, ignoring the patients' inquisitive stares.

As she wiped my lips, eyes, ears and as much of my neck as she could without moving me, I stared stony-faced at the ceiling, my insides churning in a red-hot sea of rage.

All of a sudden, she looked up and seemed to notice for the first time the presence of other people in the ward. Frowning slightly, she snapped the flimsy beige-and-white striped curtains around my bed, then yanked back the covers.

"No, Mom."

"You'll feel better." She patted my knee before leaving to go and rinse out the cloth.

I stared at a snowman-shaped brown stain on the curtains, the fabric so worn it was almost diaphanous.

When she returned she untied my hospital gown and began wiping my legs, stomach, underarms. I thought about my options: thrashing about until I brought the nurse's evil prediction to life and had to spend the rest of my tortured existence sucking food up through a straw and moving around in one of those motorized wheelchairs— if I was lucky enough to still have the use of a knuckle to operate the controls—or screaming until the psychiatrists were called in to administer an elephantine dose of a sedative, or worse, tie me to the bed—although it was painfully clear I wasn't going anywhere soon.

"Next time I'll bring a bowl and some nice-smelling soap. It doesn't look like you're going to get a wash from that lot over there." She rolled her eyes and twitched her head in the direction of the nurses' station.

I felt a potent surge of hatred for the man with the brown wing tips. Given half a chance, I'd point a gun at his temple, rip off those mirror sunglasses, and pull the trigger without a moment's hesitation. More morphine, I thought, sweet oblivion is what I need.

Again there were faces around my bed when I awoke, a sea of them, only this time they were all white, and their attention was not on me but on an elderly man with a pointed gray beard. As he spoke, he pointed at a chart with a clear plastic ruler. I was a teaching opportunity, a cursed guinea pig. I stared at them in muted hatred.

"Ah, good morning, and how are we feeling today?" the graybeard asked.

Who on earth is this *we* you speak of? I wanted to say; instead, I grunted and looked away. It was hot and sticky under the covers, and I wondered why they didn't have air-conditioning in the ward, or at least a fan.

"It's normal to feel anger and resentment," he continued. "It's a symptom of depression."

He spoke with the fake rounded vowels that screamed private English school. I knew his type: the Commonwealth Old Boy fraternity. They used phrases like *all things being equal* and *he's a fine chap,* and their offspring always got into medical and law school with the old nepotistic shoo-in.

I turned my head to the side. It was a lot less painful now. The nurses leaned in the doorway, watching the students and their teacher. They didn't bother to hide their laughter. We had something in common at last: a shared contempt for the graybeard.

Some of the students flashed me uncomfortable smiles. It was not their fault their teacher was a jerk, so I twitched my left cheek to denote a smile in return.

At last the group left and I was pleased to be able to use the newfound movement in my neck to study my neighbors. If there was a torture designed specifically for those who made their living out of observing and asking questions, lying on a bed staring at an uninteresting beige ceiling and fluorescent strip lights was it.

The lady on my left was asleep with an oxygen mask on, a shiny trail of saliva dribbling down her chin. She had tissue-paper skin and tight white curls. To my surprise, the bed on my right was empty. There were seventeen other patients in the ward, some asleep, some chatting, others reading magazines, all of them black. Not one so much as glanced in my direction. I'd never felt so out of place and utterly lonely in my life.

Chapter Six

Monica

With the province of Gauteng in the grips of a heat wave, the ward had become a major thoroughfare—for ants! Nobody did a thing about it, leaving columns of them criss-crossing the walls, floor and ceiling like a living road map. It was barely 10:00 a.m. and already my hair was plastered to my forehead; my sheets were damp with perspiration.

"I'd like to see a doctor," I said, peeling my hospital gown away from my chest and fanning it. The movement of air, slight as it was, felt good on my clammy skin.

The nurse rolled her eyes. "They're busy. I know you want to move to a private *white* hospital—" she spat out the word *white* as though it had a bitter taste "—but you're stuck here with us, you and your glamour-queen mother."

Stressful situations brought out my mother's kittenish side. When she was younger, she'd bat her eyelashes and smile coyly, and people would bow to her every wish. It didn't work as well now that she had crow's-feet and the soft beginnings of a double chin, but she tried anyway and it made me cringe in embarrassment. I told her that she relied too heavily on responses learned growing up in a patriarchal environment, but she said not to worry, I'd outgrow my feminist idealism. The funny thing is, I don't consider myself a feminist.

"I just want someone to explain what's happening to me," I said, hating my defensive tone.

"The doctor will get to you as soon as he can."

Was I being too demanding? Should I shut up and take whatever treatment I got and be grateful for it? It was hard to stay within the lines when I didn't know where they began or ended.

"I'd just like a bit of information, that's all."

"You lot are the worst." She pointed at my breastbone.

"Excuse me?"

"You English South Africans are the worst. Give me a *Boer* any day."

"But I'm—"

"If they hate us, at least we know where we stand. But you so-called liberal, English-speaking South Africans with your smiles and firm handshakes make me sick. Do you think we don't know what hypocrites you are?" Her venom landed on my right cheek in a fine spray of saliva.

"But I'm not—"

"You're not what?"

"I'm not...I mean, I am..."

How could I verbalize something I wasn't sure of myself? Children at our English school had called Luca and me *Dutchmen*, a derogatory term for Afrikaners, yet Afrikaners had never considered us one of them because our father was a foreigner. And then, when I was nine and Luca eleven, my father took us to Italy, and our cousins laughed at our pidgin Italian. With our mother's blond hair and skin that never tanned, we didn't look anything like them, either. I asked my brother once what we were: English, Afrikaans or Italian. He said I was an idiot.

"*Hase Hyatt,*" muttered the nurse as she walked away.

Although I didn't understand her words, I had a feeling I'd just been told that this wasn't a Hyatt. Fortunately for me, at that moment there was a commotion at the door as a new patient was wheeled in, and I was able to brush away my infuriating tears of frustration without anyone noticing.

"Let me out of this," complained the new patient to the porter pushing her wheelchair. "I can walk on my own."

She was a large woman, probably in her midthirties, wearing a magnificent caftan that shimmered as though it had been spun with gold. The old lady next to me raised her head, looked the newcomer over for a couple of seconds, then went straight back to sleep.

"A bit on the hard side," said the newcomer, bouncing on the vacant bed next to me.

I gave a polite smile.

"I may as well begin with you," she said, looking directly into my eyes. "State your name and illness."

"Monica Brunetti," I mumbled, taken aback. "And I was…I was shot."

"Really?" She slid off the bed, gold-beaded braids whipping her face. "I'm sorry for being flippant. Are you going to be okay?"

I felt quite limp in the face of this stranger's concern. "I'm having surgery the day after tomorrow."

"Well, I'll take your mind off it. My name's Ella." She grabbed my hand and squeezed, then stopped suddenly. "Am I hurting you?"

Her appearance suggested she could if she really wanted to. She was tall, about five-ten, with broad shoulders. With her brilliant white smile and voluptuous figure, she looked out of place in a hospital ward filled with bony, ragged bodies.

"No, you're not. What are you in for?"

"Oh, nothing really. I have a bit of bronchitis. It'll go away." She had hazel eyes that twinkled even when she was being serious.

"What do you do?" I asked, in an attempt to prolong the conversation.

"Not much, according to my boss. I'm in PR." She said it just like any Sandton princess might—Pee Aahh.

I tried not to giggle. "I'm a journalist."

"Ah, I take it you like sausage rolls then?"

"I hate them."

"Really?" She took my hand and squeezed it again. "Oh, I really am pleased to meet you, Monica."

I liked the way she said my name, with the *m* sounding like a Buddhist chant and a lilt on the *a* at the end.

"I haven't been in my job long," she continued, "and they're probably wishing they'd never hired me. But hey, what can you do?" She gave a loud, booming laugh. "Now, I'd better get into my jammies. Where's a person supposed to hang their clothes around here?"

Again the man pinned me down in the dry riverbed, but this time I saw him. He was short, slimly built, and so dark that, with the sun behind him, I couldn't make out any of his features. The sound of the approaching water was deafening in my ears. He ground his shoe on my fingers. I felt the bones crack. From their aerial vantage point the birds saw the gap closing and squawked expectantly.

A gentle nudge woke me, and I was grateful for the escape.

"Miss Brunetti, sorry to wake you from your after-lunch siesta." I must have looked dazed, because he asked, "Do you remember me, Dr. Novak, the surgery resident?" When I nodded, he said, "I need to do a neurological check."

He was tall, about six feet, with wavy dark hair, the kind that couldn't be cut into any style because it did as it pleased anyway. He looked about thirty, or maybe a couple of years older. From the way he kept yawning, I guessed he'd been on call all night. I wondered whether

I should suggest bleach for his white coat. Under it he wore a T-shirt with a logo I couldn't read because it was cracked and faded.

"You shouldn't put printed T-shirts in the dryer," I said.

"Huh?"

"Nothing."

He drummed his fingers on the top of the plastic toolbox he'd brought with him. "Are you in pain?"

I grunted.

"Tell me if you are."

I nodded.

He began to manipulate my legs, kneading them like dough. The muscles I'd gained after months of calf raises at the gym had atrophied. As a student I drank gallons of milk a day to gain weight, and I could still pig out on chocolates without too much damage. My mother said it wouldn't last; when I reached thirty it would all change. I had less than a year to find out.

He opened his toolbox, took out something that resembled a thin crochet hook, and pricked my leg with it.

"Did you feel that?"

"Barely."

He continued poking and prodding, but it was no use. I studied his movements, trying to synchronize my reactions to the stab of his needle. There, didn't I feel that? My desperation was making me delusional.

"That was seventeen," I said. "Make it an even number."

He raised his eyebrows.

"Please."

He pricked me again, his expression unchanged.

"Thanks. So what's my prognosis?"

"Well, the bullet did a lot of damage." His face became businesslike. "It tracked all over the place. It nicked your spleen...."

"Yes, yes, yes, and whizzed by my left lung and then deposited itself in my abdomen."

He yawned again. "You know, I have a lot of patients to see before the end of the day."

"Sorry."

"You didn't regain consciousness because you went into hemodynamic shock from losing so much blood. While you were in a coma, we gave you blood and fluids, put in a central line and catheter. Your X ray showed a pneumothorax, a collapsed lung, so we put in a drain. The trauma surgery removed the bullet and repaired your spleen, but we had to put you on a ventilator afterward because you developed pneumonia from a contusion to your left lung. The entrance wound was near the spine, so we did some neurological tests, but we weren't one hundred percent happy with your reactions, and they seem to be deteriorating now."

"Why?"

"I don't know. I want you to have a CT scan."

There were no frightening images anymore, just a shredded hollowness, as though someone had whittled away my mind like an old piece of driftwood.

"Monica, I take it you and Mrs. Dube have introduced yourselves," said Ella, once Dr. Novak had left.

The old lady in the bed on my left smiled at me but did not meet my gaze.

"No…not really," I said, expecting an over-the-top admonition from the larger-than-life Ella.

"Monica Brunetti, Joyce Dube, Mrs. Dube, Monica Brunetti." That was it.

"Pleased to meet you," I said, feeling chastised, even though I hadn't been.

"Hello, Miss Monica," the old lady said, her eyes still lowered.

I noticed Ella frown and cringe at the subservient form of address.

"How are you feeling, Mme?" asked Ella, pronouncing the last word, which I presumed was a respectful way of addressing an older woman, as Mmare.

"A bit better, thank you," said Mrs. Dube, visibly more at ease talking to Ella. "I didn't want to come to the hospital. I've been putting it off for many months. It's such a long way from my home to this part of Soweto. My son said he'd bring me, but he's always so busy. He's a businessman." She gave a warm, crinkled smile and closed her eyes.

Ella and I waited a few seconds, then looked at each other and shrugged. The old lady had fallen asleep on us.

"But then, one night—" Mrs. Dube opened her eyes with a start "—I collapsed when I was staying at my son's house, and my grandson had to run to the shebeen to call an ambulance. The shebeen queen is the only one with a telephone in the neighborhood. Lucky it was working."

She leaned in toward Ella and dropped her voice to a whisper. "I think she just tells people it's not working to stop them queuing up outside her house." She flopped back onto her pillow, breathing hard. "The ambulance men weren't happy to come and fetch me. They only arrived eight hours later, and my grandson had to give them beer for their trouble."

I dabbed at the perspiration on my neck with a tissue and said, "I hope you don't think me rude for asking, but why are you here?"

"TB, Miss Monica. I've had it for years, but never this bad. I'm so old everything's packing up."

I thought of the millions of airborne bacteria I could be inhaling that very moment. Why didn't they have a special ward for TB patients? Surely there was one at the hospital where my mother wanted to take me. I felt sorry for this sweet old lady, but at the same time I was terrified of catching her disease and I resented the hospital for exposing me to it.

"Your family come to visit you a lot, Miss Monica."

"Please, call me Monica." I grabbed another tissue and spread it over the lower part of my face, pretending to blot the perspiration but really fashioning a makeshift surgical mask.

"Okay, Miss Monica." She coughed, a hacking, dry rasp that shook her whole body.

Then there was a long silence. Ella and I watched her eyes widen and her arms stiffen at her sides.

"Nurse," I yelled, "come quick!"

The nurse I'd so endeared myself to earlier raised an eyebrow and lumbered over.

"There's no room service here," she said, eyeing the box of chocolates, dried fruit, nuts and spicy beef *biltong* on my bedside cabinet. "Doesn't look like you need it anyway."

My parents and Anton had brought it all in because I couldn't recognize, let alone eat, the hospital food.

"Mrs. Dube's having some sort of attack," I said.

Reluctantly taking her eyes off my food, she barked at her elderly patient to relax.

"If you hadn't been talking so much, this wouldn't have happened," she said, pressing the oxygen mask over Mrs. Dube's nose and mouth. "I don't need extra work. And you!" She pointed at me. "I suppose you've never seen a case of TB. Your people don't get it, not in your nice spacious houses where everybody has a room to themselves and the air smells like perfume. Your people don't sleep shoulder to shoulder in a dingy little room where the air's heavy with smoke from the cooking fire. Your people never have to walk two miles to collect water." She clicked her tongue and shook her head at me as though I were an intoxicated beggar asking her to spare some change.

The parts of me I could feel were shaking. I wanted to cry. I hadn't done anything to contribute to her people's poverty. What had I done? I was just a child when apartheid was at its peak. What could I have done to change things? Everything was different now anyway.

The country was ruled by *her* people. And I thought we didn't talk about "your" people and "my" people anymore. We're the Rainbow Nation. The whole world watched the election and rejoiced at the example our leaders set, at the way the transition occurred without a vicious civil war. And if she wanted to be picky, it was one of *her* people who'd put me in this hospital.

"And another thing," she continued, still pointing at me. "You think you're—"

"Leave her alone," interrupted Ella. "She was just concerned for Mrs. Dube."

"Well, she shouldn't shout like that for me. I'm not a dog." The nurse walked off, clicking her tongue.

"Ignore her," said Ella, noticing my stricken face. "She probably had a fight with her boyfriend."

"Thanks for sticking up for me."

She flapped her hands, as if to say it was nothing.

For a while we were silent, each watching the rise and fall of Mrs. Dube's bony chest. When it appeared that she was no longer distressed and had fallen asleep, Ella got out of bed and tucked the sheets up under the old lady's chin.

An hour later Mrs. Dube awoke and wanted to know if her son had come. She tried hard to hide her disappointment when Ella told her that he hadn't.

"I expect he's busy with his business," she said, shaking her head as though he were an exasperating teenager. "Did I tell you he owns a minibus taxi?" She tried to shift positions, but the struggle made her cough. "My daughter-in-law is a lazy good-for-nothing. I try to make the pap the way she likes it, but it's always too salty or lumpy or watery for her. All she wants is his money to spend in the shebeen. When my son goes on an overnight trip, he comes to fetch me from where I live with my cousin so I can watch that she doesn't harm their boy.

Those nights she comes home drunk like a man. One day my son's going to give her a sound beating." She said it without emotion, as though it were an inevitable course of events. "Miss Mo—I mean Monica, I know why you're here. I don't know what's happening to our country."

"Well, I was unlucky." I thought it best to keep things light—not that I expected a tirade from sweet Mrs. Dube, but one could never tell.

"People have gone crazy. We didn't have all this crime before, but nowadays you can't walk in the street without looking over your shoulder. People used to be safe in the villages, far away from the city thugs. But not now. Things were better in the old days." She shook her head. "I hear you white people lock yourselves up in prisons."

I thought of the high wall around my parents' home and the panic button my mother carried that would deliver an armed security force within three minutes. These businesses had become a large source of employment for ex-soldiers from the old South African Defense Force and *Umkhonto weSizwe*.

Mrs. Dube pulled herself up on one elbow and motioned for me to come closer. Since I could not peel my head from the pillow, I screwed up my face in an intent way, and it seemed to be enough for her.

"See that woman over there in the bed opposite you?" She pointed at a plump lady of about forty. "Her son's a *tsotsi*. He's in prison, and if Mr. Mandela hadn't taken away the death penalty—" she made a pulling motion at her neck "—he'd be gone."

"What did he do?" I asked.

She dropped her voice even lower. "Murdered another taxi driver. Shot him as he opened his gate to go out in the morning. I'm blessed my son's not involved in the taxi wars."

I knew about the taxi wars, a frightening, confusing battle between rival associations for rights to routes and taxi ranks. Lately, it seemed there was a shooting at a taxi rank every day, and most often the dead were innocent bystanders.

"The Lord saved you for a purpose, Monica," said Mrs. Dube, looking deep into my eyes for the first time since I'd met her. "He told me so in a dream."

Despite the heat, I felt a chill. "Do...do you know what that purpose is, Mrs. Dube?"

"*He* knows. And that's all that matters," she said, nodding emphatically.

I looked to Ella for guidance in what to say next, but she, too, was nodding and there was a knowing smile on her face.

A nurse approached. "You have visitors," she said. "It's the police." She raised the volume on the last word so that all heads turned in our direction.

Hard soles clicked on the tiles. The ward was deathly quiet.

"Are you Miss Brunetti?" The nasal, urgent voice fitted the pasty white face and red mustache perfectly.

"Yes."

I'd never had anything to do with the police, but had been brought up to believe they were there to help. This was not the attitude I sensed in the people around me; theirs was one of hostile suspicion.

"I'm Detective du Preez of the Diepkloof Murder and Robbery Squad. And this is my partner, Detective Sithole." He swung around, but there was nobody behind him.

We heard a high-pitched giggle from the corridor outside. Then a male voice said, "I'm telling you, Sissy, I've seen you before somewhere."

Detective du Preez's pale blue slit eyes narrowed, almost disappearing into his pockmarked skin. "We, I mean I, have a few questions to ask you, Miss Brunetti."

I felt the room leaning closer and wished he'd lower his voice.

"Yes, sir. I suppose that means you haven't had any success in your investigation?"

One of the patients tittered. It was clear that these women had no respect for the dull blue uniform.

He ignored the question. "Did you get a good look at the man, Miss Brunetti?"

"It's taken you long enough to come and see me, hasn't it?"

Somebody stifled a laugh, and I felt an odd sense of camaraderie with my fellow patients.

The detective studied me for a few seconds before answering. "We came here the day of the shooting, but people in comas don't talk."

"Oh."

The ward was silent.

"Can you describe your attacker?"

"He shot me in the back. I was lying facedown on the road."

I heard whispering.

"I understand this is traumatic for you, Miss Brunetti, but if you help us, we may be able to find this man. We think he's responsible for three other carjackings in the area."

"And you've probably had descriptions from all of the victims and still haven't been able to catch him."

The muffled laughs became a roar. I felt elated that the women were enjoying my performance, but, at the same time, guilty for putting one on.

Detective du Preez raised his voice. "You're the only one who's still alive, Miss Brunetti."

Silence.

"He was short—about five-six." I stopped because the detective was about the same height, but he didn't seem to take offense.

"Is that all?"

"No. He had a slim build and shaved head. He was well dressed and wore expensive sunglasses."

"Did he have any distinguishing features? A scar, a limp, fancy jewelry?"

"No, I don't think so, unless you count immaculately polished shoes."

The detective's jaw tightened. "Would you be able to pick him out of a lineup, Miss Brunetti?"

"Sure, if you're able to catch him."

My audience made its appreciation known again. I was grateful my parents weren't around to witness this.

"Thank you for your time, Miss Brunetti," he said. Then he bent over and whispered in my ear, "Take my advice and get yourself transferred before this place makes you crazy."

Chapter Seven

Monica

My father was trying to control himself for my sake. I could see this by the way he held himself—arms rigidly at his sides, fists twitching. Poor Dr. Novak. It wasn't his fault the consultant had kept my father waiting for an hour and a half.

Anybody who upset my father needed to be aware that they weren't dealing with a rational man bound by the niceties of normal life. My father's life had not been normal since that cold July night twelve years ago. People no longer dared tell him it was an unlucky twist of fate that had killed his son, not after he almost throttled the last man with his bare hands. And he'd never joined any of the support groups for those who'd lost sons in the war in Angola, because he said they would kick him out if they heard his thoughts.

Luca was just one of the thousands of white conscripts the South African government sent to the border between Angola and Namibia from the midseventies until the mideighties. With South Africa and the United States supporting the anticommunist UNITA, the National Union for the Total Independence of Angola, against the Russian- and Cuban-backed MPLA, the Marxist Popular Movement for the Liberation of Angola, it was a Cold War incubus.

From Luca's letters it had seemed that his troop wasn't doing much except waiting for orders at their base in the twelve-mile wide demilitarized zone the South African Defense Force had created along a seven-hundred mile stretch of the border. During the long, dusty days, the boys played games, kicked a ball, threw a Frisbee. Stupid as it sounded, that simple disc of orange plastic was the cause of Luca's death. The last thing he did in his nineteen-year-old life was run into the bush to intercept a long throw from his friend Karel.

The grim-faced MP who knocked at our door just after my father had put out the milk bottles for the next morning was only a boy himself. They were trying to recover as many of the bits of Luca's body as they could, he said, but it was slow going because every inch of the area had to be searched for more land mines.

He gave my parents a form letter from the army that expressed gratitude for their son's service to his country. My father scanned through it, then struck a match and held it to the bottom right corner. As the letter caught fire, my mother rushed at him, scratching, kicking and biting, but he simply held it above her head so she couldn't reach. When it had been consumed by the flame, he dropped it and walked out of the room, leaving her with a handful of ashes that her tears soon turned to a grimy stain on the carpet.

Dr. Novak was by no means short, but my father, at six-foot-four, had at least four inches on him. I knew this would make my father less respectful, more cocksure; those four inches meant more to him than the stethoscope around Dr. Novak's neck. As always, my father wore khaki pants and a green golf shirt with a navy Brunetti Tiles badge on the left breast. I noticed a bandage on his left thumb; he was always cutting himself on broken tiles. I had his genes to blame for my own clumsiness, but it was more of a liability in his profession than in mine. His shock of silver hair stood upright with static, as it did after he'd been using power tools.

The Italian in him wanted to wave his arms around in a wild accompaniment to his tirade, but my mother's frown and narrowed eyes kept them at his sides. Apparently he'd scared off most of the concerned family and friends who'd come to their house bearing gifts of cottage pie, lasagna, scones and cheesecake.

"Do you think I should call Dr. Shaw for something to calm your father down?" asked my mother.

In the years after Luca's death, Dr. Shaw had been her main supplier. She still maintained that my father should have gone to him for something to sleep, instead of drinking himself into a wakeful oblivion. I'd come home from school plays, discos and movies to find him sitting in the living room in his pajamas, the South African flag fluttering on the TV screen as the national anthem played to close the night's broadcast. The look on his face would make me afraid to kiss him good-night. Other times he'd be flipping through old photographs, or cradling one of Luca's team trophies in his lap. Sometimes he'd just be sitting. I'd try to hug him, to comfort him, but his stiff body was always unyielding. It was as though he never even saw me. I got up the courage once to ask him what he was thinking, and he said, "I curse that day in 1958 when I arrived at the port of Genoa and all the boats to Australia and the United States were full. Stupid moron me, I should have realized there was a reason the one going to South Africa still had space."

"No, Mom," I said. "I don't think you should give Dr. Shaw a call. He's an idiot."

"But your father's so upset." My mother's voice became reedy when she was trying to get her own way.

"How do you think I feel? I may be a cripple for life."

"Sweetie, don't say such things." She looked as though she might burst into tears.

"It's true. I don't know if I can face it. Yesterday I lay on my bedpan for an hour before the nurse came."

She shot a look in my father's direction. "He's got to tell the doctor we're transferring you to another hospital, with or without his permission."

"That's not my point, Mom. I'd still have to use a bedpan in another hospital. I still wouldn't be able to brush my own teeth."

"Sweetie, you're going to be fine. I know it." She picked up a comb and started working on the tangles in my hair.

I felt like telling her to cut it all off; the weather was far too hot for shoulder-length hair.

"I've brought some of that spray-on dry shampoo. We'll wash your hair, give you a dash of lipstick. You'll feel much better."

"Put on a happy face and everything will be okay. Is that it?"

"Don't pick on me, Monica. If it wasn't for my calmness, this family would have fallen apart long ago." She turned her head away from me and dabbed at her eyes with a tissue.

I held my tongue, but I wanted to say that if we'd faced things head-on together in the past, we would be the strong family she believed we were. Sweep things under the carpet, shelve them, put them in the garden shed, take a sleeping pill—they'll all go away.

My father hadn't wanted Luca to go to the army. He'd wanted him to go to university, where he could avoid conscription for a while, and had even been prepared to send him overseas afterward. My mother had other ideas.

She'd thought it his duty to his country. "Why would the government call up all these boys if they didn't really need them?" she'd wanted to know.

After Luca's death my parents' marriage crumbled, and when they tried to salvage it, the bits just didn't fit together as they used to. It functioned, but it was like a car with a blown head gasket—likely at any moment to shower an unsuspecting passerby with something hot and toxic.

Whenever he had close to half a bottle of scotch in his gut, he'd sneak up on her and whisper, "It'll make a man of him." Then, when she ran off in tears, he'd laugh as though she were a comedienne who'd just fallen flat on her face in the slapstick type of comedy he loved. Just as she'd catalogued the photographs of our childhood, he'd catalogued her words, all the reasons she'd ever given for Luca to go to the army.

Finished snarling at Dr. Novak, my father strode over to my bedside. His hands were now deep in his pockets, as though he no longer felt capable of controlling them.

"Why you have to be seen to by some East European hack, I don't know. I told him that if the consultant wasn't here in fifteen minutes, I'd pick you up myself and take you to a private hospital."

"Dad, he's good. I don't care where he comes from."

"Irritating Czechs. He said that if I wanted to risk causing you more pain, more damage, then I was welcome to do it."

My mother and I exchanged glances; we both knew he was close to cracking point. She nodded as if to say, I told you he needed something to calm him down.

"Apparently this other doctor we're waiting for is some hotshot surgeon," he said.

My father didn't hear the soft footsteps behind him. The doctor folded his arms and grinned broadly, as though he'd come across an amusing street performer.

"If he's such a hotshot," continued my father, oblivious of his audience, "why's he working in this place, huh?"

"Uh, Dad," I said, motioning with my head for him to turn around.

When he saw the doctor, he quickly removed his hands from his pockets and stood to attention. My mother's face was flushed, as though she'd been in a hot bath too long.

"I'm Dr. Wheaton, the neurosurgeon," said the doctor, "and if I'm the hotshot in question, thanks for the compliment, and allow me to tell you exactly why I'm here. I'm *here* because there's nowhere else in the world a surgeon will see the same trauma *and* have such excellent facilities at his disposal."

He was the kind of man my mother called a *vaatjie,* a vat: not more than her height, with a stocky build and barrel chest. As he unfolded his arms, I was sure he flexed his pectoral muscles, one side after the other. His white coat looked new, a dazzling backdrop for his colorful geometric tie that reeked of a younger wife's influence. The effect was impressive, but not more so than his hair, which was cut short around a bright pink bald spot. This showed spirit, a devil-may-care attitude, and I liked him immediately for it. There was nothing worse than a man who plastered silly wispy bits over his bald patch out of sad, stupid vanity.

I noticed my father staring down at the top of Dr. Wheaton's head, mortification forgotten. Other men's hair loss amused him. Thankfully, he had the good sense not to smirk.

"Why do you think there are so many foreigners working here, Mr. Brunetti?" asked the doctor, his pale gray eyes challenging.

"I didn't mean—"

Dr. Wheaton didn't give him time to finish his sentence. "I wouldn't work in any swanky private hospital if you quadrupled my salary. *This,* Mr. Brunetti, is where great surgeons and clinicians are made."

I wanted to laugh at my father's expression. He looked like a schoolboy who'd been caught smoking behind the gym.

"I'm sorry," he said. "I didn't mean to—"

"That's okay, Mr. Brunetti. You're not the first to presume that private means better. My patients believe that wealthy whites get the best doctors at the northern suburb hospitals with their marble floors, private restaurants and gift shops. The truth, is some of the finest doctors in the country are right *here* under this tin roof."

"I'm sure they are."

"Many doctors have left," continued Dr. Wheaton, "and gone overseas, where they can earn over a hundred thousand dollars a year as opposed to their paltry twenty-five here. It makes me angry when the ones who've stayed don't get the respect they deserve."

"Doctor, I *really* wasn't trying to—"

"Some, Mr. Brunetti, stay because they don't want to uproot their families, some stay because they feel they're too old to pass the entrance exams to practice medicine in other countries and some stay because they feel they owe this country something for their education."

"If we have so many good foreign doctors here already, why has the Minister of Health imported Cuban doctors?" My father had decided that attack was the best form of defense.

"To fill the gap that the exodus of South African doctors has created, and because nobody wants to work in rural areas. I'll get down from my soapbox now. I was probably up there too long this time."

"Not at all, Doctor."

I smiled at my father's deadpan face. His restraint was admirable.

"Let's get down to business," said Dr. Wheaton. "We have the results of Monica's CT scan, so we now know the reason for the slow loss of sensation in her lower limbs. She's developed a hematoma—a blood clot—that's pressing on her spine. The larger it gets, the more movement she will lose. I would like to evacuate the hematoma as soon as possible."

"Evacuate?" said my mother.

"Surgery, Mrs. Brunetti."

"Isn't that risky?" asked my father.

"Of course. All surgery is risky."

"What can go wrong?" I needed to know the worst-case scenario.

"Well, this is surgery near a vital structure, the spinal cord, so there is a danger." He was fobbing me off.

"What danger?" I persisted.

"There have been cases where the patient has permanently lost all movement of the lower body."

My mother's eyes bulged. It didn't come much plainer than that.

"But," continued Dr. Wheaton, "I assure you, it's never happened with any of my patients."

"So you think I should have the surgery?"

"Yes."

"And if I don't?"

"Well, theoretically the hematoma could disappear of its own accord. But it's expanding quite rapidly. I wouldn't wait, because it could inflict permanent damage on your spinal cord."

"You mean…" I didn't have the courage to say the words.

"Yes. There's a risk that if it gets large enough, it will paralyze you." His tone was matter-of-fact.

Perhaps I shouldn't have been so eager to learn the specifics. My parents looked at each other.

"You mean she'd be crippled?" asked my mother.

"We don't use that term, but, yes, it could happen," said Dr. Wheaton. "That's why I suggest the surgery." A faint buzz sounded, and he checked his beeper.

"Do you need to get that?" asked my father.

"It's my wife. I'll call her later—not too late though, you know what women are like." His smile was conspiratorial.

My father usually relished any talk of the battle between the sexes, but it was lost on him this time. My mother sat down on the bed with a jolt and covered her face with her hands.

"Can you give us ten minutes or so, Doctor?" asked my father.

"Of course. Are you sure that's all you need?"

"That should do it."

"I'll go on with my rounds, but I'll be back shortly." He replaced the clipboard at the end of my bed before walking away.

My mother uncovered her face and took my hands in hers. "Monica, sweetie, what do you think?"

"I don't see I have a choice."

"More surgery? I don't know. It's so drastic." Her face looked lined. She couldn't be getting enough sleep.

"Your mother's right to be cautious," said my father.

She pulled her hands away from mine. "Really?" she said.

"Why, Dad?"

"Because it's surgery of the *spine*. That's so tricky."

"But he's never messed up yet." I expected my cavalier tone of voice to attract a withering look from my mother, but she was still trying to get over the shock of her husband agreeing with her.

My father shook his head. "There's always a first time."

"What if you both change your mind, but by then it's too late? Imagine how guilty you'll feel."

They looked at each other. Blame was a game they were familiar with.

"Maybe Monica's right, Paolo."

"What? Now you've changed your mind." He threw his hands in the air. "You make me crazy."

"Oh, stop it, Paolo. You always have to be so dramatic."

"Me? Look at you, the Queen of Tragedy collapsing in front of the doctor."

"I didn't collapse. Are you blind as well as stupid? I just—"

"Enough!" I shouted.

My mother put her hands over her ears and shuddered in embarrassment. "There was no need for that, Monica. Everybody's looking at us now."

"I don't care. I've had it with your bickering."

"He started it."

"Mother!"

"Okay, okay, let's come to a decision now. Paolo, are you still against the surgery even though you know it might be your daughter's *only* chance?"

He raised his eyes skyward, as though in silent prayer, and said, "Whatever Monica thinks is best."

"Decision made. I'm having the surgery." I forced a smile to try to dispel the tense atmosphere.

And then we waited. Nobody said a word. My mother paged through a magazine, my father stared out the window and I counted the partitions in the ceiling for want of anything better to do.

It was a full twenty minutes before Dr. Wheaton returned.

"So what's the verdict?" he asked, placing his hand on my father's shoulder. "Have you decided?"

"Yes, Doctor," said my mother when her husband failed to answer because he couldn't take his eyes off the offending hand on his shoulder. "We've talked it over, and Monica's decided that if it means a greater chance of full recovery, she'll have the surgery."

I made a mental note to tease my father later about his look of horror at Dr. Wheaton's close physical proximity.

"Good. That would have been my decision, too. I'll do it the day after tomorrow at 7:00 a.m. It was a pleasure meeting you, Mr. and Mrs. Brunetti. And as for you, Monica, *we* have a date."

Chapter Eight

Monica

The beautiful girl in the bed across from mine had spent an hour applying her makeup and scraping her hair into a chignon, and was now painting her fingernails a bright fuchsia pink. She was about twenty-five and had cheekbones like razor blades, a small, pouting mouth with a pronounced Cupid's bow, and skin the color of English toffee. Her navy paisley nightgown was trimmed with a velvet collar. She looked vaguely familiar.

"I'd have thought that she would go to a private clinic," remarked Ella, noticing that I was staring. "But her parents live somewhere near here—she won't say where—and they wanted her close by."

"Who is she?" I asked.

"Faith Nkosi," said Ella. When it was apparent that the name meant nothing to me, she added, "She's on morning TV."

"Yes! That's right. I don't get much time to watch in the morning, but I've seen her. She's good. I also work for the National Broadcasting Corporation."

I didn't mention I'd been trying to move to the Corporation's television news department for years but had never even been granted an interview because I didn't fit the required affirmative-action profile.

I can still remember the day we all sat around our spanking-new television to watch the country's first news broadcast. I was only seven at the time, but as soon as I saw the lady with blue eyeshadow standing outside Parliament with a microphone in her hand, I knew that was what I wanted to do. Eager to please his little girl, my father painted a wooden tomato box black, cut a hole in it and glued old washing machine dials onto the sides. It was almost better than the real thing. I'd compile bulletins about Brownie meetings, birthday parties and Luca's soccer matches and force my family to watch me read them from behind my TV. Sometimes I'd rope Luca into presenting the weather, but he wasn't an enthusiastic colleague. "Sun, sun and more sun," was the most I ever got out of him.

After university I joined the National Broadcasting Corporation's radio news department as a junior bulletin writer in the hope that it would be a stepping stone to television. I worked my way up to senior bulletin writer and switched to reporting just before the 1994 election. Whenever a job opened up in the television news department I'd apply for it, but Le Roux, my editor and one of the stalwarts of the previous whites-only management, told me to forget about it. "You're too late," he said. "This is the new Corporation, and you don't have enough pigmentation in your skin."

Faith shook her bottle of nail polish and began painting the fingernails of her right hand.

Ella called to her across the room, "He must be special with all the trouble you're taking."

Faith's eyes lit up. "As a matter of fact, he is. He's a member of the government. He knows the president." She searched our faces for a reaction.

"Really? What's his name?" asked Ella.

Faith smirked. "I can't tell you, but you'll recognize him when he arrives."

Visiting hours were almost over and there was no sign of her mystery man. My man's no-show was a mystery— I hoped nothing bad had kept Anton away.

"Faith, I want you to meet Monica," said Ella. "Monica, this is Faith."

"Pleased to meet you," I said, and she nodded in reply.

Mrs. Dube woke up then and asked, "Did my son come while I was sleeping?"

"No, Mme, he didn't," said Ella, "but I'll be sure to wake you if he does."

"He's very busy, but I promise you he'll come. And then I'll introduce him to you both." She closed her eyes again.

"Poor old thing," whispered Ella. "The jerk has probably abandoned her here because he doesn't want the responsibility anymore."

"Do *you* have children?" I asked.

"Yes, two boys." Her face lit up with that look I'd begun to recognize as exclusive to mothers. "My firstborn is eight, my youngest is eighteen months."

"Your husband must have his hands full while you're here."

Her top lip curled into a snarl. "He's a complete waste of time. Since I chucked him out, for reasons I won't bore you with, he hasn't bothered to pick up the phone to call his kids."

It had seemed such an innocent remark. "Sorry. I should mind my own business."

"No, I don't mind telling you and anyone who cares to listen. He's a low-down, lying coward." She looked up abruptly. "Here comes a nurse. I'd better shut up, or we'll get a lecture."

I'd noticed that the night staff were active for only a couple of hours after coming on duty. Then every one of them, except the designated sentinel, would disappear behind the screens they'd pulled around two foam mattresses that were meant for patients when the ward was full.

The main lights went out. Why hadn't Anton arrived? If only he'd sent word that he was okay, that he'd just had a change of plan. There was whispering as the nurse joined her colleagues behind the screens. How did they all fit on the two narrow mattresses? None of them were slim. A faucet dripped somewhere. Now that I was aware of it, I didn't know if I'd be able to sleep. I tried to concentrate on something else, but the only thoughts that came to mind were depressing ones, like how we were all running scared, living our reduced lives looking over our shoulders, not pulling up directly behind the car in front of us at intersections so we had room to maneuver should the need arise, shooting through red lights at night, triple checking the ten locks on our doors and calling the police before we went to bed so the number would be on the redial button.

This is how South Africans live, whether it's downtown in large cities, in leafy suburbs or in sprawling townships. Some have more money to spend on buttressing their fortresses than others, but we all have the same siege mentality. We do not let our children play in the streets or parks, we mobilize ourselves into block watches and vigilante groups and we view outsiders as probable criminals.

I once cut out a newspaper article that contained the statistics: an average of fifty-two people are murdered each day in South Africa, giving the country a per capita murder rate ten times that of the United States. There's a rape every twenty-six seconds, a car stolen almost every nine minutes and an armed robbery every eleven minutes.

But we take it. We live with the tension and fear eating away at our insides. We rage in the privacy of our homes as the politicians on television try to rationalize the spiraling crime rate: It's because of corruption in the police force, inherited from the past government; it's the dehumanizing effect of apartheid; it's the impatience of people still waiting for the overblown promises of the election to be fulfilled; it's the lack of foreign financial help; it's the soaring unemployment; it's the chicken; no, it's the egg.

There was an even chorus of breathing in the darkened ward. Mrs. Dube turned over and coughed, sounding less phlegmy than earlier. Two of the nurses snored, one a high, whining wheeze, the other little staccato grunts.

I felt desperately sorry for myself, but I knew that thirty-three other people were carjacked in Johannesburg the same day I was, and most of them didn't make it to the hospital in time. Slowly, I was beginning to think that Mrs. Dube was correct. God had spared my life for a purpose. But what?

Chapter Nine

Ella

These women in the ward love the jovial, strong Ella, the one who shakes things up with a thigh-slapping joke and a breezy attitude, the one with the loud laugh, the one who has only a touch of bronchitis. I have infected them with my optimism, and now they seek it out, sucking it up as though their survival depends on it, unaware that I am hiding out here because of another contagion.

It's the day before Monica's surgery.

"Are you nervous?" I ask. A stupid question, but I feel she should talk about it instead of lying there looking like a frightened bird.

"Wouldn't you be?" she says, her tone unusually terse. "Have the surgery and you may be in a wheelchair for the rest of your life. Don't have the surgery and you still may be in a wheelchair for the rest of your life."

"At least you have hope." Immediately, I am sorry for sounding so bitter. I must not drop my guard. "I will be praying for you every minute you are in the operating room," I tell her. "I know you're going to be okay. I can feel it in my bones, and Ella's bones are never wrong."

"I'll have the *isangoma* throw some bones for you to see what lies ahead," calls the old woman in the bed next to Faith's. She is a new arrival, an asthmatic who talks nonstop, even when she's short of breath, often to nobody in particular. "I go to the
isangoma for everything," she says. Then she checks to make sure there are no nurses within earshot and lowers her voice until it's barely audible. "Don't tell the doctor, but I went to the *isangoma* three days before I came here. Oh, while she was getting her vision, she had bad troubles—such terrible pains and twitchings I thought she was dying—but she saw it all clearly. My misfortune is heavy, she said. My neighbor has put a spell on me because she is jealous that my daughter is going to university."

"Don't be silly," says Mrs. Dube, who up until now has been a silent observer. "*Izangoma* and *izinyanga* are for fools who want to throw away their money. One of my son's friends went to an *inyanga* for a private matter, you know…." She glances around. "The *inyanga* gave him *muti*—a potion of beetle juice, but he almost died in hospital the next day. You have to trust God, not witch doctors."

My mother had faith like Mrs. Dube's, as deep as the Kimberley Hole, as solid as the diamonds that came out of it. Nothing could shake my mother's faith, not broken bricks on our tin roof, snarling Alsation dogs, a long, hot trip in the back of a delivery truck, nothing. I once had faith like that, but it's been swayed by my illness. How could God allow Themba to do this to me? But then why should I merit special consideration from God when so many in Africa are suffering from this disease?

Monica has a faraway look on her face, and I hope that she is weighing Mrs. Dube's words, letting them sink in. If anybody needs to trust God with her life, it is Monica.

Mrs. Dube fidgets with the plastic name tag on her arm.

"What is it, Mme?" I ask her.

"O bolelang ka seo?" What do you mean?

"I feel you want to tell us something."

Surprise registers in her eyes, and then she gives a nervous smile. "I must be honest and tell you why I'm sick now. I was supposed to go to the clinic twice a week for six months for my TB tablets, but I stopped going after two months."

It's what I expected. TB medication is given out by the clinics twice a week in order to ensure compliance, but the practice often has the opposite effect on poor people who cannot afford the taxi fare.

"Why did you stop going?" asks Monica.

"No transport. My daughter-in-law won't give me any of my pension money."

"Does your son know?" Monica looks incredulous.

"No, I don't want to worry him. His wife told me he's not interested in my problems."

"You're silly to listen to her," I scold her. "I can tell you've been a good mother, and I'm sure your son respects you as you've taught him to."

"You're very wise, Ella, just like my son. You'll meet him soon."

"It's good you're so proud of your son, Mme. I'm proud of mine, too. Do you want to see their pictures?"

Without waiting for an answer, I grab my purse and fish out an envelope of photographs I had taken at a studio last month. Sipho hated the sailor suit I dressed him in and has his head down in all but one of the photographs. In his matching sailor suit, Mandla looks as all babies do in photographs: well-fed and pleased with life.

"My firstborn's not like his father at all. Look at him, so timid and quiet. He has a heart of gold, my Sipho does. But his father—the arrogant so-and-so…"

Mrs. Dube makes clucking noises with her tongue. "You may have picked a bad apple, but he gave you beautiful children," she says, holding a photograph two inches from her nose.

"Mrs. Dube, do you normally wear glasses?" asks Monica.

The old lady's bottom lip begins to tremble. "I got a pair in 1993 when I was still working for the Wilsons in Fairland. Mrs. Wilson took me to the eye doctor and bought me a beautiful pair with a gray frame. For the first time in years, I could see everything perfectly. She was a very good madam, that Mrs. Wilson." Her eyes glaze over and she seems lost in another world. "I just got too old to work anymore. But they were good to me, gave me a pension check. I used it to help my son buy his taxi."

"And the glasses, Mrs. Dube?" persists Monica.

The old lady sniffs. "Two years ago my daughter-in-law stood on them after one of her nights at the shebeen, and they shattered into so many pieces I couldn't put them together again. She told me I was stupid leaving them lying around, but I know I left them on the kitchen table."

"Why don't you get another pair?"

The poor girl does not know how insensitive that sounds.

"It's not that easy, Miss Mo— I mean Monica," stammers Mrs. Dube. "I don't have any money because I give my pension check to my daughter-in-law every month. And she says I don't need glasses because I only have to know my way around my cousin's shack."

"That's cruel," says Monica. "You have to get a pair while you're here. Ask one of the nurses to arrange it."

"Oh, no, I couldn't. They think I'm a whining old woman. I'm afraid to ask them for anything."

"Agh, come on." I flap my hand at her. "They're just overworked and underpaid. It's nothing personal. They'll understand that it's impossible for you to get your glasses anywhere else."

Monica bites her lip, and I feel bad about having made my point at her expense. She's well-intentioned—just ignorant of reality.

"I can't ask them," says Mrs. Dube. "I'm a waste of their time."

"I'll do it," I say.

"Thank you, my child. My son would do it, I'm sure, but with his taxi business…"

The nurses are huddled around a box of fried chicken, and I don't know whether it's their contented state or the polite way I ask, but they promise to sort it out.

"They'll send someone up to see you tomorrow," I tell Mrs. Dube.

Her eyes fill with tears. "God bless you, my child," she says.

"It was nothing, Mme, but I'll take your blessing anyway. The Lord knows I need it."

Monica's boyfriend arrives as soon as visiting hours begin. Since there are no chairs for visitors, he stands shifting from one foot to the other as though in the school principal's office. His tie is loose; his jacket is slung over his left arm. He looks like a boy caught doing something illicit.

"How do you feel?" he asks, not bothering to keep his voice down even though Mrs. Dube is asleep.

Monica gives a brittle laugh. "You know I can't feel anything, Anton."

"You're angry," he says, soothingly. "Who wouldn't be? Just remember whom you're angry with."

"Oh, I remember, Anton. Don't you worry. I can't escape him. He's in my dreams, and when I'm awake I can still see his sweating face and those mirrored sunglasses."

"It's…it's not going to work."

Monica's face freezes. Is the man going to end their relationship now? Here? What a gift for timing.

"It's not?" she asks in a small voice.

"No, this Rainbow Nation stuff is all a hoax."

Her face relaxes.

"It's impossible for us to share this country. My forefathers made it into what it is today—the strongest economy on the African continent—but it's all going to be ruined."

"Shh, Anton." She glances around and I quickly shut my eyes and pretend that I, too, am asleep.

"We'll always be watching our backs," he continues, ignoring her plea, "and scrabbling to keep what we have."

"Keep your voice down."

I'm afraid to peep.

"Think about it. What did your attacker call you?" He does not wait for her answer. "White scum! He didn't care what sort of person you were, just saw the color of your skin and hated you for it. They all do. Do you think that's going to change?"

I chance a peek. Monica has covered her face with her hands.

"Think of the Lost Generation, Monica—all those kids who didn't go to school because they were fighting the Struggle. Do you think they'll ever know any other way except violence? Do you think they'll ever stop hating us?"

Again Monica refuses to answer him.

"Do you?"

"No," she says finally.

"And it's going to get worse, because the economy's never going to improve."

"Anton, please. Not here."

"Nobody's listening, but all right, I'll stop. Did the nurses tell you I phoned yesterday afternoon?"

"No."

He curses. "I wanted you to know I wouldn't be able to come last night because I had an important meeting. I didn't want you to worry. I'll have a word with them now."

"Don't. They'll just tell you this is not the Hyatt or something."

"I wish you'd never been brought here." He purses his lips and puffs out his cheeks before blowing the air out noisily. Sipho does that when he's tackling a particularly tricky math problem. "Monica, there's something I want you to consider. It's important."

"Not now, Anton, please. I can't concentrate on anything but the surgery. If I make it through that, I'll consider anything."

"You promise?"

She ignores the question. "What was the important meeting you had to go to?"

"It's related to what I wanted to discuss with you. But you're right—you have enough on your mind at the moment."

Mrs. Dube stirs, and Monica's voice becomes bright, too bright.

"Ah, Mrs. Dube," she says.

With great effort, the old lady pulls herself up into a sitting position.

"Anton, I'd like you to meet a new friend, Mrs. Dube. Mrs. Dube, this is Anton."

They stare at each other, not saying a word. Finally, Anton leans forward and sticks out his hand. The handshake barely lasts a second before Anton turns away and bends to kiss Monica—twice—on the forehead.

"Think about what I said," he tells her.

He waves from the doorway and disappears down the hall.

"I see problems ahead for that boy," I say.

Monica flushes deep crimson. "I thought you were asleep." Her voice is shaky.

"You're going to break his heart one day." What's the point of letting her know I heard every word?

A nurse approaches, and for once Monica looks pleased. I suspect it's because she knows she'll escape me when the curtain is snapped shut around her. Her guilty conscience could not be plainer if she spelled it out on a sign and hung it around her neck.

"Please give me a few minutes of privacy," I hear her say to the nurse within her curtained-off sanctuary.

"I'm busy," comes the reply.

"Two minutes, that's all."

"Agh." The nurse slips out through a slit in the curtain and gives a theatrical shrug for my benefit.

She will not get a conspiratorial nod in return from me. A full forty minutes passes before the bedpan is removed.

Chapter Ten

Monica

The solemn early morning gathering around my bed reminded me of Luca's funeral. Anton might have understood my fear if I'd shared this observation with him, but I dared not upset my mother and father; their composure was a finely wrought balance of resolve, alcohol and prescription drugs.

The body bag had taken up only a third of the casket, and the funeral director himself had stood guard over it so my father wouldn't look inside, an action more than likely motivated by compassion, but one that he probably regretted later when it almost got him strangled. The police came, but all they did was make my father a pot of coffee and tell him to take it easy. They were young themselves, and the only reason they weren't wearing the chocolate-brown uniform of the South African Defence Force was that they'd chosen the police force's blue one for four years instead.

I couldn't feel even the slightest twinge in my legs. They weren't numb, more like missing, as though my body ended at the waist. What if something went wrong during the surgery? This was how I would be for the rest of my life. I took deep breaths, in, out, in, out, concentrating on this simple function rather than on what lay ahead.

"Last night they had cricket on TV," said my father, "and just before the end of play they had technical difficulties. Now we have to watch the rest of the match on Friday. Can you believe that? I can't watch your Corporation's channels anymore. They're pathetic."

My mother rolled her eyes.

I thought of how much late-night television he'd watched in the past, a bottle of scotch in the crook of one arm, a rugby trophy in the other, the flicker of dated documentaries giving his face a ghostly hue. The mating habits of mountain gorillas, the life cycle of the fruit bat, the strange symbiosis between the tick bird and the white rhino—he'd watched them all with dull, dead eyes. While the jungles and grasslands resonated with the eternal rhythms of a teeming continent, and slick, shiny new life dropped onto the veld on spindly legs, or tapped its way out of freckled shells, or shoved its pink, wet nose out the ground to take its first sniff at the world, my father sat like a living corpse in our lounge.

Across the ward, Faith muttered a string of insults. She'd heard my father's comments about the National Broadcasting Corporation.

"No more about the Corporation," I told him.

"But it's true. I don't know what's happening in this country. I'll have to get satellite. It'll cost me a fortune, but I don't have a choice."

"Paolo, you're disturbing the other patients." As usual, my mother was embarrassed.

"Like you're not with your sniveling."

For once I was pleased with their bickering; it was a distraction. Anyway, I'd given up trying to stop the constant low-grade attrition between them because the effort did nothing except wear me down, too. I closed my eyes.

"You see?" said my mother. "You've upset your daughter. Are you happy now?"

"Me? You're the one upsetting her. Can't you get off my back for one minute? We're sending our daughter off to surgery, for goodness' sake."

"It's okay, honey," whispered Anton. "They just don't know how to deal with this."

They're my parents, I thought, I don't need you to make excuses for them.

At six-thirty the anesthetist gave me a sedative. He smelled of stale cigar smoke and spoke in staccato, unfinished sentences, as though his mouth couldn't keep up with his mind.

When the time came to say our goodbyes, the preop shot had already kicked in, and I was numb to the surging emotion around me. As the porter pushed my gurney toward the door, I was relieved to see my father put an arm around my mother.

Strip lights whizzed by on the ceiling like the center line of a road, and the porter's flirtatious greetings to nurses along the way sounded like the distant cackle of an unattended CB radio. When we finally stopped, I found myself in a white tiled room filled with masked people setting out instruments on trays, adjusting the monitors, tweaking, straightening, scurrying about.

I recognized the anesthetist fiddling with knobs on a machine.

"It's a matter of…what a fool to…I'll show them," he said to nobody in particular.

As I grew sleepy, it seemed that everyone shifted into a lower gear. I felt myself being lifted onto a table under hot lights. Then two pairs of hands turned me over onto my stomach and placed my arms out at my sides on narrow extensions of the bed. With my head resting on something that resembled a padded tennis racket without strings, I stared at the floor, at the white clogs and sneakers moving in slow motion around me. My hospital gown was open at the back. I thought of my dress blowing up as I'd lain facedown on the road, of the hot asphalt beneath my cheek.

Someone crashed through the swing doors and everybody froze.

"Good morning, Miss Brunetti." It was Dr. Wheaton's voice, only it sounded like an answering machine greeting on a stretched tape.

His shoes were conservative black lace-ups, soft and well-worn. I bet the young wife who bought his ties had tried to turf these.

"Nice to see you again," he said. "Come here often?" He whispered in my ear, "Everything's going to be A-one." I felt a prick on my left arm. "I'm the best surgeon there is, but shh—" his voice began to disappear into the blackness "—don't tell them I said that...."

Chapter Eleven

Monica

When I regained consciousness, I was lying on my side in the sanctum of the Intensive Care Unit, the faces of my mother, father and Anton hovering over me as had those of the nurses that first day. Searing flames engulfed my body from the neck down. I groaned, and the vibration only increased the pain.

"Sister, there's something wrong," my mother said. "Hurry! Get the doctor!"

"He's coming, Mrs. Brunetti. But you must remember, she's had major surgery. Merely being awake is an excellent sign."

The nurses in the ICU were different from those on the general wards. Ella would say it was because they were better paid.

The pain was unlike anything I'd ever experienced. Now I understood why wounded soldiers in Vietnam movies begged their comrades to end it all for them.

Dr. Wheaton arrived a few seconds later. "Monica, it went well. And if I might say so myself—" his voice dropped to a whisper "—I was brilliant."

What was the man trying to do? I couldn't smile.

"We're going to give you a lot of morphine. As your body recovers, we'll slowly bring down the dose."

"Dr. Wheaton, are you saying the operation was a success, that she'll recover…umm—" my mother stole a nervous glance at me "—completely?"

"It's too early to say. We'll conduct neurological tests every day to see whether or not her movement is returning."

Whoever said wine is the nectar of the gods was dead wrong—it's morphine. Straightaway, the pain subsided to a dull ache, and then sweet numbness took over, allowing me to slip into a deep, dark nothingness.

I had no idea if it was day or night when I awoke, because there were no windows in the ICU. The machines hummed softly like a distant hive, and every now and then I heard the squeak of rubber soles as a nurse did a quick survey of the blinking screens and silent drips. There was far more space here than in the ward, enough for four or five visitors to fit around each of the twelve beds. And there were chairs, too.

The calm was eerie. I missed the bedlam of the ward and the faces I'd come to know: Mrs. Dube's meek expression that made me feel inexplicably melancholy, Ella's combative grin, Faith's perpetually made-up readiness. I wondered if Mrs. Dube's son or Faith's lover had turned up, or if Ella's children had been brought to see her yet.

Did any of them miss me? Likely not. Nobody missed a novelty toy. For all I knew, at that very moment they were sitting on Ella's bed telling funny Monica stories, laughing about how hysterical Monica had been when she discovered she was the only white patient in the hospital. I could kick myself for not having been more discreet, less emotional. Was fear a justifiable excuse for such behavior? Would they forgive me, or understand me any better if they could see what I saw when I closed my eyes: that blue-black face spitting out the words *white scum?* Maybe. But they'd never understand what I'd just come to realize myself: that my attitude toward black people had not been created by my attack; it had merely been exposed by it.

We pointed fingers at right-wing Afrikaners with their khaki uniforms, naked racism and steaming hatred, but I had no right to claim moral superiority. No wonder that nurse said *Boere* were better because at least she knew where she stood with them. But if I was a racist, why did I want to go back and be with Ella and Mrs. Dube? And was this curious attachment any more, or any less, than I would have felt toward a ward of white women?

Five days later Dr. Wheaton pronounced me fit enough to go back to a general ward.

The nurse sighed loudly when he ordered her to grant my request to return to my old ward. "Doctor, she was in that medical ward because the surgical wards were full. But there's space now."

"If it'll make Miss Brunetti happy, please arrange it." She walked off without another word to him.

"Thank you, Dr. Wheaton. I've made some friends there and they make it more bearable."

Friends? Did I just say friends? How could I be so presumptuous? I was sure that word didn't enter their minds when they thought about me.

Chapter Twelve

Ella

The new patient, a skinny woman with bleached yellow hair, has been shrieking for hours in a voice high enough to shatter glass.

"Tloha mona Moleko!" Get away, Satan, she screams at every nurse or orderly who tries to go near.

Mrs. Dube sleeps through it, but Faith looks about to throw something at the woman. And me? I'm floating high after a visit from my children. Thandeka brought them in a taxi—she said she knew the driver, so he gave them a lift for free. I was so happy I didn't ask any questions. Mandla bounced in on Thandeka's shoulders as though he were a journeyman surveying new land; Sipho refused to meet Mrs. Dube's eyes and stuck to me like a burr to socks. He didn't want to leave when Thandeka said it was time to get their lift back home. The doctors have to discharge me—I'm feeling a whole lot better. More important, though, my family needs me.

The wheels of a gurney rattle outside in the corridor, and there is a crash as the porter misjudges the distance to the doorjamb. He curses loudly, but the patient does not complain. With her mad grin, blond hair fanned out on the pillow behind her and lower body swathed in sheets, she looks like an inebriated mermaid.

"My prayers have been answered," I tell Monica, rushing up to pinch her cheek. "I knew you'd be okay. Didn't I say so?"

"You did. I made it through the surgery, but we won't know if it was successful until these useless sticks on the end of my body start working again." She rubs her cheek.

"I say you'll be up and about in no time. I can feel it in my bones, and you don't want to mess with those, do you?"

"Absolutely not."

The porter pushes past me, a mischievous grin on his face. He rolls the gurney back to Monica's old bed and lifts her as though she weighs no more than a bag of sugar. Thankfully, the new patient stops screaming.

"Sissie, come for a walk," he tells me.

I laugh at him, and, in his hurry to get away, he almost rams me with the gurney.

"You're happy today," says Monica.

"My little ones came to visit this morning."

"Oh, I wanted to see them."

I wanted her to see them, too. "Never mind, there'll be other times."

"I hope so. I'm glad for you, Ella." She offers me a chocolate from an ornate tin. "Take two, four, six or eight."

"Huh?"

"An even number."

"And you *look* so normal."

The new patient starts up again, and Monica groans.

"Psych ward's full," I tell her.

"What about you, Ella? Have they discovered why you keep getting bronchitis?"

I'm glad my mouth is full, because it gives me a few seconds to think. "I'm feeling a lot better. It's not as painful when I breathe anymore. But enough about sickness. I have something for you." I hurry over to my bed and retrieve the brown paper bag Thandeka brought this morning at my request.

"What's this?" asks Monica.

"You're a journalist, right? And a journalist shouldn't be without these things."

She peers into the bag.

"The notebook and pencil are new, but the tape recorder's old," I tell her. "I thought you could use it if your back hurt too much to sit up and write."

She runs her finger down the notebook's metal spiral. "I don't know what to say."

"Agh, you looked so frustrated, lying there with nothing to do, I thought you should start being a journalist again. And writing things down might help you understand your own feelings, too."

"A new take on occupational therapy. This is so kind of you."

"I know your big dream is to be on TV, but you mentioned something about freelancing for magazines."

"Yes, Le Roux allows it because our salaries are so pathetic."

"Well, then? Write some stories about this place, about the people you've met."

She has that same delighted look on her face Mandla gets when I give him chocolate or a bowl of ice cream.

"But don't forget to mention how beautiful and intelligent I am," I tell her.

She grabs my hand. "Thanks. This could be just what I need. I don't deal with things very well."

"Like what?"

"For instance, I know that even if the police catch my attacker, he won't be appropriately punished. Criminals nowadays walk in one door of the prison and straight out another. And if people don't fear the law, chaos is the obvious result."

I sit down on her bed and resort to a bad habit, cracking my knuckles. "The apartheid government left the justice system in a mess. But there are lots of reasons for the increase in crime—one being starvation."

She shakes her head. "Do you really think the guys in the carjacking syndicates are starving?"

"Fine. But what about muggers and burglars? Do you know the unemployment rate in this country—the real figures, not the official ones? In some places it's eighty per cent. Wouldn't you steal from a rich man if your family were starving?"

"But why *shoot* the person?"

"People have become brutal, but apartheid was a brutal system. Treat the man like an animal, but don't be surprised when he turns around and bites you."

She studies my face, searching for something—a hint of humor, maybe. "You don't mean that, do you?" she asks.

"I do."

Her eyes narrow. "Well, whites feel targeted."

"They shouldn't. More blacks are murdered and carjacked. This is not about race. It's about the haves and the have-nots, and you whites have so much—too much in some cases."

"All I had was an old hatchback," she says in a small voice.

I feel a weariness that seems to go right to my bones. "The old Ella would get into a debate with you about democracy being worthless if the wealth of the country remains in the hands of one group, but Ella the exile is worn out."

Something is biting our resident television personality—she almost falls out of bed, such is her hurry to get to the nurses' station. After a brief discussion with the group there, she comes back with one of them in tow.

"What's going on here?" asks the nurse. "You're disrupting the patients. Go back to your bed, Ella."

As she turns her back, I jump off Monica's bed and onto Faith's.

"Didn't you hear her?" says Faith, pulling the blanket up to her chin.

"Yes, but I want to know why you're so upset."

"Because you're going on and on and on."

"So's the new psychiatric patient. What's the real problem here?"

"Fine. I'll tell you. To hear you exiles talk, you'd think you were gods, not people. You'd think that what you went through in Zambia, Botswana, Russia, Cuba, the United States or wherever you were makes you superior to the ones who stayed behind. Don't you think we deserve credit for putting up with all we did here?"

"Faith! It's not a competition to see who suffered the most."

She glares at me. "I'm tired of you exiles and your stories of glory."

"Tell me, Faith, where are your parents from?"

"Mmabatho," she says, eyes downcast.

"Aha. And what did your father do?"

She fingers a hole in the blanket. "He worked for—" she sighs "—for the Bophuthatswana government."

"Your father worked for one of apartheid's puppet states, and I bet you didn't know anything of the Struggle except what you read in the newspapers. And we know in those days reporters weren't allowed to quote the ANC, so what you were reading was biased rubbish. I'm right, aren't I?"

She pulls on the blanket's weave. A thread comes loose and starts a long ladder that obliterates the first *O* in Hospital Property.

"Oh, Faith! I don't resent you. We couldn't all leave. Some of us had to stay, or we'd have made the Nationalist government far too happy."

She raises her head. "You mean you don't think I'm a sellout?"

"No." This is my chance to broach the subject that's been bothering me since I met her. "But I do think you are selling yourself short going out with a married man."

She freezes, then shrugs her shoulders as if to say she doesn't care that I've guessed her secret.

"What do your parents think about it?"

She shakes her head.

"You haven't told them, have you? Why? Because you know it's wrong."

"He's going to divorce his wife," she snaps.

"And that makes it right? Come now, Faith, you know better. A pretty woman like you—there must be tons of other men you could go out with."

Her pout reminds me of Mandla's when I've taken away a glass, fork, stick or other dangerous object toddlers find so enticing. "But he's important."

"Yes, to his wife and children," I say quietly.

This is the first and last time I will mention it. Whether or not she does what is right remains to be seen. It's her choice...but I hope she'll be guided to make the right decision.

Chapter Thirteen

Mrs. Dube: A Domestic Servant Looks Back On Life
by Monica Brunetti

Lying in her hospital bed, as small and frail as a child, Mrs. Dube does not look capable of carrying a bucket of water on her head. But that is exactly what she did every day until she was admitted to the Soweto Hospital for tuberculosis, and what she will do the very day she is discharged. The early morning trip to fetch water, she says, is the one thing about her home she doesn't miss.

The line at the faucet is always long, even before the morning mist has begun to lift off the ground and the dawn is still pale and weak. There is never a blade of grass in sight, just red dirt, packed hard by months of no rain, and rocks that pierce the soles of even the stoutest shoes. Because the water pressure is not very strong, the line moves slowly, like a lazy *rinkhals* snake on a hot summer day. When the buckets are finally filled, the women hoist them onto their heads for the walk back to their shacks. There are no accidents here. Every drop is precious. Mrs. Dube never fills her bucket, or it will be too heavy. If the woman behind her in the line is not too busy talking, she might hand Mrs. Dube her walking stick and help her lift the bucket onto her head. Mrs. Dube is thankful that her home is one of the shacks closest to the faucet, even if it means she's kept awake at night by the chatter of people fetching water to wash the dishes from the evening meal.

Her neighbors have never known the luxury of waking up in the morning and turning on a faucet in the bathroom or the kitchen, not in this mushrooming squatter camp on the southwestern tip of Soweto. Mrs. Dube has, but she does not offer this information for fear of being labeled a braggart. Up until last year she lived with her son and daughter-in-law in a two-bedroom house with a tin roof in the rural town of Zuurbekom, west of Soweto. She rather enjoyed sharing a bedroom with her young grandson, and many a night he would leave his mattress on the floor and climb into bed with her.

But then alcoholism turned her daughter-in-law violent, and her son, Edward, sent her to live with her cousin.

"It's for your own safety," he told her.

It pained Mrs. Dube deeply to be asked to leave her son's home. The years she'd spent raising him had not always been easy. When the children rioted, the government shut down the school where her husband, Elijah, taught, and they had to live on cabbage soup for weeks on end. But even on the worst day, she'd never considered sending her son away to live with someone else.

Now she lives in a shack made of corrugated iron, with a bucket outside for a toilet. Her cousin's son was picked up many years ago by the police for being in a white area without his passbook, and hasn't been seen since. He drinks, too, this cousin—home-brewed beer made from sorghum—but Mrs. Dube has not mentioned this to her son. If he has sent her there, it must be for the best.

Mrs. Dube doesn't know how old she is, but she remembers many strange things happening in her lifetime,
like thousands of South African men going up north in
Africa to fight a European war; the decree by Prime Minister Hendrik Verwoerd in the late fifties that blacks and
whites should be "separate but equal"; the time the mad
Greek stole into the government building in Cape Town
and stabbed Verwoerd; the many prime ministers and
presidents afterward who could not find it in themselves
to undo what Verwoerd had started. She remembers a
young Nelson Mandela being sent to Robben Island for
treason, children throwing stones at policemen, then
being sprayed by water and rubber bullets, sometimes
real ones. She remembers the Bantu Education Department running her husband's school because the government believed white and black children should learn
different things, and bombs killing white people in bars,
churches and town centers, and men jumping out of
windows at the John Vorster Square Police Station when
they could no longer endure their beatings, and the sanc-
tions that upset the white people because their rugby
team was no longer welcome overseas. In the weeks
before the election, when right-wingers planted bombs
and militant blacks talked of "one settler, one bullet," she
wondered whether the great day so many people had
fought and died for would ever come in her lifetime.

But it did, and she awoke at 4:00 a.m. that day to put
on her very best dress, the one she'd worn to her son's
wedding in 1987 and had kept in tissue paper in a box
under her bed ever since. Her son had wanted to take her
to Johannesburg to choose it, but her cough was so bad
at the time that she told him anything he chose would
be perfect, so long as it covered her old-lady arms and
knees.

By 5:00 a.m. the line for the special buses the ANC had

organized went all the way down to the old quarry. The young people sang political songs and *toyi-toyied,* and the old people muttered under their breath because all the foot stomping was raising clouds of red dust and they'd spent the previous evening polishing their shoes. Babies seemed especially well behaved that day. With so much to look at from under the blankets on their mothers' backs, they didn't make a sound.

When the buses arrived, men and women in ANC T-shirts began barking orders at the crowd to start boarding, and the young people swelled past the elderly, eager to get to the polling station as early as possible. A young mother with a baby on her back took Mrs. Dube's elbow and helped her up the steps and onto a seat in front. The seats were soon filled, but the men in ANC T-shirts kept shepherding people onto the bus until the aisles were jammed and condensation began to form on the inside of the grimy windows.

Mrs. Dube wished her son was with her, but business would be good that day, so he planned to vote late in the afternoon. As she'd feared, her daughter-in-law was too hungover to get out of bed.

The bus shivered into motion, sending the crowd in the aisle swaying backward, squealing with laughter. Mrs. Dube helped the young mother take her baby off her back and wrap it up again in the blanket. She prayed that her coughing would not start and scare this nice girl with her fat little baby, but, just in case, she took a clean white handkerchief out of her handbag.

She thought of the time she'd traveled to Soweto with Elijah to see the classrooms the teachers and parents had built with bricks begged from building sites in white areas. Elijah was always the first to help someone in need.

"Joyce," he'd say, "it's the smallest actions that bring the greatest change."

After her son left home to do his mechanic's apprenticeship in Ermelo, she took a job with the Wilson family in the Johannesburg suburb of Fairland. It wasn't easy being separated from Elijah, but the law forbade him to stay with her in the white neighborhood. In any case, though, he'd never have made it to school in time each morning—Soweto was two unreliable bus rides away.

Thursday was maids' day off in Johannesburg. Mrs. Dube would make the family's beds, wash their breakfast dishes, and then she'd be free for the rest of the day. It was too far to go home just for an afternoon, so the neighborhood domestic workers would sit on the grass sidewalk playing cards, chatting about their last visit home and laughing at things their bosses and madams had done. Mrs. Dube would listen and join in the laughter, but she never said a word about the Wilsons. It wasn't their fault they were wealthy and she was a poor woman with no rights, she told Elijah. Besides, hadn't the Lord promised that the meek would inherit the earth?

Some of her friends' families lived hundreds of miles away and they'd only see them for a month at Christmas. The cars and minibus taxis would depart before dawn, roofs piled high with boxes of sweets, biscuits, coffee, new shoes for the children, clothing bought at the white madams' jumble sales. But often their employers would ask them to accompany the family on a beach holiday instead to look after the children. The women with their own children would try and get out of it, but they nearly always had to give in and delay their time off until January, which was useless, because their children were back at school by then. But the unmarried women loved it, because they got to stay in a hotel—even if it was in the black employees' quarters at the back—and they met men from a completely different province. Strangely enough, none of them ever contemplated meeting a man who'd take them away from this life of servitude—that just didn't happen in their world.

Mrs. Dube left the Wilson family when she became too frail to get down on her hands and knees to scrub the kitchen floor. The very unexpected pension check they gave her went toward buying a minibus taxi for her son.

As the bus rumbled through Soweto, Mrs. Dube wondered what her husband would have thought of the day's events if he'd lived to see them. The greatest change of all was about to happen.

Ten years to the day before the election, he was struck and killed by a car as it ran a red light in downtown Johannesburg. The driver didn't stop, and the police never bothered to ask if any of the bystanders had taken down his registration number. Ironically, Elijah had gone into town to deposit money into their burial fund.

The bus groaned to a stop, and the young people pushed their way forward from the back. Mrs. Dube took the hand that the young mother offered and tried not to lean too heavily on it as they made their way down the steps. Before she could thank the girl, they were separated by a crowd surging up the road to join the line that was already almost half a mile long.

After three hours standing in the hot sun, Mrs. Dube watched, horrified, as the doors of the polling station were shut. Word traveled down the line that they'd run out of ballot papers and were waiting for a truck to arrive with more. It was almost an hour before the doors opened again.

At last she got to the front. The official at the door checked her identity book, stamped her hand with invisible ink and told her to proceed to the first box behind the black curtain.

"Move along, Mme," said a man in an ANC T-shirt, and she shuffled as fast as she could into the cubicle and closed the curtain behind her.

There were pencils on the wooden desk, but before

picking one up, she put on the glasses Mrs. Wilson had bought her. Although there'd never been any question in her mind as to which party she'd vote for, she studied the list of logos as a show of respect for the election process. Then, with a slow, careful hand, she made her cross. A whole lifetime of waiting and it was over—just like that. She smiled at her cross. It was a good one, not too spindly. That had worried her, because her hands trembled most of the time now. She'd wanted her cross to be firm so the counting people would have no doubt about it. It was peaceful in the cubicle, and she wished she could look at her cross a while longer, but there were thousands of people still waiting their turn.

Parting the black curtain, she followed the other voters to where they were stuffing their papers into a large box. She folded hers so the official sitting next to the box wouldn't see it.

"Hurry up, Mme," he told her.

The box was already full, and she was afraid to force her ballot in, in case it wrinkled.

"It won't go in," she said.

He grabbed the ballot out of her hand, jammed it into the box, and waved her on.

Out in the sunshine again, she made her way down to the buses and climbed aboard the one in front. For two hours she seemed to be the only person ready to go home. The counting hadn't even begun, but everyone was out there singing and dancing as though they were at the victory celebration.

Four years after the election Mrs. Dube says her cross may have been a good one, but it has let her down. The single faucet near her cousin's house is still the only running water in the squatter camp; their shack made of corrugated iron, wooden planks and stolen bricks has yet to be replaced by a proper house with windows and doors to keep out the cold night wind that gives her a stiff neck;

and, as far as she can tell, the men in the squatter camp still sit around smoking and swearing because there aren't enough jobs to go around.

Chapter Fourteen

Monica

Anton looked as though he'd been up all night studying for an exam; his eyes were bloodshot, his skin even more sallow, with an outbreak of fine red spots on his forehead, and he was not wearing his tie or jacket. My mother, however, in a new navy silk dress with high-heeled sandals to match, had never looked better. For her, shopping was a release valve. There was a fresh bandage stretched across the back of my father's right hand.

Dr. Wheaton stood at the end of my bed, his hands clasped in front of him, his expression unusually grave.

Go with the flow, I told myself, go with the flow. You can always get a second opinion if you don't like his prognosis.

My mother held my hand so tightly it went numb.

"After an exhaustive examination…" Dr. Wheaton stopped to clear his throat.

My scalp prickled with perspiration.

"Excuse me," continued Dr. Wheaton. "The dust seems to be especially bad today. As I was saying, after an exhaustive examination, my conclusion is that the operation went as well as it could have, given the circumstances."

Even though my mother had removed my hospital gown this morning and dressed me in one of my own, much cooler nighties, I suddenly felt hot all over.

"It didn't work then?" asked my father in a small voice.

"I'm not saying that, Mr. Brunetti," said Dr. Wheaton, raising his voice as though my father were hard of hearing. "Technically, the surgery was a success. We've evacuated the hematoma. Monica has a seventy percent chance of regaining all movement in her lower body."

The marvelous statistics again. But they weren't so marvelous. I had a thirty percent chance of never walking again.

My mother let go of my hand. "I don't understand," she said. "After the surgery, you said everything went well."

"It did. But you didn't expect her to walk out of here, did you? She still has a long way to go. You might say that the hardest part is yet to come. We've done all the work in here, and now it's up to her."

"How long do you think it will take?" My mother's tone was impatient, as though she'd just bought a piece of furniture and was being told that she had to assemble it herself.

"Mrs. Brunetti, she'll need months of physical therapy. How many? That's up to Monica."

"So where are the streamers and party hats?" I asked.

My parents exchanged uncomfortable glances.

"You heard the doctor. He said it's up to me. Have you ever known me to give up easily?" It was ridiculous that I had to cheer *them* up.

"No," said my father.

"Well, let's have some enthusiasm then."

I caught a whiff of perfume—the one she used for special occasions—as my mother bent down to hug me. Suddenly, I was a little girl again, sitting on her bed, watching her brush her long blond hair with slow, graceful strokes. I felt a hand on my shoulder.

"Congratulations," said Anton, breaking the spell.

After Dr. Wheaton had left, they told me they'd known all along it was going to be okay. I didn't believe them. Out of the corner of my eye I noticed Ella grinning at us as she filled her water jug at the sink.

"What are you doing?" whispered Anton, as I waved her over. "I'm sure your mother and father don't want anybody else around."

Ella charged up, but there was no room for her to get close, so she stood at the foot of the bed, stroking the blanket over my feet. I watched the movement of her hand, but could not feel it.

"I prayed for you, and God told me you'd be okay," she said.

I believed her.

"Everybody, this is Ella, one of the Games Organizers here at the Soweto Club Med. Her portfolio is nightly entertainment."

My mother tittered, and Anton and my father both made grunting noises that sounded like they had postnasal drips.

"Honestly, Monica," said my mother with a tight little mouth. "Pleased to meet you, Ella." She shook Ella's hand. Ella kept hers extended to shake my father's and Anton's, but they shoved theirs in their pockets and murmured, "Pleased to meet you."

"They don't give us much room for socializing here, do they?" said Ella, as though she hadn't noticed their snub. "See you all again soon." With her braids bobbing up and down on her shoulders, she hopped across the tiles and bounced back into bed.

"She seems a nice type," whispered my mother.

My father pulled off his bandage and examined his cut.

"I don't trust her," said Anton.

He didn't even bother to lower his voice. Who was he to judge Ella when he didn't even know her, hadn't made any attempt to interact with her since I'd arrived here? Where was my sweet Anton, the one I thought I loved? Suddenly it was clear to me—Anton was being difficult and impolite because he felt deeply insecure. Why? Because the Monica who had come into the hospital was not the same one he saw lying here now. I had changed. A sense of relief filled me as I turned the words over in my brain.

No longer were my thoughts those of a confused and frightened little girl. I recognized the life I didn't want—a superficial one like Faith's. Her obsession with hair, makeup and clothes and her dead-end affair made her a rather sad example of how a life lacking a spiritual element was ultimately unsatisfying, even if one did get to be on television. Ella, on the other hand, had an integrity and substance that I wished to find for my own life. Just how was unclear, but I knew now in my heart that God had saved me for a purpose, and I would wait patiently for Him to reveal it to me.

Chapter Fifteen

Monica

All eyes were on Glory, a new patient. I smiled when the others laughed at her story, nodded when they clapped, but I didn't understand any of it. The words were bold, confident, pronounced with shifting pitch and volume. I looked for clues in Glory's body language: the jut of her chin, the widening of her eyes, the way she shook her hand as though she'd just touched something hot—all of it nonverbal punctuation, but none of it helpful. I still didn't get even the gist of the story. I'd never contemplated learning an African language. Rivers empty out in the sea, summer afternoons bring thunderstorms, objects fall downward, black people speak languages we can't understand—it was one of those things I'd accepted without thought. And now Glory's words lapped around me as though I were a lone rock in a swirling current.

Ella looked over at me and winked. My initial fear had been ridiculous; I was safe here.

When I saw Tanya enter the ward, I knew that safety had been an issue for my colleagues, too; instead of

coming to visit en masse, they'd sent a single represen-
tative. Tanya had been with the Corporation for fifteen
years and, although hardworking and loyal, she'd been
overlooked for promotion time and again because of her
interpersonal skills—or lack thereof. We'd never been
particularly close, but then she'd never been close to
anybody; Tanya often mistook honesty for an excuse to
be rude.

"So how's the food?" she asked, jumping onto my bed
without asking whether it would cause me discomfort.

"To be expected." I was purposefully vague, as I didn't
want to be drawn into a cheap offensive against the hospital.

"Wat? Pap en amahewu?" What? Porridge and fer-
mented maize meal? She was using Afrikaans as though
it were a code only she and I shared. But Tanya was not
stupid or naive, just arrogant; she didn't really care if
anyone understood. Her laugh was loud, shiny. "I brought
you—" she dropped her voice to a stage whisper
"—white man's food—*biltong.*"

Faith slammed her magazine down on her bedside
cabinet. "And I suppose dried pieces of raw meat are civ-
ilized?" she snapped.

The smile on Tanya's face froze. "Listen, *poppie,* I
wasn't talking to you."

I wanted to pull the sheets over my head and hide until
Tanya left.

"I don't care," said Faith, swinging her legs over the
side of the bed. "You were insulting and racist."

"Agh, here we go with the racism story again. Just
because I don't like *pap,* it doesn't make me a racist."

"Faith also works at the National Broadcasting
Corporation," I said brightly. "Don't you recognize her?
She's on *Sunrise South Africa.*"

"And how did you get your job, Faith?" asked Tanya.
"Never mind—" she looked Faith up and down "—I can
guess."

Faith slipped off the bed and charged over so that she was face-to-face with Tanya. "What is that supposed to mean?"

"Faith, Tanya," I said. "Don't be silly. We can sort this out."

"Stay out of this, Monica," said Tanya.

"What is that supposed to mean?" shouted Faith, waving her finger in Tanya's face.

"It means I could also get a job if I dressed like a streetwalker and—"

Faith rushed at her with her nails out, but, before she could scratch Tanya's face, Ella stepped between them.

"That's typical of you people!" shouted Tanya. "TV star or not, violence is all you know."

"Faith, Tanya, stop this!" I said.

"What's going on?" asked Ella.

"None of your business," replied Tanya.

The nurses had edged closer, but showed no inclination to put a stop to the confrontation.

"Tanya, please just apologize," I said.

"Apologize? Monica, are you crazy? She attacked me."

"Both of you say you're sorry."

Faith shook her head.

"What on earth's happened to you, Monica?" asked Tanya. "Have they brainwashed you in here?"

I knew exactly what everybody had to be thinking: that we were close, that I was probably just like her.

"It was an insulting thing to say," I told her.

Then, in Afrikaans, Tanya asked, in extremely offensive language, when I'd become so friendly with black people.

There was a sharp inhalation, as though the room itself had taken a breath. She'd used the most villified of words, a forbidden word, an insult aimed at me, but one whose collateral damage was far more extensive.

"What did you say?" asked Ella, folding her arms. She was still sandwiched between the two women.

"You heard me—and what are you going to do about it?" replied Tanya, unintimidated by Ella's physical size and proximity.

"Tanya, say you didn't mean it," I told her. More than her outright racism—which I was used to—it was her blinkered sense of entitlement and superiority that amazed me. Didn't she realize where she was?

"Shut up, Monica," she said. "You've shown your true colors."

"I think you'd better leave," said Ella.

"Oh, is that so?" said Tanya. "Well, I don't take orders from *ousies.*" From maids.

"Tanya," I said. "You're insulting people you don't even know."

"What's to know?" She pointed at Ella. "This one's probably got housemaid's knee from scrubbing other people's floors." She pointed at Faith. "This one's a high-class hooker." She pointed at Mrs. Dube, who hadn't said a word the entire time. "This one probably can't even write her own name."

"Get out," said Ella, "before I pick you up myself and throw you out."

"Aren't you going to try to hit me, too, big mama?"

"You're not worth the energy," said Ella.

Tanya grabbed her bag. "Honestly, Monica, can't you see what's happening? These people are robbing us blind, killing the farmers, taking our jobs, ruining our country. What's the matter with you? Pull yourself together, girl."

She pushed past Ella, then elbowed her way through the group of nurses, who looked disappointed that the show had come to an end. I burst into tears.

"Don't cry, Monica," said Ella, patting my hand. "It's not your fault."

"I never knew it was so ugly close up," I sobbed.

I didn't expect her to understand, but she nodded as though she did.

"She doesn't even know you…and poor Mrs. Dube, what has she ever done to anyone?"

"Shhh," said Ella. "There'll always be people like her. You're not like that."

"How can you be so sure? How do you know I don't just hide it better than she does? You weren't here when I arrived. You didn't see how upset I was that I'd been brought to this hospital. Ella, my attacker called me 'white scum.'"

"Yes? And should I hate all whites because of the indignities I've endured from white policemen? Should I hate all whites because my family had to leave our country of birth on account of our politics? I could be a racist, but I'm not."

I'd heard insults like Tanya's countless times before, but always aimed at groups, never at individuals I knew personally. In that way their poison had seemed diluted, and I'm ashamed to say that I was never outraged.

Growing up in our whites-only, blue-collar neighborhood, the only contact I had with members of the majority of the country's population was when one of them mowed our lawn, washed our dishes or clinked down the milk and juice bottles on our doorstep at sunrise. Of course, that's an exaggeration; there were others, too: the garbagemen in rag bandannas who sent the neighborhood dogs into a frenzy with their whistling, the printer man who delivered the news circulars to our classrooms in a long white doctor's coat, the groundsmen who kept the flower beds at the school free of litter, the cashiers at the grocery store and the teenage boys who pushed my mother's shopping cart out to the car for a fifty-cent tip. Every one of them was known by function, or at the very most, first name.

Then there were the faceless, nameless hordes of black terrorists I learned about when my class went to Veld School in the Eastern Transvaal. These killers were waiting to creep into white households at night to slit the throats of the parents and run off into the bush with the children. We were told how to recognize a terrorist: He was blacker than the night, wore khaki camouflage, and had a look of hatred in his eyes. But he was also weak, and one day the South African Defense Force would crush him like a tin can. After the camp I slept with the light on until my father told me to stop my nonsense, the South African police knew what they were doing and would always keep their people safe.

As a teenager, I read of protest marches, boycotts and a state of emergency that gave the SADF and police unlimited powers. But the reports always said that the authorities had everything under control. I had no idea at that time that everything I read and saw was being screened by the South African censorship machine.

I told my father it was wrong that black people couldn't vote. He said it would change, but just not as quickly as black people wished. Nobody wanted anarchy, which was what would happen if the president woke up one morning and decided to give every black South African the vote that very same day.

My first social contact with black people was at the University of the Witwatersrand, a liberal English university my father was reluctant to let me attend because the student body was politically active and racially mixed. The alternative in Johannesburg was a smaller Afrikaans university, but he'd ruled out Afrikaans schools when Luca and I were growing up.

From the coffee shop across the road I'd watch the crowd of students surge forward, taunting the police to set foot on the university grounds, then scattering when they did just that. I'd watch white policemen beating students with rubber truncheons while their dogs ripped at denim jeans and bare black and white legs.

I sympathized with the protesters' cause but wished there was another way to bring about change, a way without mobs, beatings, bombs and killing. It wasn't difficult to obey my parents and stay away from the protests. I never felt the bravado of so many of my fellow students. I just felt frightened.

It was clear to me now just how sheltered my life had been. The critics who painted apartheid as a massive bungle were wrong; it had been one of the most chillingly effective examples of social engineering in the history of the world, one that had succeeded so thoroughly that, although I'd lived less than an hour's drive away from one of the largest black townships in South Africa, I may as well have been in Scandinavia.

Now, for the first time in my life, I had a sense of the real South Africa. And it was where I wanted to make my home. All I had to do now was find the right road.

Chapter Sixteen

Ella

As much as Mrs. Brunetti irritates me, I have to admit she's good to her daughter. She's threaded a sheepskin under Monica to prevent bedsores, and every day brings her food and gives her a sponge bath behind the curtain. Monica says the dry shampoo makes her scalp itch, but it's a lot more than the rest of us get.

As each day passes without a visit from her beloved son, Mrs. Dube grows more and more subdued. Monica and I try to make conversation with her, but she doesn't respond, and whenever somebody else gets a visitor, she seems to shrink a little more into her shriveled skin. Three times a day a full plate of food is set down next to her, and removed—untouched—two hours later. She hasn't even worn the new glasses the nurses brought her.

Monica believes Mrs. Dube wants to die and has asked a nurse to call a psychiatrist, but so far nobody has come. From what we've seen, they don't have enough time or space for the seriously mentally ill, never mind the merely depressed.

And so we've decided to try an intervention of sorts.

"Mme, how are you feeling?" I ask, nudging the old lady awake.

She stares at us with wide, blank eyes.

"We're worried about you," says Monica. "You don't eat anymore."

"Come on, Mme. You come to a hospital to get better, not worse."

Her eyes fill with tears. "I see it all clearly now. First he sends me to stay with my cousin, now he leaves me here. I'm a burden to him, and he's going to leave me here till I die. Who knows if he'll even give me a decent funeral? That wife of his won't want to spend the money."

"How can you say that about your son, Mme?" I ask.

"Then why hasn't he come?" She begins to sob.

"He could have a good reason for not coming," says Monica.

"Like what?"

"He could be sick, or maybe his taxi was stolen and he doesn't have money for transport."

She stops crying. "Do you think so? I hope nothing horrible has happened to him, but do you think there could be a good reason for him not coming?"

"Of course," says Monica, squeezing her hand. "We'll think of a way to find out. When I first came here, you told me there was a telephone at the shebeen in your son's neighborhood."

Mrs. Dube's face brightens. "I asked my grandson to write the number down on a piece of paper and put it in the inside pocket of my handbag, just in case the doctors wanted to send a message to my son. If you look in the cupboard of my bedside cabinet, you'll find my bag."

I open the cupboard and pull out a neatly folded burgundy dress with a cream lace collar.

"My church dress," says Mrs. Dube.

Right at the back of the cupboard is a fifties-style handbag with worn edges. Mrs. Dube's grandson is an obedient child. In the inside pocket, in a rounded, childish handwriting, is the telephone number.

"Now, Mme, I want you to eat every bit of food the nurses put in front of you. Do you hear me?" I wag my finger at her.

She gives us a feeble smile. "I promise I'll try. Thank you both for caring about me."

Monica turns her head, but not before I see the tears on her cheeks.

Chapter Seventeen

Monica

Stalactite, stalagmite,
Pie, chips and gravy,
Lucky fish, make a wish,
Lead us to the dawn.

Luca's childhood rhyme had been spinning around in my head like a broken record ever since Dr. Wheaton told me I could go home tomorrow.

Things were going right for a change: I was going to learn to walk, even if it took the rest of my life, and my mother had confided in me that she and my father had gone out for dinner together like two normal people. The rhyme was working.

Being the older sibling, it was Luca whom Agnes chose to confide in about her brush with the terrifying *utokoloshe*. After that he considered himself quite the expert on things supernatural.

"It's not God who makes bad things happen in life,"

he lectured me. "It's the *utokoloshe*. He's out to make mischief."

In retrospect, he'd probably simplified and confused the details, but, to me, his wide-eyed young convert, it was delicious relief to a question my Sunday school teacher had never been able to answer. Of course God didn't make mischief. He was too busy delivering babies, making sure everybody was fed and getting the clouds to stick together long enough for it to rain. Mischief was the *utokoloshe's* domain, and he had plenty of time for it. Because he was a very short creature, the only way to protect yourself was to put your bed up on bricks. Not surprisingly, my mother forbade this in her house, so Luca had come up with a rhyme which would keep the *utokoloshe* away if recited over and over as though praying.

Strident voices on a patient's radio hurled insults at each other as the soap opera reached its daily climax. Barely noticing the jolts against my bed as the cleaners swilled dirt around on the floor with their mops, I stared up at the ceiling, hands behind my head, thinking how it felt as though I'd been in this ward forever. It was hard to believe that my flat and the life I knew were a mere twenty miles away.

"So you're out of here tomorrow." Faith had to shout to make herself heard over a radio commercial for detergent.

"Yes. And you?"

"The day after. I got my test results back. It's only anemia. All I have to do is take vitamins and iron tablets."

"If only they'd discovered that sooner."

The doctors had taken so many blood samples Faith's arms looked like those of a junkie, and she'd even suffered the pain of a bone-marrow biopsy.

"Tell me about it," she said. "But I'll be back on TV within a week. When are you going back to work?"

"A few months. It depends."

"Maybe I'll see you around, although you're in the radio building and I'm up at the television center."

Was she gloating or was I being paranoid because her career was moving at a rapid gallop and mine had gone from a slow donkey clip-clop to a dead stop? I pushed the thought aside.

"It must be tough getting up at three or four to be in time for the—"

"Try two-thirty," she interrupted.

It was beginning to sound less like glamour and more like torture.

"But I'm finished by ten-thirty," she said. "Sometimes I hang around to do voice-overs. Sometimes I go to the boutique in Rosebank to choose outfits for the show." She closed her magazine.

"Hey, that's you," I said, pointing at the cover.

Nodding, she hopped out of bed and brought it to me.

"You look fantastic." I flipped to the inside story on her rise to fame.

"Thanks. Tell that to my boyfriend."

"Maybe it's too risky for him to come. He might find a curious radio journalist in the bed opposite yours." It was my guess that he'd moved on to fresher pastures, but I didn't have the courage to say it, not as she lay there in her expensive nightie, face perfectly made up, a new tortoise-shell grip in her hair.

"He could have sent flowers."

It seemed that Ella's words had not had any effect on her.

My mother planted a kiss on my cheek. "Sweetie, I just bumped into Dr. Wheaton in the corridor and he told me the good news." She had another new outfit—a charcoal linen shift dress with a matching short-sleeved jacket—and she was wearing the black pearl necklace my father had bought for her fiftieth birthday.

"I'm so happy you're coming home," she continued, rubbing the lipstick mark off my cheek with her thumb. "Your dad and I had a look at that new medical center near us yesterday. It's like NASA crossed with a resort spa."

I hadn't seen her looking so purposeful, so animated, for years.

She lowered her voice. "I'm glad you're leaving this place. I was just accosted in the corridor by a madman asking me for money. Never mind, tomorrow it'll all be over. I'm sure Anton will be able to take time off work, and your dad will close the business for the day. We'll have your favorite meal, Vienna schnitzel. It'll be like a party."

Suddenly, I became aware of Mrs. Dube listening to us, and I was overcome with guilt. I had a family that had supported me throughout my ordeal, and things like private physical therapists and heated pools were readily at my disposal; she had to go home to her cousin's shack and fetch water outside every morning.

"*Oh no,*" said my mother, slapping her hand over her mouth.

"What?"

"I was supposed to give you a message from Anton. He can't come today because he has something to take care of."

"It's okay. You can tell him he needn't come here again."

"He'll be ecstatic about that. The poor boy has lost about ten pounds over the past few weeks."

"Mom, what's this hush-hush stuff he's involved in?"

As she fanned through the pages of the fashion magazine she'd brought in, I caught a whiff of floral scent from the samples inside.

"I don't know, sweetie. It's none of my business."

She knew. My mother thought everything was her business. There was a time when I would have persisted, but whatever it was could wait until Anton and I had a heart-to-heart. Painful as it was, there was no denying that I was growing away from him, and it would be dishonest, even cruel, for me to pretend otherwise.

Chapter Eighteen

Ella

Plain pap is a staple, something hot to fill an empty belly, but heap steaming-hot tomato *bredie* or lamb stew onto it and it becomes a meal fit for a tribal king. Just as a chef can dress up his creation, so can the bearer of news. The Americans call it *spin;* I call it the *Ella Nkhoma shake and bake.*

"I'm glad Mrs. Dube's asleep," I tell Monica, as I climb onto the end of her bed.

"Oh, no, bad news," she says. "I don't know if I want to hear it."

I tried ten public telephones before finding one with a dial tone in the canteen. The shebeen queen was a *kgarebe,* a real lady. She phoned me back when I ran out of change and didn't mind repeating herself when I couldn't hear her over the lunchtime noise.

"There is some good news, too," I say. "Mrs. Dube's son planned to visit her. The bad news is that he's in jail."

"Oh, no!"

The two nurses at the nurses' station look up from the classifieds section of the newspaper.

"Why?" asks Monica in a softer voice. "Mrs. Dube said he was a straitlaced guy."

"The police picked him up in a roadblock with a loaded gun in his possession three hours after a shoot-out at a taxi rank in Braamfontein. The taxi driver who was shot died before the ambulance arrived, and they're charging Mrs. Dube's son with his murder."

"She told me he wasn't involved in the taxi wars," says Monica.

"How can a mother know what her son does half the time? But he may be innocent—who knows?"

"Do we have to tell her? By the time she's discharged, he may have already been tried and acquitted."

"And all that time she'll be thinking he doesn't want to take care of her anymore."

"But this might put her into an irreversible depression, and then…"

"Monica, you're not a mother. I am. And I know that a mother would rather deal with her son straying from the straight and narrow than with him abandoning her. Believe me, that would be my choice."

"She's been so hopeful lately." Monica chokes on the words.

She's right. Poor old Mrs. Dube has been polishing off her food as though her son's loyalty depends on it.

"The question is not *if,* but *how* we tell…" I cannot finish my sentence because of a sudden, searing pain in my lungs.

"Ella! Are you all right? Do you want me to call a nurse?"

The pain begins to subside. "No, I'm fine."

"You're not. Look at you."

"I'm just getting used to new medication, that's all. I think we'd better…tell Mrs. Dube now."

"Are you sure you're okay?"

I nod.

"Well, if you're sure," she says. "Mrs. Dube, wake up. Mrs. Dube?"

The old lady opens her eyes and wipes a shiny patch of dribble from her chin. "Is it dinnertime? I'm starving."

"Mme, we have news of your son." As the pain returns, I cannot help but wince.

Seeing the expression on my face, Mrs. Dube begins to whimper. I look at Monica pleadingly.

"Mrs. Dube," she says, without hesitation, "your son planned to visit you at the hospital, so you must blot out all those doubts about him deserting you. He's a good son."

Without any instruction from me, Monica is relaying the news exactly as I would—with a good dash of *Ella Nkhoma shake and bake*.

Mrs. Dube lets out a sigh of relief. "I knew it all along. I don't know what got over me, what evil got into my head to make me think such things about him." She gives a little gasp. "He isn't sick, is he? He isn't…?"

"No, Mme," I say, relaxing as the pain disappears again. "He's healthy and safe, thank God. It's just that, well, he's had some trouble with the law."

"Not my son." She shakes her head vigorously.

"It must be a misunderstanding or a case of mistaken identity," says Monica. The girl is a pro. "There'll be a trial, and it'll all be sorted—"

"What are they accusing him of?"

"There was some violence at the taxi rank," explains Monica. "They say he was involved."

That was a mistake. She shouldn't have used the word *violence*.

"Violence?"

I was right—the word is a trigger.

"Not my son, never. I don't believe that. He's never been involved in any violence, not even when the other children were throwing stones at the police during the

Struggle." She slams her fist down on the blanket with surprising force.

"You know your son, Mme," I tell her. "And that's why I'm sure you're right. But he and his family need you now more than ever, and that's why it's important for you to get strong."

She thinks about this for a while. Finally she says, "You're right. I feel bad for behaving like a child when all along my son was going through something so terrible. I hope you two will forgive me."

"There's nothing to forgive, Mrs. Dube," says Monica.

"Bless you, my child. And thank you, both of you, for finding out about my son. If it wasn't for you, I'd rot in this place."

"Stop it, Mme," I say. "I don't want to hear any more of that. I'll give you my number. The three of us will keep in touch, won't we, Monica?

Monica smiles at me as though I've given her a gift tied up with a bright red bow.

Chapter Nineteen

Monica

It was not yet dawn, but I could hear the night shift's sentinel rustling packets, setting out plates for her colleagues' breakfast. I knew by heart what they'd be having: thick slices of fresh white bread, apricot jam, bananas, hot mugs of tea. The sentinel would wake the others up in about ten minutes—they'd sleep through a riot.

My eyeballs felt too big for their sockets. I hadn't slept well with the alkie in the next ward moaning the entire night for another drink. Soon he'd be hallucinating and in full-blown DTs if they didn't hurry up with his medicine. Mrs. Dube was sleeping soundly, but I could hear Ella tossing and turning, smacking her pillows.

It was the day of my release, and I ached to lie down on the familiar comfort of my own bed and drift off into an uninterrupted sleep.

At nine o'clock my parents arrived with a change of clothes for me. My mother was on her haunches in front of my bedside cupboard, packing up my stuff, when I noticed her freeze.

"What's wrong, Mom?"

"Nothing, sweetie." She didn't get up.

"You look strange."

She stood up, holding a bloody rag between two fingers. It was my dress, the one I was wearing when I was shot.

"Throw that away," said my father. His face had taken on the same off-white hue as his most expensive range of marble tiles.

"I can't believe they just threw it into the cupboard and left it there. Why didn't they wash it?" said my mother.

"What for? They should have thrown it away," said my father.

He made a grab for it, but my mother held on, and there was a ripping sound.

"Look what you've done now," she said.

"Stop it!" I told them both. "Throw it away. I don't want to see it."

My mother glared at my father as she dropped the torn dress into the garbage can.

"Mom, I think you'd better put some clothes on me."

She shook her head slowly, not taking her eyes off her husband's face. My father snickered.

"Mom?"

"Okay, Monica," she said, finally turning away, "but I wish you wouldn't order me about like that." She heaved the overnight bag they'd brought with them onto the bed.

"Careful," said my father.

She wagged a finger at him. "And you, too. I don't need you speaking to me like that, either."

I caught my father's eye over her head as she unpacked the bag. "What's wrong with her?" I mouthed.

"The wedding dress," he mouthed back.

Aha…the ritual. So the dress had not fitted.

He pointed at his temple and made a circular motion.

"I know you're talking about me, so stop it," said my mother, holding up a clean set of underwear.

My father's gaze dropped to the floor. "I'll wait for Dr. Wheaton in the corridor."

"Don't come near me while you're in that mood, Mother."

She clicked her tongue. "Don't be ridiculous. Do you think I'd hurt my own daughter?"

Luckily for me, she'd used foresight and brought a short-sleeved shirt with buttons; I don't think I'd have managed anything that would have required me to lift my arms above my head. The skirt was easy to put on, too. It was one of my wraparounds—last summer's fashion. I looked down at my fully clothed body, and Dr. Wheaton's words came to me: "The hardest part is yet to come."

"Tonight I'll give your hair a proper wash," said my mother, brushing it now with long, gentle strokes.

"With water and all?" I asked, and she laughed, the unyielding seams of the wedding dress forgotten.

She placed my makeup bag in front of me and waved a hand.

"Oh, no, Mom." I pulled my most pained expression: cheeks puckered up, eyes narrowed into slits.

"It's your coming-home party. You have to look nice."

"Do you think people won't notice the wheelchair if my face is made up?"

She frowned. "Just do it, sweetie. For me, please."

"Oh, all right."

I picked up the brightest lipstick I could find. Rose Fiesta it was called—a suitably tawdry name. After applying that, I stroked on some blush and mascara, dusted it all off with matte powder, and then gave my mother a smoldering model look. She raised her eyebrows slightly. I could tell she was itching to get me to change the lipstick.

"That's better, sweetie."

I grabbed her hand. "Thanks, Mom. I love you."

She bent down and hugged me.

My father returned with Dr. Wheaton, and we caught the tail end of a discussion on rugby.

"This new coach has to go," said Dr. Wheaton.

"No, no," replied my father, looking grave as he always did when the subject of debate was the national team. "Just give him time."

"It'll be too late then," said Dr. Wheaton. He picked up my chart and scribbled his signature on four or five pages. "So today's the day, huh, Monica?"

"Yes. I can't wait to get home."

"Don't overdo things now. Mrs. Brunetti, I'm relying on you to see that she takes it easy at first."

"She'll do exactly as you say," said my mother, giving him a demure smile.

Dr. Wheaton's beeper buzzed. "Goodbye, Monica." He extended his hand to me. "And good luck."

"Thank you for…well, for everything." My gratitude sounded banal and inadequate.

"Dr. Wheaton," said my father, pulling an envelope from his top pocket. "I have two tickets for the test match against the All Blacks at Ellis Park on Saturday. I'd like you to have them."

Dr. Wheaton's pale gray eyes lit up. "You managed to get tickets? Thank you very much." His beeper buzzed again. "Sorry, but I've really got to go now." And with a wave he was gone.

"Time for us to go, too," said my mother, clapping her hands like a ballet teacher.

"Can you give me a couple of minutes to say my goodbyes?"

"Sure," said my father. "We'll go and settle your account in the meantime."

"I'm off now, Faith," I said, after they'd gone.

She took her nose out of the magazine she was reading, the cover of which promised an earth-shattering lead story on "Where to Meet Men with Money."

"Guess who's taking me home tomorrow," she said.

"Him? Really?" I hoped she had enough cash for a taxi. "Maybe we can get together at work sometime for a coffee."

"Yes, we might bump into each other," she said.

Before I could say another word, she gave me a quick wave and went back to her magazine story.

I turned toward the bed on my left. "I have to say goodbye now, Mrs. Dube."

"Oh, Monica, I'm going to miss you. You've been very good to me." She sounded so forlorn.

"You've been a great neighbor, Mrs. Dube. Do you have any news for me?"

"Yes, the doctor said I can go home on Friday. I'm impatient to leave. I want to talk to my daughter-in-law and see what's happening with my son's trial. I feel so cut off."

"How will you get home?"

"Taxi. I have some money, but I might have to walk the last couple of miles."

From the way she said it, I knew she'd done it many times before. But this time would be different; it would be straight after her discharge from hospital. I pulled some notes from my purse and pushed them into her hand. "This is so you can take the taxi all the way home."

She looked at the money. "You're so kind, my child, but I can't accept it."

"I'll be offended if you don't. You'd do the same for me if the situation was reversed."

She pondered this for a few seconds. "That's true. Thank you."

"I'd like your permission to give you a bit extra so you won't miss any more appointments at the clinic."

"Thank you, but that won't be necessary," she said, shaking her head. "As soon as my son's home, I'm going to have a talk with him about my pension money. I'm sure he doesn't even know that his wife is taking it all."

"But what if…?"

Her eyes flashed. "He's coming home. He didn't do it."

"Of course, Mrs. Dube. Look after yourself now."

"You'll be in my prayers, Monica."

I was touched, because with all her troubles, Mrs. Dube's prayers were going to be jam-packed. I looked across at Ella's bed. It was empty. Was she one of those people who avoided goodbyes?

"So, you're leaving us, are you?" said a voice behind me. It was Ella.

I nodded. "The nurses seem happy."

"Oh, come on," said Ella, but, by the way she laughed, I knew it was the truth.

"The usual greetings like 'It's nice to have met you' or 'Glad to have made your acquaintance' seem absurd now, don't they?" I said.

"Nobody means it anyway." She rolled one of her braids between her forefinger and thumb.

"If I hadn't been shot, I wouldn't have met you."

She nodded. "Yep, a Laundromat or bookstore would have been preferable, but what can you do? I *am* glad to have met you, though, Monica."

I looked around. "My parents will be here any minute. They've got a welcome-home thing planned for me. As long as they don't expect me to get up and do a cartwheel or something, I think I'll manage."

"You're going to be fine. I can feel it in these…."

"Ah, the bones, not to be toyed with."

"You'd better believe it. I don't know when I'll be out of here, but I meant it about staying in touch. Give me your number and I'll call you when I'm home."

"You can come for dinner."

"Agh," she said, flapping her hand as though chasing away a bee. "Your father and boyfriend wouldn't appreciate that. They might even make me eat in the kitchen."

"You're too harsh on them."

"Maybe so, but lunch would be better. I'd rather take my chances with your mother."

I scribbled my number on the corner of a piece of newspaper and tore it off. "Bring your little boys with you."

"Ha! Mandla will destroy your parents' place."

"No, he won't, but if you'll feel more comfortable, bring them over when I'm back in my flat. In a few weeks I'll need my own space again. Mind you, the idea of not having to cook, clean or wash dishes is appealing."

"Yep, once it starts, it never stops." Her face grew serious. "Monica, don't push yourself too hard. It'll all happen in good time."

I loved it that her hazel eyes twinkled even when she was being stern.

"Yes, Ma'am," I said, giving a salute. "I'm trading you for my mother now. From one bossy lady to the other."

"You need bossing around sometimes."

"Before I forget—" I handed her a brown paper bag "—your tape recorder. I can't tell you how much your idea helped me."

Ella put up her hand. "Keep it."

"But you'll need it again—maybe not now, but sometime in the future."

"Mmm. Wouldn't that be nice." There was a faraway look in her eyes.

"What do you mean?"

"Nothing, nothing at all." Her beads tinkled against each other as she shook her head. "Please keep it."

I heard my mother's voice in the corridor.

"Goodbye, Monica." Ella put her arms around me. Her skin smelled like camphor cream. "It's going to be quiet here without you."

"In your dreams, Ella. The psychotics will more than make up for my absence."

I could still hear her booming laugh as my parents wheeled me down the corridor.

Chapter Twenty

Monica

The sun was already high in the sky, rendering everything stark and textureless like an overexposed photograph. A lawn stretched all the way to a high concrete wall that was topped with barbed wire in which old newspapers, chip packets and wrappers fluttered like flags at the Durban July horse race. Clusters of patients lolled about, smoking or sleeping in the short late-morning shadows of three giant oak trees and the overhang provided by the corrugated iron roof of the open corridor. Every four days the nurses shunted the able-bodied patients out of the ward so they could change the bed linen. Today was laundry day.

Despite the dry heat that assaulted us, I found myself getting goose flesh from the breeze on my bare arms. It was the first time I'd been outdoors in five weeks.

On the other side of the wall, voices hummed and a vendor cried, *"Greeen mielieees."* A vehicle, sounding distinctly like a bus, revved its engine, and the smell of diesel fumes drifted over on the breeze.

My parents navigated the forks in the corridor without hesitation, and before long we were in the parking lot alongside the familiar midnight-blue BMW.

I could smell the antacid on my father's breath as he lifted me out of my wheelchair and arranged me on the back seat.

"That's better," he said, straightening my skirt so that it covered my knees.

As he was fastening my seat belt, something knocked against the back of the car.

"Paolo," called my mother. "I can't seem to…"

My father was there in an instant. "Let me do that." He gave her a gentle shove out of the way so that he could fold the wheelchair into the trunk.

I'd waited until he'd had the car for a week before telling him he'd made himself a prime target for a carjacking. How ironic. My Toyota was five years old, with fading paint, and still somebody had wanted it so badly they'd shot me for it.

"Have we got everything?" My mother used her special leaving-on-a-holiday tone of voice.

"Yes. You checked the cupboard and under my bed six times."

My father pulled out of the parking lot and followed a winding route past low-slung, brown-brick buildings to the security check at the main gate. He slowed down, but the guard was lighting a cigarette and waved him through without looking up. Dr. Novak had told me that these guards searched the doctors' cars every night for pilfered drugs. Apparently they'd even handcuffed one after he refused to open his trunk because he was in a hurry.

"I'm so glad we don't have to see this place again," said my mother with a shudder.

Outside the gate, vendors hawked fruit and cigarettes and offered on-the-spot haircuts and braiding in the shade of a pedestrian bridge. Behind the open patch of litter-speckled red dirt, rows of tin shacks started a methodical tangle. I'd heard that there were sections of the township where the houses were nice, some of them even large, but these were cramped little hovels, vulnerable to the elements, smog, other people.

Although the traffic light was green for us, my father stopped and looked up and down the street. Then he trod heavily on the accelerator.

"Do you have to do that?" asked my mother, clutching the dashboard as the car lurched forward.

"I want to get away from this intersection. You never know when some idiot's going to come careening through the red light."

"Are you all right, Monica?" It was a familiar ploy of my mother's to make him feel guilty.

"I'm okay, Mom. Relax."

Nearer the highway, there were fewer houses and denser bush.

"Paolo, where are you going?"

He shrugged. "Home. Where do you think? Sun City?"

"But, Paolo…" She furrowed her brow and screwed her mouth into a tight grimace to show that he should know what she was thinking.

"Come on, what's the matter?" My father had never mastered the mental telepathy required of spouses.

"Do you have to go *this* way now? We'll go right by the place where *it* happened."

My mother loved euphemisms. She thought they made her sound refined, but it was really because she was a coward and couldn't face things head-on.

"Mom, that's all right. I can handle it. Leave him alone."

"I'm sorry, Monica," said my father, "but I don't know any other route home."

"That's fine, Dad."

"You see what you've done?" said my mother. "If you'd just thought ahead, we could have avoided this."

Her stupid obsession with fitting into her wedding dress had obviously ruined their recent cease-fire. Hopefully it was only a temporary flare-up. I watched my father's eyes in the rearview mirror. He'd shut his wife out and was concentrating on driving his beloved machine.

I didn't remember the area well, but I realized we'd reached the spot when my mother swung round and looked at me with soulful eyes.

"Don't look if you don't want to, sweetie."

But I wanted to. The entrance to the highway was busy. Maybe if it had been that day, too, I wouldn't be driving past now, viewing it like a veteran paying his respects at the site of a battle. A young boy with a radio under his arm and a placard around his neck that read Fifty Cents for Bafana Bafana Scores stood on the exact spot where I'd lain, facedown, dress blown up around my waist. The little entrepreneur's pockets were bulging with change.

"Are you okay, Monica?" My father's eyes searched out mine in the rearview mirror.

"It all looks so normal, as though nothing happened here."

I didn't know what I'd expected. In other countries people erected crosses or placed wreaths on the side of the road where their loved one had died. Had I expected a similar monument? I imagined thousands of white crosses dotted alongside South Africa's roads—all carjacking victims.

The traffic began to move down the on-ramp, onto the highway, and then I was being bulleted away from the scene, away from the hospital, away from Soweto, in the direction of my parents' home, of everything that was familiar and comfortable to me.

After twenty minutes we exited the highway and entered the leafy, irrigated calm of my parents' suburb. It was a weekday morning and, except for a couple of gardeners mowing the grass outside their employers' gates, the streets were deserted. The drone of the lawn mowers followed us as we turned into my parents' street. Two more people had put razor wire on top of their walls; another had topped his with broken glass.

"It brings down the tone of the neighborhood, but what can you do?" said my mother.

Most of the houses bore signs announcing the name of their security firm. Mrs. Dube was right—they did look like prisons.

As my parents' white, flat-roofed, Mediterranean-style house came into view, a cerise bougainvillea billowing over the front wall like cotton candy, my mind went back to the weekend we spent drawing designs for our dream home in the back of my school accounting ledger. Luca never saw it finished.

Our previous neighborhood wasn't anything like this one, but none of us had cared—none of us that is, except my mother. She'd hated the way men worked bare-chested on their cars in the street, beer bottles in hand, radios blaring rugby commentary. She'd hated it that children didn't knock on the door asking her to buy raffle tickets to raise funds for a school pool or tennis court, but for money to buy bread and milk because their mother had spent it all on alcohol. She'd hated it that every house was a brown box, designed for function not form. And she'd hated seeing her neighbor's underwear flapping in the wind on the clothesline. Considering my father's humble beginnings in this country, the fact that we had a roof over our heads was an achievement.

My father had arrived from Italy with five hundred Rands in his pocket, not a word of English or Afrikaans on his lips, and a letter offering him a job on an East Rand gold mine. He thought he'd come to the good life, but deep down in the dusty bowels of the earth, his six-foot-four skinny frame doubled over, he longed for the sweet sea air of his hometown. Nobody wanted him. To the

Afrikaners, he was an *uitlander,* an outlander, and to the black miners, he was just another unwelcome white guest in their colonized motherland. Surrounded by strange languages—Afrikaans, Zulu, Xhosa and *Fanagaló,* a fabricated language used by the white shift bosses to communicate with the black workers—he longed to go home, but his mother and brothers needed the money he sent them, and he hadn't yet reached the unofficial five-year milestone a man from the old country had to pass before he could return.

My father not only hung on until then, he learned to speak English and married an Afrikaner, causing great unhappiness to his father-in-law, who was outraged at having an *uitlander* in the family. On the day of my grandfather's funeral, my father got as drunk as a conscript on his first weekend leave.

We were home. My father activated the automatic garage door and parked next to my mother's three-year-old navy Honda Ballade. Shelves laden with tools, jars of nails, insecticides and old newspapers lined the side walls. Bicycles and lawn mowers were parked along the back.

Anton opened the door from the kitchen and bounded up to the car. "It's okay, Mr. Brunetti. I'll carry her," he said.

My father scowled as Anton pulled me from the back seat.

A huge Welcome Home sign hung across the oak display cupboards that housed my mother's best china, and the island hob was crowded with simmering pots. I could smell the Vienna schnitzel frying. My mother had probably woken up early to prepare the veal, leaving Francina in charge of the vegetables because she hated peeling. Ebony, the fluffy Persian-cross my father doted on, lay next to the oak table and chairs in a pillar of sunshine that streamed down from the skylight. She opened one eye to see what all the commotion was about, stretched and went back to sleep.

Francina ran in from the scullery, making wild oohing noises, her arms outstretched. "You're home, you're home. Thank the Lord, you're better." She grabbed both my hands in her soapy ones and squeezed. "I prayed for you every day, and the Lord answered my prayers."

"Thank you, Francina. I needed your prayers."

Her scarf matched her tent dress, which told me she'd made the outfit herself. She said she could make four dresses for the price of one store-bought one, and every weekend you could hear the old sewing machine my mother had given her whirring away until late at night.

"It was an evil man who did this to you," she said.

"Francina, we don't want to talk about that now," interrupted my mother. "Come, Anton, bring her to the living room."

"There's no hurry, Mom. Francina, come and have a cup of tea with us, and I'll tell you all about it."

Francina's jaw fell open. So did my mother's.

Francina's eyes flitted nervously to her employer's face. "I'll bring Madam the tea now."

"Fine," said my mother in a hard voice.

Anton shifted my weight in his arms.

"Anton, put her down in the recliner. I think she's over-tired," said my mother.

I caught a glimpse of Francina over Anton's shoulder. She had a mischievous grin on her face.

My mother had redecorated the living room four years ago in what she called "Santa Fe Chic." She'd never been to New Mexico—had never even set foot in the United States—but she read every American home decorating magazine she could get her hands on. The interior design writer had referred to it as "Southwestern Simplicity," but my mother had worried that this was too vague.

"I don't want people asking me 'southwest of what?'" she'd said.

She'd painted the burnt-yellow walls herself, but my father hadn't allowed her to give them the faux distressed finish she'd wanted. He hadn't left his country, he said, to end up watching soccer in a room that looked like the inside of his mother's barn. There was no persuading him, so she gave up, leaving that creative urge forever unfulfilled. The two sofas were caramel leather three-seaters. She didn't like the traditional Southwestern sofas she'd seen in the magazine. With their straight backs and wooden armrests, they'd reminded her of the hideous *plaas,* or farm, furniture her family had owned when she was growing up in the Karoo. My father's recliner used to be hunter green with gold piping, but it had been reupholstered in leather, a few shades deeper than the sofas.

The base of the coffee table was made of old railway sleepers, and my mother had arranged her collection of antique snuff boxes and imported magazines on its glass top. Under the table was a hand-woven Navajo rug with a geometric design in russet, caramel and the same burnt-yellow of the walls. Although my father had wanted marble floors, my mother had won that particular battle and the floors were terra-cotta tile, in keeping with her Southwestern theme.

Two photographs in pewter frames stood on top of the television cabinet, which was also made of railway sleepers. One was of Luca holding the Victor Ludorum trophy, the other was of me sitting behind a desk in my school uniform.

One day, after a business trip to Phalaborwa, a town near the northern tip of the Kruger National Park, my father brought home a massive soapstone hippopotamus, which he'd bought from a young boy on the side of the road.

"Are you stupid?" my mother asked when he walked in with it under his arm. "I don't want ethnic curios here."

"You have those sandpaintings," he said, pointing at three Navajo works of art on the wall. There was a *yei,* or Navajo spirit, a stylized desert landscape and a bear.

"Yes, but those are American. I don't want this place looking like an African market. Put it in the garage."

He'd taken it to his office instead, where it now sat between a shield from the Johannesburg Chamber of Commerce for the Best Import Company of 1990 and a photo of Luca kicking a drop goal.

All over the living room were vases of my favorite flowers, yellow roses, and bowls of Quality Street chocolates. In honor of the occasion, nobody had touched the purple ones. I unwrapped two and popped them in my mouth.

"Hmm. I should go to hospital more often."

"That's not funny," said my mother, straightening the pile of magazines on the coffee table. "And don't talk with your mouth full."

Anton sat back on the sofa with a smile. It had only been two days since I'd last seen him, but it felt like ages.

"So how are you?" I asked.

"Much happier now," he said, placing his hand on mine in a rare display of affection in front of my parents.

"Where's Francina with that tea?" said my mother, hurrying off to the kitchen.

I lay back on the recliner, shut my eyes and took in the familiar smells of potpourri and furniture polish. I felt stiff, as though I needed a good stretch. Strangely enough, I looked forward to the physical therapy sessions—or as Dr. Wheaton called them, torture sessions. It was time for me to take charge of my body. No nurses, no doctors, just me and the exercise equipment.

My mother entered the room carrying a tray of teacups, and Francina brought up the rear bearing a large chocolate cake, thickly iced and decorated with glazed cherries.

"I'm going to get fat," I told Francina, as she began cutting thick slices.

She handed me a plate. "You need some meat on your bones. If you were a chicken, I wouldn't even bother to cook you."

I looked down at the two Popsicle sticks poking out from under my skirt. All those dawn sessions at the gym had gone to waste.

"Never mind," said my mother. "We'll soon fatten her up. Francina, you forgot a cake fork for me."

Francina looked confused. "But Madam told me to keep all sweet foods away from Madam."

My mother's ears reddened. "Don't be silly. Today I'm celebrating my daughter's return. I'll start my diet tomorrow."

"Where's your tea, Francina?" I asked.

She looked nervously at my mother. "In the kitchen. I'm too busy to sit down and drink tea with you."

A little smile spread across my mother's lips.

After lunch I lay on the recliner and looked through the box of get well cards my mother had put on my lap. Everybody had sent one: relations, friends, colleagues and about fifty strangers who'd heard about my attack on the radio. I passed each one to Anton.

"Did you see the one from my parents?" he asked. He looked tired, and my mother was right—he had lost weight.

"Yes, thank them for me."

The phone rang—again. My mother had told everybody I was coming home, and there wasn't a third cousin or uncle twice removed who hadn't called to find out how I was. There were also the calls from my friends, none of whom had visited me at the hospital. Presumably, they'd been too frightened to drive into Soweto, or maybe they'd assumed that only family were allowed to visit. Whatever their excuse, a quick phone call now was just not good enough. Even if I was the embodiment of their worst nightmares, friends were supposed to care about one another. I was disappointed, but I knew I couldn't be angry; in their position, I might have done the same.

My mother had been instructed to tell everybody that I was too tired for visitors on my first day out of the hospital. It was selfish to be so aloof in the face of such kindness, but I dreaded the concerned looks and the questions about how and where it had happened. I didn't want to see how thankful everybody was that it hadn't happened to them. I didn't want to hear them tell me I should be grateful I'd survived. I knew it. And I was.

"Look at this beautiful one, Anton."

His head had fallen forward, his eyes were closed.

"Anton?"

"Huh? I'm sorry."

"Why don't you go to the spare bedroom? You'll get a stiff neck sleeping like that."

"Okay," he said, and dragged himself off.

A short while later, my father came in. His business was closed for the day, but he still wore his green golf shirt with the Brunetti Tiles logo.

"Has Anton gone?" he asked.

"No, he's sleeping in the guest bedroom. Dad, what's the latest from the police?"

He hesitated, as though he couldn't make up his mind whether to sit down or walk out. Eventually he sat down on the sofa opposite me.

"They've found your car."

"Where? I thought it would be across the border by now."

"It's at the Krugersdorp Police Station. It's being used as evidence."

"You mean they caught the guy who shot me?"

"No. This is another case. It was used in an armed robbery of a late-night supermarket. There was a gunfight. The police just happened to be driving past, but by then the supermarket owner and one of the two robbers were already dead."

"How do they know it wasn't him?" My face felt flushed, my palms sweaty.

"He and his buddy were both in prison when you were attacked."

"Are they doing anything at all to catch him?"

"Yes, but these things take time. Or that's what they keep telling me. They think he's responsible for at least three other carjackings in the area."

"So I heard. It takes more than one to make them interested."

He made a fist with his right hand and watched the bandage tauten across his knuckles. "I didn't want to tell you." He looked up. "But you're so difficult to put off." His forehead was creased with concern—or were those wrinkles? When did he get so old?

"I'm glad you told me." I put my hands on my cheeks. They were still hot. "It seems so unreal. Like a movie. First me, then that shopkeeper. I don't know why, but I feel as though I'm connected to that poor dead man in some way. It's all around me—violence, crime, murder. In the past, it was something I read about in the newspapers. Then it was something that happened to a friend of a friend. Now it's happened to me. Dad, I could have died, too."

I squeezed my eyes shut, but the tears spilled over. In the hospital, I hadn't cried at all over my attack. Now, I couldn't stop.

"Shh," said my father, rubbing my hand in a circular motion.

Seeing the helpless expression on his face, I sobbed even louder.

My mother, who'd been in the kitchen washing the tomatoes she'd picked in her vegetable garden, stormed into the living room.

"What did you say to her, Paolo?"

"I just told her about the car." He stopped rubbing my hand.

She sat on the armrest of the recliner and put her arms around me. "Your father shouldn't have told you that story, sweetie. Don't think about it. Come now, don't cry."

"I'm glad he told me, Mom. Don't blame him. I just feel so…I don't know. That man died. I could have died, too."

"I know, sweetie, but you didn't. So why think about what could have happened?"

I couldn't help myself. It was as though all the red-hot anger licking away at my insides had suddenly condensed, filling me with enough tears to cry for days. My mother began to rock me like an infant, and my father stood watching us and fingering his bandage. And I, feeling as if I had been given permission to let loose the floodgate, sobbed until all the tears were spent.

Chapter Twenty-One

Ella

Yes, my son is older than his years, but does he deserve to be burdened with knowledge that I, an adult, am not able to deal with? Am I failing him by keeping the details of my disease from him? Am I betraying him by not telling him that I won't be around to see him through primary school? Nobody has told me how long it will be, but without antiretroviral drugs there will be no surprises.

People in the West take antiretrovirals soon after the disease is detected, but we have other priorities here on the bitter tip of the African continent. Our concerns are more rudimentary: running water, electricity, food. It's a joke really, because, by the time they sort that all out, there aren't going to be many people left to use the running water.

The irony has not escaped me that I wouldn't have met Themba if I'd not left South Africa. Granted, I'd have a second-class high school education and no advanced degrees, but I wouldn't have this cursed virus rousing up a slow, bubbling mutiny in my body. Perhaps that's not logical; whoever I married might have done the same thing—it seems my life is destined to be a series of trials. Look at the evidence: First my mother dies before making it home to South Africa, then my father, who does make it home, slowly becomes a child again, and now I am about to leave my children without a home. Is God testing me? Or has He abandoned me altogether? My mother said that all we needed was faith, but I'm starting to have my doubts.

The doctors aren't sending me into battle totally unarmed; I have been discharged with a two-week supply of antibiotics to fight my broncho-pneumonia. As I exit the hospital gates to wait for my bus under the shadow of the footbridge, I feel like those brave Zulus who took on the gunpowder of the British with *assegais,* slender spears. The comparison gives me strength, for we still celebrate the whipping those *Brits* suffered.

Even though there are open seats all over the bus, a mother with a baby stuck to her breast comes to sit next to me. Here's something for my list of things to be grateful for: I don't have any of those hideous Kaposi's sarcomas, which give it away as surely as the weeping sores of a leper.

By the time the second bus comes to a pneumatic halt a block away from my flat, I have to shout at the bus driver to give me extra time to get off. All my energy has gone. It's after two—Sipho should be home from school. And there he is, number one on my list of things for which I'm grateful, sitting on the low perimeter wall of our building reading a book. He hears me dragging my feet and drops the book to come running.

"Mommy, you're back," he cries, throwing his arms around my waist.

"What are you doing outside?"

"Thandeka said I could wait for you."

I will have to speak to her; he should never be allowed outside alone. Thandeka cannot live her life like an ostrich with its head in the sand.

"I was waiting to help you up the stairs, Mommy," he says, taking my arm.

I try not to lean on him too heavily as we go up. How is it that something so pure came out of a marriage as destructive as mine and Themba's? Was Themba ever the sunrise, sunset, noon and midnight of his mother's existence? I wonder what he was like at eight years old. Did *he* ever bring his mother water at night, as Sipho now does for me? Did *he* ever feel his way to the bathroom in the dark so that he wouldn't wake her? Nothing he did for me could ever be considered sweet or touching, yet I have nobody but myself to blame—I, too, was once impressed by that olive-green uniform, that fire in those remarkable eyes.

"I have one for you," says Sipho.

"Good. A chance for me to catch up."

"I'm gray and fat and I love being in the river."

Before I can take a shot at it, he gives me another clue. "At night I walk very far to find food."

"You're a hippo!"

"You got it, Mommy," he says, clapping his hands.

I have a feeling I've just been given a sympathy point.

Although Thandeka tries to keep from showing it, she is overjoyed I'm back. So is Mandla; there are tears on his cheeks, but as soon as he sees me, his whole face lights up, whatever it was that was upsetting him forgotten.

"Tlo ho nna thope." Come to me, baby.

"English, Mommy," says Sipho. "Or he won't know what they're talking about when he goes to school."

"Can I go now?" asks Thandeka.

"Of course," I tell her, "and thank you very much." I hand her an envelope with her pay.

She takes the money out and counts it aloud. Sipho looks at her with solemn eyes.

"Twenty short," she says. She motions with her thumb in Sipho's direction. "You said I'd get an extra twenty for walking him to school."

He looks at me to see what I will do next.

"Of course, I forgot. Here, have forty."

She takes the money without a smile. "Thanks. Will you need me tomorrow?"

I sigh. "Unfortunately, yes."

Sipho looks alarmed.

"I have to go back to work."

"Okay, see you tomorrow." She closes the door behind her, and Sipho hurries over to lock the security gate and slide across the dead bolts.

Oh, my sweet little boy. What is to become of you and Mandla? How can I leave you both when you are so young? I will not live to see you lose all your baby teeth. Who will put one-rand coins in your slipper on those nights? Who will teach Mandla the songs I taught you? There is so much I will miss, so many birthdays, Christmases, graduations—milestones and every days. So many firsts, so many lasts, so many in-betweens. Ah, my sons, it is those in-betweens that make up life, and like fools we let them slip away, we wish them away, we lose them in the bustle of this world. And when we are facing the end, as I am, we wish that we could have them back, but then it is too late.

Dear God, I pray, *help me be strong for my boys so that they have nothing but happy .nemories of their mother's final days.*

I sit down on the sofa with a pen and writing pad. The last time I heard from my cousin was when my mother died. Seven years is a long time, but she is my only family, and I would not hesitate if she asked the same of me.

Chapter Twenty-Two

Monica

With her tanned, sculpted muscles, short hair slicked back with gel, and no-nonsense air, Laura was my own personal drill instructor. She didn't pity me, nor did she want to know any of the gory details of my attack. She was interested in one thing only: seeing me walk from one end of the rehabilitation center to the other. I liked her the minute I met her.

She'd increased my twice-weekly sessions to daily ones, and, each morning at nine, Francina would help load me into the car for the three-mile trip and Laura would off-load me on the other side.

The rehab center was a fake Art Deco building in pastel-blue with yellow trim. Sago palms filled the white marble lobby, and from behind her spaceship console the elegant receptionist looked as though she were navigating a tropical universe. There were two floors of exercise equipment, most of it computerized, and glass cubicles that served as offices for the physical therapists. Black wooden gangways crisscrossed the charcoal-colored carpet, giving wheelchairs access to the exercise stations. Each basin in the white marble bathroom was surrounded by a collection of imported bath soaps, creams and perfumes, and the four saunas, five steam baths and six massage rooms were clinically clean. I wanted to move in.

Most mornings I had the center to myself, but sometimes I shared it with an elderly man who was learning to walk again after a stroke. Once I saw a little boy being taught how to use his new artificial leg. Laura said he'd been knocked down by a car. For almost an hour he did nothing but fall over, but each time he brushed away his frantic mother and pulled himself up again with the parallel bars. Watching his freckled, eager face, I'd wanted to cry.

"Okay, we're going to try something here," said Laura, lifting me out of my wheelchair. "Grab hold of the parallel bars."

I propped myself up between them, with my legs dangling beneath me like a marionette's.

"Straighten your legs and plant your feet firmly on the ground."

Slowly, I did as she commanded.

"That's it. See how easy it is. You're standing."

I was. I was really standing, even if I was holding all of my weight up with my arms. My mother applauded. After a few minutes my arms started to shake, and Laura plucked me down like a cat from a tree.

"I'm so weak," I said, massaging my triceps.

"What did you expect?" she asked.

I stop at a red light. There's nobody around. I should shoot through, but my foot won't move. I can't press down on the accelerator. There are footsteps around me, lots of them. Suddenly, my car begins to rock. There are no faces in the dark night, just hands, hundreds of them, rocking

my car as if they want to turn it over. Then they start
pounding on it with their fists. The windshield shatters,
and the hands reach for me....

I woke up, still rocking, and looked at the clock radio:
1:00 a.m. This happened every night. I went to bed at
around eleven and woke up at one or two, damp with
sweat, sheets rumpled.

The house was still. I could hear the wind rustling
the yesterday, today and tomorrow shrub outside my
window. If my window were open, I'd get a whiff of
the shrub's heavy night perfume, but I'd rather suffo-
cate in the heat than worry about someone putting their
hand through the burglar bars to touch my face as I
slept. I heard a gurgle and then a loud sucking sound:
the automatic pool cleaner riding too high up the side.
I listened to the noises, trying to sort out the familiar
from the unfamiliar. A car drove past and slowed down.
It stopped. My body felt hot all over again. If I shouted
for my father, would he have enough time to get his gun
from the safe? Would the intruders be able to disarm
our alarm? The car moved off again and stopped at
another house a few doors down. It was probably a
security company patrol.

I needed to go to the bathroom. My mother had told
me to call her, but I didn't want to wake them in the
middle of the night. I could probably swing myself into
the wheelchair, but then I'd need help once I got to the
bathroom. It was humiliating enough that my mother had
to take me there during the day, but calling for her during
the night was even worse. I tried thinking of something
else. Ella hadn't phoned yet. I suppose kids kept one
busy, especially with no husband to help.

I drifted back into a shallow sleep, but at six o'clock,
when I heard my mother getting up to collect the newspaper on the driveway, I thanked God she was an early
riser.

* * *

For a while I didn't have to think about facing the world again. The days rolled into each other and, little by little, I became stronger.

I took time to talk to Francina, to ask questions I'd never even thought of before. This was the woman who'd made my bed, washed my lingerie, scrubbed the ring around my bath for years, yet I didn't know the names of her parents, the whereabouts of her husband, why she didn't have any children of her own. I didn't even know whether she liked white bread or brown, tea or coffee, local or American music. She'd always just been there. Good-old Francina—as strong as a tractor, only more dependable.

When I was eleven years old I saw my father handing her a pay packet one Friday afternoon, and I sulked for ages. I'd been under the impression she was with us because she loved us.

Chapter Twenty-Three

Francina: Far From The Valley Of A Thousand Hills
by Monica Brunetti

Those meeting Francina Zuma for the first time know there is something different about her face, but cannot say what. With her high cheekbones, aquiline nose and flawless complexion, she has the kind of face one could call elegant, even aristocratic, but there is something unnerving about the way her left eye stares without blinking. Only her family and the people of her village know that her husband once beat her so badly the doctors had to remove her left eye and replace it with a glass one.

She wears homemade dresses with high necklines and no waist, men's lace-up shoes, and a scarf wrapped around her head. There is not a formal dress or pair of high heels in her closet, and she never uses makeup. Never again, she says, will she allow a man to get close to her, and if she looks nice, they'll only be tempted to try. On Sundays she goes out in her red-and-black church uniform, but always with her head covered and lace-up shoes on her feet. Men cannot be trusted, she says, even in the house of God.

Growing up in Jabulani, a small rural village in the Valley of a Thousand Hills, KwaZulu-Natal, Francina attracted the attention of Winston, the oldest son of the local tribal chief, and when she was sixteen, he paid her father a handsome *lebola* of twelve cows for her hand in marriage. After the festivities he went to Johannesburg to work on a gold mine and moved into a compound with hundreds of other mine workers. Barely literate with only four years of education, Francina followed him to *Egoli*, the city of gold, and got the only job she could, as a domestic servant in a white family's house.

Having grown up with three brothers, she was unfazed by a naughty eleven-year-old boy and a moody nine-year-old girl. She even hoped more babies would come, but they never did. She washed and mended the family's clothes, cooked their meat, potato and three-vegetable meals, coaxed spoonfuls of medicine into stubborn mouths, disinfected grazed knees, smoothed fevered brows, picked up toys and books, vacuumed, made beds and washed the dishes, all the while dreaming of the day she'd do the same for her own children.

Winston visited her regularly in her small room at the back of the house. With his passbook in his back pocket he was permitted to be in the white neighborhood during the day, but staying overnight was prohibited by law because he was not an employee of the family. The plan was that Francina would go back to the village to live with his parents as soon as she got pregnant, and he'd continue working on the mine for a few years before returning to take over as chief from his father.

After taking the gardener his lunch one day, Francina was walking back to the kitchen when Winston appeared out of nowhere and grabbed her by the braids. He usually only drank on weekends, but he'd won a hundred Rand on Farfi, the numbers game, and had spent it on beers for his friends. She was flirting with the gardener, he said, and deserved what she was about to get.

The African ambulance took her to the nearest black hospital—more than twenty miles away—but there was nothing the doctors could do to save her eye.

Francina sent word of what had happened to her parents, and a cousin returned ten days later with a message from her father that she was not to bring shame on the family by showing her face in the village. Winston was back home and had told everyone that she was sleeping around. Her cousin almost forgot to hand her the small parcel from her mother. Inside was a beaded necklace patterned with tiny black shields. Her cousin said her mother must be going senile, but Francina knew the shields symbolized protection from attack, and this was the only way her mother could secretly convey her heartfelt hope that, alone in a far-off city, her daughter would be safe.

Five years later, when Francina braved a visit back home, her father was not able to reject her in the flesh. She understood that he wouldn't confront Winston, who by then was the new chief of the village, but it was enough for her to know that he believed her side of the story.

At times she wishes she could move back to Kwa-Zulu-Natal, where her people, the Zulus, live. But it has become a place where women and children hide in their huts while supporters of the African National Congress and the Zulu Inkatha Freedom Party, IFP, fight each other with *knopkieries*—short clubs with one knobbed end—*pangas*—machetes—and machine guns. The green, rolling hills that once saw the mighty warriors take on the white settlers, and later the British Army, now resound with cries of anguish as whole families are massacred in the night.

Francina watches the news on television in her room. She sees the flashing images of burned-out huts, wailing women, men with fear in their eyes. Her own village has so far been spared, but a cousin who recently moved to Johannesburg to find work says one of the residents has been accused of helping to massacre a family in a neighboring village, and there are rumors of an imminent revenge killing.

She doesn't believe those who say that the South African Defense Force armed the IFP hoping they'd derail the first democratic elections in the country; nor does she believe those who claim that President Mandela is the savior of the nation. Just last week she accused the packers down at the grocery store of having cabbage for brains. "It's four years since the election," she told them. "Forget about Mr. Mandela giving you a big house, a new car and a job with a pension."

Like many of her Zulu family and friends she's not happy being ruled by a central ANC government and predicts it will attempt to broaden its control until the provincial authorities have no power at all.

"That's why we need an independent homeland," she says. "But it won't happen with the leaders we have now. They're not real men like those of long ago."

Until that day comes, she says she'll stay in "ANC-infested Johannesburg." She loves the family she works for—they, too, have experienced great sorrow through the loss of their son. Besides, there are no jobs in Kwa-Zulu-Natal anyway, and what's a single woman to do without a job? She doesn't care if she dies cleaning another family's house, as long as they send her body home to the Valley of a Thousand Hills so her spirit can rest easy.

Chapter Twenty-Four

Ella

My illness separates the runts from the litter, the bad-tempered, mean-spirited creatures nobody should have the misfortune to take home. Small observations like these, no matter how painful, give me comfort, not because I feel any moral superiority over these weak and prejudiced people, but because I'm just so happy I can think clearly, that the disease hasn't affected my mind. My greatest fear is that I will become like my father in his last days.

My boss no longer communicates with me verbally; his instructions come by way of a memo, and he is always too busy behind his computer screen to answer my cheery "Hello" or "Have a good evening." Today I had an urge to scream, "You won't get it because I'd never sleep with you in a thousand years anyway, you spineless toad." The men from sales who used to perch on my desk and chat about music and movies no longer come. Do they really think I'm interested in getting physical with them? My latest memo says: *"Please be informed that all leave from now on will be unpaid. Yours sincerely, Bob.*" It's sad that the only time he truly is sincere is when he's threatening me.

I've been ordered to update our directory of products, a job any junior with a high school education could do. I see it taking weeks and weeks. It's his way of chaining me to my desk, keeping me away from clients.

I open the Yellow Pages at the legal section and dial the number of the Legal Aid Clinic at the local university. A girl answers with the bright, sympathetic voice of indignant youth. Although she's young, she sounds confident of her facts. If Themba has never paid child support, or made an attempt to see his children, I can divorce him *in absentia*. I like the snappy way she says the Latin words, like the whiz of deadly arrows. When I first contemplated divorcing Themba, I felt a pang of sadness, but when I considered how lightly he had taken our marriage vows, it soon passed. Even the Bible permitted divorce in cases of adultery. She tells me she'll start on the paperwork and I should come in as soon as I can to sign. There is no fee, but I can make a donation toward the clinic's operating expenses if I want to. It sounds too simple; there has to be a catch. But she assures me she's told me everything. As long as Themba doesn't appear with a child-support check, I can be rid of him within weeks. She advises me not to sell property or conclude any transactions of any sort until the divorce has been granted by a magistrate. I take it that doesn't include appointing a guardian to take care of my children when I'm gone. This, my most important task, is yet to be finalized, but I'm hoping that it won't take much longer.

I feel like asserting myself at work, as well. I tidy my desk, pack my bag and walk right up to my boss as he sits hunched over columns of figures on his computer screen. He almost jumps out of his chair.

"There's a home-improvement trade show on at the moment," I say.

He nods. Of course he knows; two of my colleagues are there, and until he gave me the "urgent" task of updating the directory, I was scheduled to be there, as well. Beads of sweat start to form along his hairline.

I lean closer, as though I'm about to straighten his tie, and he pushes his chair back so hard it crashes into the filing cabinet behind him.

"Yes, go," he says. "Check out the competition."

"Thanks." I pick up his coffee mug and run my finger along the rim. I Love New York, it says. "Nice. When were you there?"

"N-ninety two," he stammers.

"Special trip?"

"My fortieth birthday."

"Nice," I say again, enjoying the banality of the word. "Okay, see you tomorrow."

As I get into the elevator, I see him picking up the mug with a tissue and tossing it into the trash.

Chapter Twenty-Five

Monica

The early evening news was not so much watched in our house as picked apart, and tonight was no exception. My mother thought the newsreader's gelled chignon resembled a camel's hump; my father laughed at her mispronunciation of the French president's name, and swore that if he heard another story about the Truth and Reconciliation Commission, he'd take a golf club to the TV; and Anton scoffed at the airtime given to a professor from an obscure American university who declared that the South African government was on the right economic path.

I imagined the same ceaseless chatter going on in homes across the country. Ours was a nation stuck between radio stations and buzzing with static. Who knew how long it would be before we moved on?

"Why are you pulling a face, Mirinda?" my father asked my mother.

Out of the corner of my eye, I noticed her raised eyebrows.

"What?" he asked.

"Paolo," she said through pursed lips.

"Oh. I forgot. We're going to bed early tonight." He gave an affected yawn.

"Good night, Monica. Good night, Anton," said my mother.

"You can lock up and give us the keys tomorrow. We have an extra set."

And then Anton and I were alone for the first time in what seemed like years. Looking at him, I noted that his skin was no longer sallow, and he'd put back on the weight he'd lost.

"Monica, I've been waiting for this moment for ages." He slipped his fingers through mine and squeezed. "We need to talk."

Those should have been my words. Had he, too, noticed the change in our relationship? Was he about to say the very words I had been rehearsing for days and was now too nervous to try?

He brushed his lips against mine, and I realized that I was mistaken—he was not about to make this any easier for me.

"Anton," I whispered. "What if my parents see us?"

"They won't."

"Aha! You arranged this with them, didn't you?"

He studied his sandals.

"You did! I can't believe you arranged for them to go to bed early so you could kiss me." I started to laugh.

He blushed again. "I did arrange it with them, but not for that. I missed you so much, I got carried away."

"I'm irresistible, aren't I? Let's see if you still think so when you have to help me to the bathroom."

"I'll do that for you, you know I will." He looked around the room as if searching for something. "Monica, about those meetings…"

"You've joined Weight Watchers, have you?" I teased, nudging him in the ribs.

"This is serious, Monica. For some time I've been thinking about our future in South Africa."

"What do you mean?"

"Don't tell me you've never thought about going to another country and starting afresh. Everybody has."

"Well, my dad wanted to go back to Italy after Luca died, but my mother refused."

"Ever since you were carjacked, I can't think of anything else. This country is not safe anymore. None of us are safe." He took both my hands in his as though he were about to give me bad news. "The statistics for violence in this country border on those of a war zone."

"What are you saying, Anton?"

"The other day I went to a seminar given by a visiting American lawyer on how to emigrate to the U.S." He seemed coiled with nervous energy, a big cat about to pounce. "Do you remember my uncle, the one who married an American woman he met on holiday in Cape Town?"

I laughed. "They got married after a week, didn't they?"

"Yes, but the point is that he's an American citizen now. And listen to this—he has his own construction company in Las Vegas, the fastest-growing city in the country."

"So?"

"I phoned him the other day, and he offered me a job. Isn't that great?"

"Is he allowed to offer a foreigner a job?"

"It's not simple," said Anton. His voice had become testy. "He'll have to prove that no American can fill the position."

"I hate to burst your bubble, but they have accountants in America."

He scowled. "He's advertised the position, but none of the replies have been from suitable candidates. The good ones don't want to work for a company that builds strip malls when there's a high-tech revolution going on. He wants my answer *tomorrow*."

I was sure he'd stressed the word tomorrow as punishment for my reaction to his news. If it was alarm he wanted to see on my face, he was not disappointed.

"You're moving fast."

"That's why I had to speak to you today," he said, his expression and voice gentle again. "Monica, I want you to come with me. We can start a new life in America. We have to think about the future of our children."

"Our children!" I leaned away so I could get a good look at his face.

"Yes. I want to spend the rest of my life with you." He fumbled in his pocket and handed me a small velvet box. "Monica, will you marry me?"

I opened the box. Inside was a gorgeous ring with a diamond surrounded by an even number of emeralds.

"Anton, I…"

"So, what do you say?"

Whenever he gave me a birthday or Christmas present it was with a shy look, as though he wasn't sure he'd bought the right thing. There was no such look now. His eyes were fixed on mine, waiting, serious.

"Anton, it's beautiful."

"Yes, and…"

"I'm not sure what to say."

He stood up. "I need one word, *yes* or *no*."

I ran my finger over the diamond. "But this is a loaded proposal. You're not just asking me to marry you. You're asking me to leave my family, my home, my job."

He shoved his hands in his pockets and walked to the kitchen door. Then he turned around and came back again. "I want to look after you for the rest of your life, Monica. As we've seen, I can't do that here."

"Oh, Anton, you couldn't have prevented what happened to me."

He shrugged, and there was a look of such defeat on his face I wanted to jump up and give him a hug. But, of course, I couldn't.

"Can I have some time to think about it?" I asked. As soon as the words were out of my mouth, I knew that it was not necessary. The answer was no. But *no* was such a cruel word on its own. What I needed to think about was how to let him down gently. I caught hold of his hand as he turned around to continue pacing. "Anton, come here, please."

He looked pale, but more angry than upset. It was as though a strong, almost hard streak had surfaced in him, one I'd never seen before. I tugged on his hand to make him sit down next to me, but he wouldn't.

"Anton, what is it? What are you thinking?"

"You don't want to know." He'd never used this bitter tone with me before.

"I do."

"Okay, then." He pulled his hand away with such force it made me gasp. "I don't think you ever loved me." He grabbed the little box out of my grasp, snapped it shut and threw it onto the coffee table, where it clattered against an empty teacup.

I caught my breath again. "Anton, don't. Come and sit next to me."

He walked to the sofa on the other side of the coffee table and dropped down next to Ebony. She meowed loudly, glared at him for disturbing her sleep and hopped onto the floor.

"If you loved me, you wouldn't need…" He covered his face with his hands, and I couldn't hear the rest.

My stomach lurched. Was he crying?

"I can't hear what you're saying, Anton."

He took his hands away from his face. His eyes were dry. "I said if you loved me, you wouldn't need time to think about it." His voice was loud and harsh.

"Shh, Anton. My parents will hear you."

"I don't care." He stood up and grabbed his car keys from the coffee table.

"Anton, don't go. Let's discuss this." I started to cry.

"What's to discuss? You need time to think about it. I'm giving you two days." He jangled the keys as he spoke.

"You know it's not as simple as it sounds."

"No, Monica, I don't know that. I love you. I want to marry you. To me that's simple." He opened the front door and unlocked the security gate. "Two days, Monica."

The door closed and he was gone, without even saying goodbye.

I wheeled myself to the front door and locked the security gate and both locks on the door.

Switching on the light in my bedroom, I caught sight of a skinny, blotchy-faced woman in the dressing table mirror. Who was going to help this pathetic creature out of her wheelchair and into bed? Ten pairs of beady black eyes watched from my antique wrought-iron bed as I began to cry again. The two giraffes, three elephants, two hippos, overweight ostrich, threadbare lion and red-faced monkey looked wrong on the pink sweet-pea comforter, but Anton had brought them over from my flat so I'd have company at night. Gifts of love over many years, they now seemed to regard me with reproach.

When I was a teenager, I made one nervous attempt to get my mother to reduce the amount of pink in my room, but she was offended because she'd sewed the matching comforter, curtains, and Dolly Varden dressing table skirt herself, and so I dropped the issue. As a show of independence, however, I'd replaced the enlarged photo of myself in a pink ballet tutu with a Boy George poster. The moss-green wing chair she'd recently picked up at an antique store brought out the green of the sweet peas' stalks, but she insisted it would look better in pink. Its fate remained uncertain.

After positioning the wheelchair next to my bed, I grabbed hold of a wrought-iron post with my right hand and pushed with my left against the armrest of the wheelchair. All that work on the parallel bars had strengthened my upper body, and I was able to shift my right hand another post across with relative ease. Then, as I reached for the bed with my left hand, the wheelchair tipped over, and my legs were left dangling over the side of the bed like wet jeans on a clothesline. A minute went by, and another, and still my parents did not come rushing in to see what the noise was. I would have to do it myself. Pulling my body upward, as though doing a chin-up at the gym, I managed to drag my legs onto the bed. I couldn't help smiling.

There wasn't much space among all the animals, but I couldn't bring myself to throw them off and pushed them to the foot of the bed instead.

I peeled off my clothes, slipped my nightie over my head and slid under the comforter. Then I realized that I'd forgotten to turn off the light, and the switch was all the way across the room next to the door. I covered my eyes with the T-shirt I'd just taken off, but I couldn't sleep anyway, because I kept seeing Anton's bitter expression.

I understood his reasons for wanting to go. His father, Hendrik, had been planning his own move for almost a year now, ever since his elderly neighbor was tied up by intruders and forced to watch his wife being raped. Afterward, while she lay bleeding on the floor, the men sat around drinking beer and eating the food from his refrigerator. His ten-year-old truck was found the next morning on its roof in a ditch, a mile down the road.

Hendrik was about to join the Second Great Trek. The first, which began in 1836, saw Boers leaving the British-ruled Cape colony in ox-wagons to set up republics of their own in the north. Farmers were on the move again, but they were going further north this time, to Zambia. And this time it was in convoys of trucks and trailers.

"It's the beginning of the end," said Hendrik, "when citizens can no longer rely on their police force to keep them safe."

Like his neighbors, Hendrik believed the violence against farmers was an orchestrated plot to drive them from their land, and for this reason he'd joined the local self-protection unit that patrolled at night with loaded rifles.

"I know exactly how my forefathers felt," he said, "when they placed their ox-wagons in a circle to defend themselves against the marauding tribes."

A group of twenty people had already invaded a farm ten miles south of his own, assembling rough shacks of corrugated iron in the middle of the night on the land they claimed was stolen from their forefathers. The farmer, who had only owned the property for ten years, tried to evict them, but the government said they had squatters' rights and could remain. Every morning as the farmer passes the makeshift settlement on his way to the fields, he notices one or two new huts have sprung up overnight.

Anton tried to get his father to sell his farm years ago when the ANC first started talking about redistribution of land as part of their election platform. Now that farmers were being murdered at a rate of five per month, Hendrik was ready to join the forty families who'd bought land in southern Zambia claiming to feel safer and more welcome there.

Of course, there were farmers who beat their workers, paid them a pittance, fired them for no reason, but Hendrik was not like that. He'd built houses for his employees, had started a class for those who couldn't read and write. Some of them had been with him for forty years and would soon be receiving the pensions he'd paid for. Even though he knew he shouldn't, it was hard for the old man not to take the changing tide personally.

Anton's mother, Sara, believed that whites would have a better chance if they weren't split down language lines, and for this she blamed the British.

"They brought their hateful class system with them when they landed in 1820," she was fond of telling anyone who would listen, "and it led to the oppression of the Boers, and later, the Boer War."

Sara's grandmother died after eating porridge laced with glass in a British concentration camp.

There was nothing Sara hated more than a liberal English South African. They just hid their racism under pretty manners and posh accents, she said. Sara was all for leaving.

"We didn't have a civil war," she told Anton, "but they're picking us off one by one instead."

If they couldn't sell the farm, she proposed setting fire to the house and crops before leaving.

"I won't stand by," she said, "and let someone else benefit from our forty years of hard work." She'd even volunteered to light the first match herself.

The peaceful nights Anton knew growing up, when only the chirp of crickets and the occasional hoot of an owl disturbed the quiet of the bush, were no more. That was the quiet of the past. Now the quiet was sinister. In it lurked danger: men with guns and beer on their breath. His parents had burglar bars right around the house, but still slept with the windows shut, even in the hot months of December and January. And they would not take him up on his offer of an air conditioner.

"Why make the house comfortable," his mother said, "when we might have to burn it to the ground anyway?"

They hadn't asked Anton to go with them to Zambia. Hendrik was a sensitive man and didn't want to add to the guilt Anton already felt for having left the farm to take up another profession.

Unlike his mother, Anton did not despise Afrikaner leaders for not insisting on an independent homeland for

Afrikaners at the 1991 constitutional negotiations in Johannesburg. What he despised them for was being stupid enough to institute apartheid in the first place.

"If only they hadn't made it law," he said, "society would have divided itself of its own accord anyway, as it did—and still does—in all countries. But that's Afrikaners for you—sticklers for putting everything in writing and going by the book."

And now Anton wanted our relationship formalized, and I'd weaseled out of giving him the answer I should have. It was mean of me to allow him to leave thinking that I needed time when my mind was already made up. *Please God*, I prayed, *let me use these two days to find a way to tell him...without breaking his heart.*

But then I remembered Ella's prediction that I would do just that, and I hoped she hadn't felt it in her bones.

Chapter Twenty-Six

Monica

The physical therapy session was not going well. I'd already fallen on an exercise I thought I'd mastered and had dropped the weights on the leg extension machine with such a clang Laura thought I'd injured myself.

This morning my mother came into my room carrying a cup of tea and wearing a poorly disguised look of anticipation. Sweet, old-fashioned Anton—of course he'd asked my father's permission beforehand. She was strangely subdued when I told her I hadn't given him an answer.

"Then I may as well let you know," she said. "I've given in to your father—we're moving to Italy. We want you to go with us. America or Italy—the decision is yours." Her tone was so casual, her body language so neutral, she might have been asking me to go with them to the movies.

Laura was pulling my feet; Anton and my parents were doing their own kind of pulling. I felt like a carcass thrown to a pack of greedy dogs. And the strange thing was that the only direction I wanted to be pulled in was the one God decided, yet I still had no idea where that was.

Twenty minutes of halfhearted effort later, Laura asked my mother to leave us for a while.

"What's up, Monica?" she asked, hands on hips, triceps standing out like knots on a tree.

"Just a bad day."

"I don't care what's going on in the rest of your life. It can't possibly compare to what you've just been through. When you're here, I want your full attention."

Her arrogance reminded me of Luca's. In the years immediately after his death, it was this quality of his I missed most of all. It had made him seem strong, invincible, and without him it was almost as though the backbone of the family had disintegrated.

"Right," Laura said, slapping her thigh. "Back to work."

She lifted me out of the wheelchair and waited until I had a comfortable grip on both parallel bars. Out of the corner of my eye I saw that my mother hadn't been able to stand her banishment.

Sliding my left leg out in front of me, I readjusted my grip on the bars. Then I slid my right leg forward. I took another of these weak, wobbly steps, then two more. An intense pain shot up my spine like a Roman candle. Each time I seemed unsteady, my mother would make a move toward me, then stop herself and cover her face with her hands instead. My arms shook. I took one more step and reached the end of the parallel bars. I'd made it.

I let go and heard my mother's sharp intake of breath. I took a step forward, away from the bars, and stood for a full four minutes adrift on a sea of plushly carpeted quiet. Suddenly my knees buckled and I began to fall backward, but Laura got to me just in time, and I fell into her arms like a baseball into a mitt.

My mother dashed over. "Sweetie, you did it. You can walk again."

"Okay, girl. Next time, no bars at all," said Laura.

I grinned at them both. My bravado about it taking merely a bit of hard work on my part had been just that—bravado. In that tiny part of the brain where one stores thoughts and memories too painful to examine had lurked some serious doubts. But I had really done it. On a whim I'd taken a chance and let go. How exhilarating it had been to put out my arms and feel nothing. No bars, no wheelchair, no arm of support—nothing but cool air. My broken body was almost fully healed. I was truly blessed.

Luca and I had always chosen Vienna schnitzel as our special meal for our birthdays, and over time it had become a family celebration standard. Anton liked it, too, but he hadn't arrived for dinner, and I was ashamed at the relief I felt. My father said nothing, just stabbed Anton's Vienna schnitzel with his fork and transplanted it to his own plate. He was telling the story of how he used to smear a ring of grime around the tub when he was a child so his mother would be conned into thinking he'd already bathed. We'd heard it many times, but my mother cried with laughter each time he told it. Before he got to the part where his mother found him out, the telephone rang.

"Who on earth is that at this time of night?" said my father.

"Relax, Dad, it's only eight."

"If it's for me, I'm not here," he shouted, knowing full well that whoever it was would hear him as my mother picked up the phone.

There was a frown on her face when she returned. "It's for you, Monica. It's Ella. Should I bring the portable phone?"

"No, thanks," I said. "I'll wheel myself there."

It wasn't helpfulness on her part; she wanted to hear my conversation.

* * *

My mother appeared out of nowhere as I put down the phone. "Monica, you should have consulted me first."

"Were you here all the time?" I asked.

She pointed to an oil painting of Table Mountain on the wall behind me. "I was dusting that. Honestly, I don't know what Francina does all day. It was filthy."

"Dusting? At this time of night?"

"I have no objection to you being friends with a black woman, but…"

"What are you afraid of? That she'll contaminate the tea-cups?"

"You know your father wouldn't approve."

"Don't shift this onto him, Mom. And how do you know he won't approve? Have I ever brought a black person home before?

"No. So why now?"

"Because she's my friend."

"But Ella's an ex-ANC exile. Have you forgotten why your brother had to go to the army? To protect us against terrorists like the one she's married to. You know how your father feels about black people."

"Mom, Luca's death didn't have anything to do with the ANC. He was killed by a government that sent him to a war we shouldn't have been involved in. Blame them."

Her eyes widened. "Don't you dare say such things in this house, my girl." Then she dropped the sharp tone and her voice became wheedling. "Come on, sweetie, invite some of your old friends around instead."

She felt so bad for me that none of my old friends had come to visit that I suspected she'd engineered last week's surprise visit from Nina, a classmate from university. Poor Nina. She'd fidgeted with the snuff boxes on the coffee table, studied the sandpaintings on the wall—paint-ings she'd seen many times before—and remarked over and over how much she liked the Navajo rug. The only thing she hadn't taken a good look at was me in my wheel-chair.

"Mom, Ella's visit shouldn't be an issue."

She shook her head slowly. "Maybe. But I'm not going to tell your father."

It was unreasonable of me to expect my parents to have changed their attitudes just because I had. Ella and Mrs. Dube had been magnanimous with the patience they'd shown me in the hospital; surely I owed my mother and father the same generosity of spirit.

Chapter Twenty-Seven

Ella

Five teenage boys sit on the low perimeter wall of my building passing a hand-rolled cigarette around and nodding in time to American rap music that blares from a sticker-emblazoned boom box at their feet.

Like every block of flats in the area, this one is hopelessly equipped for the disabled, which is why I'm waiting for Monica on the sidewalk. Just as well, too, because there aren't any open parking spaces.

I'm wearing my floor-length green-and-gold caftan with a matching headdress that, for some reason, just won't sit right today. Anyone watching me would think I had lice, with all the fiddling I'm doing.

A navy Honda pulls up, and Monica waves from the passenger seat before reaching round to unlock the back door.

One of the boys shouts an insult at my companions as I climb in.

Monica and her mother don't realize they've just been insulted, but I shake my fist at the boys. They laugh and whoop like lovesick baboons.

Monica doesn't look like a pathetic bag of bones anymore, but she's short of a few good steak meals.

"Do I go back the way I came?" asks Mrs. Brunetti. She has pulled up at a red light, leaving ten feet between us and the car in front.

"I'm sorry, Mrs. Brunetti, in all my excitement to see Monica, I forgot my manners. How are you?"

"I'm fine, but I'd be better if I knew which street to take." Her eyes flick back and forth from the rearview to the side mirror as though she's a spectator at a tennis match.

"If we turn left," I tell her, "we can take a shortcut to Barry Hertzog via Hijackers' Avenue."

She whips around. "What?"

I'm not trying to scare her; people do call it Hijackers' Avenue. "Well, the other option is taking a right, but then we have to drive under that bridge where those tourists were killed by kids throwing rocks onto the cars down below."

Mrs. Brunetti turns back to face the intersection, her knuckles white on the steering wheel.

"Don't worry, she's joking. There's no such thing as Hijackers' Avenue," says Monica, putting her hand on her mother's arm. "Turn left here."

Mrs. Brunetti presses her lips together. The light changes, and we shudder into motion.

There are no children riding bikes or playing soccer on the quiet, shaded streets of Monica's neighborhood. No mothers pushing strollers. No old women sitting on benches, watching the parade of life. An ice-cream truck trundles past broadcasting its tinny tune from a rooftop speaker, and not a soul appears from anywhere. The signs on the high stucco walls have illustrations to go with their threatening messages. Beware: Vicious Dogs, says one, and there is a drawing of a rottweiler with fangs bared. Armed Guard On Patrol, says another, and it has a picture of a man taking aim with a rifle. Underneath the signs are rows of cacti: further deterrents to those still intent on climbing over.

Mrs. Brunetti pulls up in front of a white, flat-roofed house that reminds me of picture postcards of the Greek Islands. As I'm admiring the cerise bougainvillea that billows over the white perimeter wall like a ceremonial headdress, automatic sprinklers start up and splatter my window.

Mrs. Brunetti leaves us in the American movie-set living room and goes to her bedroom, ostensibly to rest. Monica insists on fetching the tea to show me how well she can maneuver her wheelchair. While she's in the kitchen, I hear her asking someone to join us. She returns balancing the tray on her knees. But the heavy teapot is off center and the teacups slide down and crash into it. As I help her put the cups back onto their saucers, I notice a black woman peeking at us from around the corner. She disappears when she sees me looking.

Sweet Monica can be such a nag. She insists I tell her what the doctors said about my prognosis. I try changing the subject by commenting on how tense she seems, and, thankfully, it works. Sighing like a prisoner on her way to the gallows, she tells me that Anton has proposed. Did I not tell her she was going to break his heart one day?

She refuses to believe me when I tell her that millions of South Africans would jump at the chance to go to America.

"Don't you think they're traitors?" she asks, eyebrows swooping upward.

"Not if they're worried about their children. I understand that. Do you think I enjoy keeping my kids cooped up in the flat because it's too dangerous to play outside? Remember, *I've* lived elsewhere. I can picture what it would be like for them growing up somewhere like Canada. But all this crime won't go on forever. The Rainbow Nation—"

"Anton says it's a hoax."

"More like a PR ploy—and a good one, too. If we believe it, we'll start to live it. The problem is that we *all* have to buy into it."

Monica looks thoughtful, but does not reply.

Mrs. Brunetti appears suspiciously quickly when Monica calls for her after a couple of hours. She doesn't like her daughter's idea one bit.

"Have you gone mad?" she says. "You haven't driven since, well, since you went to the hospital."

"I have to start sometime," says Monica.

"Please don't worry about me," I tell them. "I can get a taxi." If I don't leave now, my neighbor's husband will beat me home, and with his temper after a long day at work…I don't want him around my boys.

"I'll drive you, Ella," says Monica, eyes fixed on her mother. "Please, Mom. If I leave it too long I may never drive again."

Despite the frigid air-conditioning in the car, Monica rubs her palms on her skirt as if to dry them. We stop at a red light, and she flicks the central locking button, eliciting a horrible buzzing sound because the doors are already locked. Her gear changes are rough because she can't apply sufficient pressure to the clutch, but I pretend not to notice.

For some reason the Bible verse about perfect love casting out fear comes to me, and I say a silent prayer that Monica's fear will be cast out.

Chapter Twenty-Eight

Monica

Like a silly child who'd climbed to the top of the slide and now refused to go backward or forward, I'd taken on more than I could handle. It was all right when I was driving, but each time I had to stop...

Ella had gone upstairs, and I was about to start the car when I felt the vibration of a steady, pounding beat. Immediately my dream came to me—the hundreds of hands rocking my car, shattering the windshield. Sweat trickled down my sides and soaked the waistband of my skirt.

The group of teenagers we'd seen earlier rounded the corner with their boom box and one of them kicked over a trash can, scattering soda bottles and broken glass across the sidewalk.

As I pulled away from the curb, I saw Ella outside on her balcony shaking her fist and shouting at the boys.

My father was lying on the sofa watching a children's program when I arrived home. There was a cushion under his legs, which meant his back was bothering him. Even though he hadn't worked underground for twenty years, there were still times his back hurt as though he'd been bent over for a ten-hour shift.

"Monica's had a big day," said my mother. "She drove her friend home."

I noticed she didn't identify my friend.

He frowned. "I wish you'd waited for me. Something could have happened to you."

"Dad, something already did."

His face fell. "I know, I know, I know. I haven't done a good job of looking after—"

"Daddy, don't say that." I maneuvered my wheelchair until it was flush against the sofa. "There was nothing you could have done to prevent it."

He shrugged.

My father, Anton, his father—they all wanted to look after their families but felt they couldn't do it here. The country emasculated them, so they wanted to leave.

"Do you remember when I cut my knee falling off my bike?"

My father smiled. "Such waterworks. But you forgot about it as soon as you were riding again."

"Exactly. You made me get straight back on."

"I'm off to see if Francina needs a hand," said my mother, stooping to pick up my father's empty scotch glass.

On the television screen a fuzzy green bear serenaded a chameleon with long, curled eyelashes. My father shifted uncomfortably in our silence, then decided to sit up.

"What do you think of Anton's proposal?" I asked, as the signal tune for the evening news began.

He studied a graze across his knuckles as the newsreader began the headlines. It was a few seconds before he spoke.

"When I left my mother in Italy all those years ago, I vowed that if I ever had a family, I'd never let it split up. I never, ever wanted to go through—or put someone else through—the pain of parting again."

He pressed the mute button, and the newsreader's head began to bob around comically.

"I've never told anybody this, but I promised my mother I'd return to Italy for good one day with all of you." He stared at the flickering screen. "But every year your mother refused, and now my mother's passed on."

"Mom's certainly done a complete about-face."

He nodded. "Luca would've loved it. He could have gone to university in Milan and come home to us on weekends. My son would have showed them all."

He sat silently for a while, head bowed, chin resting on his chest. When he looked up, there were tears in his eyes. "Things don't always work out the way they're planned."

I leaned out of my wheelchair and put my arms around his neck, once again the little girl trying to comfort him. Once again he stiffened and pulled away.

"What do you want, Dad?" I asked, wishing my voice wouldn't quaver so much.

"I want Luca here. I want us to be a family again."

"We *are* a family. Luca's dead. He's not coming back. But I survived, Daddy. I'm still here." I began to sob loudly.

My mother rushed in but, after communicating silently with my father over my head, stopped and didn't say a word. With this decision to move to Italy they'd become a united force, a regular UN army. She put her arm around me, but I felt utterly left out.

My father didn't explode, didn't break anything, as I expected him to. He just looked at me with glassy eyes and pressed the mute button, bringing the bobbing head to life again with its litany of civil strife, natural disasters and political intrigue.

I hadn't expected the new path I'd chosen in life to be so hazardous to my relationships. With Anton it was unavoidable, but I hoped the distance growing between me and my parents could somehow be closed.

Chapter Twenty-Nine

Monica

Anton was forty minutes late, which made me wonder if he was going to arrive at all—punctuality was something he prided himself on. He couldn't stand the concept of "African time," calling it a sorry excuse for laziness and disrespect. I hadn't heard from him since the night he'd proposed, which was also unlike him, as he was normally the first to cave in when we had a fight.

My parents were outside at the pool enjoying a cool drink in the indigo summer twilight with their panic button. I heard Anton's car and then the buzzer at the gate. My mother's sandals clattered down the brick path.

His hair was wet, and as he walked past me to the opposite sofa, I caught a whiff of the cologne I'd bought him for Christmas. We looked at each other like strangers in a doctor's waiting room.

"Would you like something to drink, Anton?"

"No, thanks. I've just had coffee."

My mother had been telling him for years to help himself to whatever he wanted from the refrigerator, but the one time he did, his face went so red you'd have thought she'd caught him stealing the silver not drinking a soda in the kitchen.

That seemed such a long time ago, an uncomplicated time when the future was a distant speck on the horizon. Now it was here, looming large and fearsome in the living room, and I felt the passing of time so acutely it frightened me. I was an adult now—almost thirty years old. Only a while back that had seemed ancient.

"Are you sure?" I persisted. "We've got juice, sparkling mineral water."

"I'm fine."

"How's work?"

"I've taken time off to organize the documents for the immigration lawyer." He was maddeningly calm, as though this visit were purely a formality.

"So you're going through with this?"

For a brief instant there was panic in his eyes, but then he said in a low, flat voice, "You're not coming, are you?"

"Anton, I…"

"Yes, or no?" He leaned forward, as though to catch my answer.

It was only one word, yet I couldn't get my tongue around it. From the kitchen came sounds of water running and plates being stacked. Francina had finished her dinner in her room and was now at the sink washing our dishes.

"Can we at least discuss this?" I said.

He drummed his fingers on the coffee table. "What's to discuss? I asked you to marry me. You answer yes or no. It's as simple as that."

"But it's not simple. You're asking me to leave my home, my parents…."

"You do know they're also leaving, no matter what you say?"

He was lashing out at me because he was hurt. I knew that. But there was something odd about his reaction. His face was strangely expressionless, as though he'd known all along what the outcome of this would be and had already come to terms with it.

I started to cry, not because I didn't want to break up with him, but because I should have done it long ago. To marry Anton would be to choose an inauthentic life, one devoid of substance and purpose, and I couldn't do that. Not now. Not after all I'd been through.

He stopped drumming on the table and stood up. "So, this is it then?"

I caught my breath at his matter-of-fact tone.

"Anton, after all these years… Let me explain myself. I've changed, Anton. I'm not the person you fell in love with. I—"

He wouldn't let me finish. "I should know in a week when I'll be going."

He stared at me for a long time, as though trying to make up his mind about something. Finally, he picked up his car keys, walked over to me and put his hand on my shoulder. I expected him to say something meaningful, something about us, but he just kissed me on top of my head—twice—and walked out.

I heard him talking to my parents outside. Then his car started up and roared off at an uncharacteristic speed.

Suddenly, the cuckoo jumped out of my mother's hideous heirloom clock and gave a horrible cry. I hurled the television remote at it, but it popped smugly back inside and the little doors shut with a victorious click. What audacity to choose this moment to reappear after a mysterious absence of ten years.

The end had not gone as planned. Anton would leave South Africa thinking me a heartless, spineless fraud—and with good reason. I'd meant to let him down kindly, to thank him for the time he'd spent at my hospital bed—for all he'd ever done for me really, and to ask his forgiveness for not having told him as soon as I realized that our relationship had no future. But he'd denied me the opportunity. The only thing to do now was to put it all in a letter. My words might land up in the trash, unread, but it was a chance I was willing to take.

My mother came in from the garden and gathered me into her arms. Then my father joined us, which surprised me, because we hadn't spoken since my emotional outburst.

"Anton told us you said no," said my mother, stroking my hair.

I'd never actually said the word.

"There are plenty of fish in the sea," said my father, looking pleased with himself for finally finding what he thought was an appropriate context for the cliché he'd been repeating to me ever since I'd started going out with Anton.

My mother did not understand my decision and my father didn't even care to. To him Anton was an obstacle that had been dragged from the road, leaving the way clear for me to go to Italy with them. Would they be angry or upset when they discovered what I'd made up my mind to do? Probably both, but I'd prayed about it and knew in my heart that God was guiding me to the purpose He'd had in mind when He'd saved my life alongside that busy highway.

Chapter Thirty

Monica

Rookie stuntmen had their first fall from the top of a building, trapeze artists their first somersault without a harness, Formula One drivers their first race; I had this. There was no danger in what I was about to attempt, but my body didn't know that—my mouth was as dry as the Kalahari, and my stomach fluttered queasily.

Seizing my chance when Laura was called to the telephone, I let go of the parallel bars and took a step.

Three more, I told myself. Four steps, one after the other, constitute walking.

I took three, and then another, and another. Everything, except for the carpet in front of me, became blurred. Each fiber in that charcoal Berber, each speck of lint the vacuum cleaner had missed, seemed magnified. My legs began to feel stronger. With my arms stretched out as though I were a tightrope walker, I felt myself floating, being passed along from one warm current of air to the next. The only sound I heard was my own breathing, coming fast and shallow.

"Laura, Laura!" I called. "Look at me! I'm doing it. I'm walking."

"Keep going, girl," she shouted back.

The carpet was spongy beneath my bare feet. I'd walked the entire length of the parallel bars without holding on, plus another twelve steps. I felt I could walk forever, out to the car, down the street, and, if nobody stopped me, all the way to Pretoria. I was an athlete, a well-oiled machine ready for anything: walking, jumping, running, kicking. I was an invincible, mighty, supernatural wonder girl who could walk up walls, fly across the rooftops, flit through the trees with the grace of a ballerina.

"Don't overdo it," said Laura, grabbing me from behind.

I tried to slip out of her grasp.

"It's the adrenaline," she said. "Wait till tomorrow and I'll let you double your distance."

"I walked. You missed it," I shouted to my mother as she entered the rehab center with clothes from the dry cleaners draped over her arm.

"About fifteen feet," said Laura, looking proud and just a little surprised, as though she'd invented something but hadn't really expected it to work.

"Not again," said my mother. "I missed your first steps as a baby because I left you with the maid to take Luca to the public pool."

She'd missed more than that. While she was lying in her darkened bedroom after Luca's death, drugged up, barely moving for months on end, I had soldiered on, going to school, studying for exams, researching the application process for university. My father had shuffled around, sweating alcohol and malevolence, but doing just enough to keep the company running and the bills paid. He even managed the grocery shopping, but it was Francina who bought me my tampons, because how could I have asked him for those?

Like a butterfly breaking out of its cocoon, my mother emerged one day from her bedroom. With her new pills, she'd flit around on a crazy high, never stopping long enough to take notice of anything. Then, all of a sudden, she'd fold in on herself, shutting us out again while she took a rest from life, from her family. When I was studying for my matric exams, she decided to play every record in her huge collection full blast, repeating her favorite songs six or seven times, as though trying to end a siege. When the two-week-long exam period began, she was back in bed with one of her "bad heads." I don't think she even knew it was that time of year.

Sensing an awkward moment, Laura put her hand on my mother's arm and said, "Never mind, Mrs. Brunetti. Tomorrow you'll see her do thirty feet, and by Friday, the hundred-yard dash."

My mother tightened the belt on her long silk dressing gown as she watched me apply mascara at my dressing table.

"Are you sure you want to go back to work?" she asked. "You've only been out of that wheelchair for a couple of weeks now."

"Dr. Wheaton said it was a good idea, Mom, so why wait any longer?"

He'd actually gone so far as to tell me I was in better shape than he was. He was being kind; I had a pronounced limp in my right leg that made it impossible for me to run. Laura said it might go away over time, but I should learn to accept that this may be as good as it got.

"Let me drive you," said my mother.

"I'll be fine," I told her, rifling through the drawer for my favorite lipstick.

After finding it, I turned back to the mirror and caught

sight of my mother's reflection in the glass. She was staring at the back of my head with a look of pure panic.

"Mom," I said, swiveling around to face her. "I have to return to work sometime. I'm on unpaid leave."

"Money isn't a problem," she said, collecting the tissue I'd used to blend my foundation. "Why pay rent for your flat when you can move in here permanently?"

I didn't answer, and she didn't push the issue as she followed me into the garage.

"Let me drive you. I'll slip on a sweat suit," she said, watching me lower myself into the driver's seat of her Honda.

My father had sold my car without ever bringing it home because it was riddled with bullet holes from the botched supermarket robbery.

I turned the key and put the car in Reverse. "No, Mom. But thanks. I'll call you when I get to work."

She peered up and down the street as I backed out of the garage and, as the door slowly closed, she ducked lower and lower to wave until she was almost crouching on the cement floor.

As soon as she disappeared from sight, I lost coordination of my movements and stalled the car. The same thing could happen again, couldn't it? I could stop at a light and find myself again staring up the nose of a gun.

Don't be silly, I told myself. Lightning doesn't strike the same place twice.

A bad example. An old oak tree in our neighbor's yard recently keeled over after being hit twice in two years. It just missed their house.

The traffic thickened as I approached the on-ramp to the highway. There were a few people milling about the intersection on foot: a teenager selling the morning newspaper, two men handing out flyers for a new town house development, someone hawking steering wheel covers and a small beggar boy in a bright orange jersey with sleeves that hung to his knees. There were four other men at the intersection, waiting for a taxi, a bus, or who knew what. My attacker might have been loitering at the intersection that hot afternoon. If I hadn't been so busy concentrating on my tape, I might have noticed him. I studied the men, trying to memorize their faces in case one of them tried anything.

How absurd. I was hanging on to the steering wheel with trembling hands because a few men were waiting for a bus. The light changed, and the cars inched down the on-ramp before accelerating to merge with the flow on the highway. I sat bolt upright, my back not even touching the seat. I'd tried to be nonchalant with my mother, but this *was* a big deal.

Twenty minutes later, I pulled up at the automatic door of the Corporation's parking garage and fell back into my seat like an unwound top. Because my entrance card had disappeared along with my car, I had to call security on the intercom to let me in, and it was five whole minutes— I counted them as the polite hoots behind me became an aggressive chorus—before the door went up.

My workday was as expected: sympathetic nods and smiles, questions about minute details from the less sensitive, and, of course, flashes of brilliance on how everybody else would have handled the situation. And not to neglect the anecdotes: the same thing happened to my aunt, my neighbor, my friend's father, my brother's girlfriend's parents, a friend of a friend, a friend of a friend of a friend. I sat listening to the grim chronicles, wishing I'd obeyed my mother and stayed home. The thought of her sitting in the kitchen with a crossword puzzle made me feel like a child on her first day of school.

At lunch I saw Faith chatting to a chic, good-looking group in the line at the cash register—TV people slumming it in the radio canteen. One of the men placed his hand in the small of her back to steer her out of the path of a woman carrying a tower of polystyrene boxes. Faith flashed him a smile over her shoulder. Emboldened, he slipped his arm around her waist and pulled her toward him, but before he could plant a kiss on her neck she wriggled out of his grip, giggling, and gave him a playful slap. About twenty sandwiches poised midair as the women in the vicinity stopped eating to watch. The man was the arch villain on the hottest soap opera in the country. He was gorgeous, from a wealthy and politically connected family, but most important in my estimation, he was as free as a bird—there was no wife or children on the sidelines. Faith seemed oblivious to the malignant stares being directed her way. I couldn't have been happier for her.

Around midafternoon I was called in to Le Roux's office.

"Sit down, Monica," he said, guiding me into a low-slung canvas director's chair.

My limp made people uncomfortable; they kept wanting to take my arm.

"I called you here," he said, walking around to the other side of the desk to sit down, "because I wanted to tell you that if you ever need to—" he made the sign of quotation marks in the air with his index fingers "—go on a story at two in the afternoon, that's okay with me. And if you're ever on a story—" he made the sign again "—in the morning and can only come in late, that's also okay. Don't strain yourself until you feel one hundred percent."

This was the first time I'd seen Le Roux acting human. The surprise continued; he apologized for the personnel department putting me on unpaid leave and promised to have them send me a check.

His telephone rang as he was asking me where exactly my attack had taken place.

"I'm busy," he barked into the receiver. "What do you want?"

He listened for less than a minute before slamming down the phone.

"Agh no. Joe's just read the news in a fake Cockney accent, and Vusi claims he did it to make him look bad."

I knew Joe. He'd probably taken a swig too many from the flask he kept hidden in the potted palm outside the men's bathroom. I could just picture him watching Vusi's face contort with helpless rage on the other side of the soundproof glass. Joe was always looking for ways to "brighten his day."

"You go ahead," I said. "I'll see myself out."

Alone in his office, I burst out laughing; there were some good things about being back after all. A minute later Le Roux's secretary flounced in to see what the noise was. Seeing the tears streaming down my cheeks, she scooped me up into a motherly hug.

"There, there," she said, rocking me as though I were a colicky baby. "It'll take time, but you'll get over it."

That stripped away the last vestiges of my self-control, which, of course, only resulted in my being held hostage even longer. Finally, I was saved by a ringing phone in her office.

I was genuinely touched by Le Roux's offer of reduced hours, but I'd come back to work with a list of story ideas as long as my arm. I'd sent the profiles I'd done of Mrs. Dube and Francina to a few magazines and was in the process of drawing up a proposal for a radio series titled *Everyday People,* in which people from all walks of life would talk about the major issues on their minds. If Le Roux protested, I'd remind him of the National Broadcasting Corporation's new policy that interview subjects should reflect the demographics of the country's population.

My proposal for a series on Gauteng hospitals was complete. The cuts in their government subsidies were well reported, but I wanted to follow individual patients, from their long wait in admissions, to their assignment to a ward, their treatment and eventual follow-up in their local areas. I wanted to investigate the impact of primary-care clinics on the community. Were they really alleviating the burden on cash-strapped hospitals? And were the Cuban doctors the government had brought in to work in rural areas being accepted by the local people? I could not forget what Dr. Novak had told me—that babies were often found abandoned in the hospital's waiting rooms. Were there enough adoptive parents to go around? And what about the elderly people who were dumped at hospitals because their families could not, or would not, look after them any longer? Were they permitted to spend their last few weeks, or months, in a clean, comfortable hospital bed, being fed, bathed and given medication to dull the pain? Was Ella right: Were some of the nurses at the Soweto Hospital indifferent, even callous, toward their patients because they themselves were being abused and overworked by their employers?

The hospital had provided me with a wealth of material for meaningful stories that might make our white, affluent listeners sit up and take notice. Of course, there'd be cynics who'd say I was only trying to keep my job in the stringent affirmative-action environment of the new National Broadcasting Corporation, but I didn't care. This was something I felt called to do. It was part of my new purpose in life.

Chapter Thirty-One

Ella

The breeze billowing my blue gingham curtains smells faintly of car fumes, but I do not mind because it is cool and my skin feels as though it's crawling with a million red ants, all biting into me with their hot little mouths.

Thandeka has left a pile of clean laundry on my dressing table. The poor thing left in such a hurry to get the taxi that I wonder if she remembered to take the cold meats and rolls I bought her for the journey. It's a long way to Lesotho, but her grandmother has had a bad fall and needs her.

A woman's voice, shrill and exhausted, floats up from the concrete courtyard below. I'm guessing some inconsiderate fool has backed his car into her clean sheets on the clothesline. Or worse—her washing may have grown wings and disappeared. It happens all the time.

Bob the Nervous is making noises about letting me go, so I'm considering asking that nice girl at Legal Aid to put in a sweet, little lawyerly call to him—crank his blood pressure up a few points.

The doorbell rings and Sipho runs to my bedroom, wide-eyed, breathing heavily.

"Mom, it's a lady. I stood on a chair to look through the peephole."

I pull on my dressing gown and drag myself, barefoot, to the door.

"It's Monica," I say, undoing the locks. Sipho cowers behind me. I hear Mandla laughing at something on television.

"Come in," I tell her, and quickly clear a path through Mandla's colored wooden blocks with my foot.

"I hope I'm not disturbing you," she says.

"Of course not. This is Sipho, my firstborn." He will not come out from behind me. "He seems busy at the moment, but I hope he'll come and introduce himself later." I motion for her to follow me to my bedroom, and Sipho makes his escape to the living room.

"You look terrible," says Monica, watching me open the curtains before crawling back into bed.

"Thanks. You look great, too." I try to laugh, but it hurts my chest.

She seems agitated. "Have you seen a doctor?"

"Yes. This morning. He gave me more antibiotics and told me to rest. But it's difficult."

Something changes in her face. It's as though she's at the scene of an accident and can't turn away, even though what she sees makes her sick to her stomach.

"Are you telling me everything?" she asks.

The moment has finally come, but I cannot bring myself to say the words.

She shakes her head. "No, no...don't tell me that. I don't want to believe..."

"I knew you were too sharp for me to hide it from you forever."

The clock next to my bed ticks loudly. From the

living room comes the sound of Sipho reading a story to his baby brother.

"Yes, Monica, I have it."

She exhales loudly. "How long have you known?"

"About three years."

"And…and Mandla?"

"No, thank the Lord. That in itself is a miracle."

"Those drug cocktails—antiretrovirals, I think they call them—are supposed to be so good. I've read that if you start taking them early enough, the infection can be controlled, and you can live a normal life."

"Yes, but with a hefty price tag."

"What about your Medical Aid?"

"They won't pay. If I were still living in Canada I'd probably get them for nothing, but this is Africa, my dear. Those drugs are completely unaffordable to us in the Third World."

"How…?" She shakes her head. "No, never mind."

"How did I get it? Is that what you wanted to ask?"

"It's immaterial."

"No, it's not. I got it from that jerk husband of mine. When we came back to South Africa he did the rounds, and I reaped the rewards."

"I can't believe you've managed to keep this from me."

Anger is a strange companion. It can have you spitting with energy one minute, and so tired the next you can hardly open your lips to speak. "I wasn't trying to," I tell her in a flat voice. "It just never came up. You had other things to think about."

She has a sheepish expression on her face, and I have the feeling she came here to unburden herself of something but has since changed her mind. She looks at the floor so I won't see a tear trickling down her cheek.

"Look at me," I tell her. "What are you doing?"

She refuses to lift her head.

"There'll be no tears around me. I'm not dead yet."

"I'm sorry. You'll never see that again."

"Good. Now can you do me a favor? I know it's Friday night and you probably have a date or something…"

"*Ja,* sure."

"Well, you never know. There's a container of chicken stew in the refrigerator that Thandeka cooked before she left. Would you heat it in the microwave for the boys' dinner?"

"Are you going to have some, too?"

"I don't feel like eating."

"We'll see about that," she says in a voice that tells me I'm dealing with a will as strong as my own.

Chapter Thirty-Two

Monica

Sipho was sitting on the chocolate-brown corduroy sofa reading a story out loud, but the cartoon on television was far more alluring to his baby brother, Mandla, who was pressed against the screen trying to poke the wily cartoon cat with his chubby index finger.

Sipho was a slender boy with eyes the size of the old fifty-cent coin. He must have got them from his father, because Ella's were small and almond-shaped.

"Do you like soccer, Sipho?" I asked.

He looked down at the South African soccer team logo on his T-shirt. "Not really. My mom gave me this for Christmas. She says I should watch the games on TV and she'll watch with me, but I prefer wildlife programs."

"Me, too," I said.

He looked at me skeptically.

Mandla giggled.

"Come away from the TV," Sipho told him, but was flatly ignored. With a weary sigh, he put a marker in his book and went to get his brother.

"No," he said firmly, as Mandla tried to slip out of his grasp. "The TV is heavy, and if it falls on you you'll be squashed like an *ishongololo*."

The toddler didn't care if he'd land up like a flattened millipede; he wanted to get back to poking the cat on television. He didn't seem to care about my presence, either.

I put on my best friendly-adult voice. "Are you hungry, guys? I'm going to have your dinner ready in two ticks."

They both stared at me.

"Why are *you* doing it?" asked Sipho.

"Because your mommy's not feeling well. I'll try to do it the way she does. Is that all right?"

He studied me with his solemn eyes, then nodded. Mandla was back at the TV, having taken advantage of the distraction I'd provided.

It was a large kitchen for a flat. The old-fashioned tin cupboards had been repainted avocado green, and the curtains and tablecloth were a matching gingham. Ella was obviously fond of checks. There was a mathematics workbook on the table next to a small vase of bright red pansies. I opened the cavernous old fridge and searched among the cans of soda, grape juice cartons and assortment of fresh fruit until I found the container of chicken. The microwave was digital and far more sophisticated than my mother's, but I finally located the reheat button. There were three plates on the drying rack, but the knives and forks were more elusive. A search of the drawers turned up carving knives and serving forks, but nothing the boys could eat with.

"They're in the cupboard. My mommy has them hanging up on a thing that goes round so you can choose your own knife and fork."

I hadn't noticed Sipho leaning against the doorway.

"Tell me, sweetheart, do you and your brother have something to drink *with* your dinner or *after* your dinner?"

"Mommy says if we drink while we're eating we won't finish our food. She gives us apple juice after dinner before she watches the news. Is my mommy going to die?"

"What?" I whipped round, knocking over an egg timer. It bounced onto the floor and rolled under the table.

Sipho picked it up. "Lucky for you it's plastic." He stood staring at me, waiting for an answer.

I pulled out a kitchen chair and motioned for him to do the same, but before I could sit down, the microwave beeped and flashed a Stir command.

"Where did you get such an idea, Sipho?" I asked, turning my back on him to open the microwave door.

"Nomsa's mother was sick in bed, and then the ambulance took her to the hospital, but they never brought her back. Now Nomsa lives with her granny."

"Your mother has been to the hospital, and she did come back."

I didn't know how to handle this and tried stalling by handing him the pile of plates to set out, but he was far too astute to fall for my ploy.

"She isn't better," he said.

I glanced over my shoulder at the digital timer on the microwave, hoping to be saved by a beep and a Done message, but Sipho would not take his eyes off my face. He was waiting for some sense to come from this grown-up.

"Sipho, I won't lie to you. Your mother is very sick. But the doctor has given her some pills, and hopefully they'll make her feel better."

He seemed buoyed by that idea. "When I'm big, I'm going to be a doctor. And then I'll look after my mother and Mandla."

I turned around and blinked the tears from my eyes. If Ella was not allowed to see them, neither was this sweet child.

He sat down to eat, and I went to get Mandla from in front of the television.

"E-e," said Mandla as I picked him up. From the distressed look on his face, I gathered that it meant no.

He stopped moaning as soon as he saw the food on the table. I put him in his high chair, placed the plate in front of him and handed him a fork.

"He's too little for that," said Sipho. "Mommy says he'll hurt himself."

Of course. What was I thinking? I snatched the fork away from the child, who'd already started stabbing at his food, and replaced it with a spoon, which he found far less exciting.

There was so much I didn't know about children. Mandla then proceeded to transfer the contents of his plate onto the high chair's tray.

"Mommy lets him play for one minute and then she feeds him," said my tutor.

"Okay, fun's over," I said to Mandla. "My turn."

It wasn't difficult; he loved his food. No games like "Open wide, here comes the train" were necessary.

Sipho finished eating and informed me that the apple juice was on the top shelf of the refrigerator, the glasses in the cupboard over the sink.

I settled Mandla back in front of the television with his sippy cup and took Ella a small plate of chicken. She was asleep, so I shook her gently.

"I don't feel like eating," she said, covering her face with her hands.

"Come on, you probably haven't had anything the whole day. You need your strength."

"You're so bossy," she said, trying to pull herself up.

"It's my turn now." I helped her sit up, then plumped the pillows behind her.

When she'd cleaned her plate, I asked what else had to be done.

"Nothing, don't worry," she replied.

"I've left Mandla watching TV. But what about their bath?" I didn't have a clue where I'd even begin, but Ella was in no condition to do it.

"They'd love nothing better than to skip that."

"I don't mind, Ella."

"Sipho can wash himself, but it would be great if you could bathe Mandla. I'm sure you've noticed that he gets into everything."

"Well, he managed to keep the stew off his eyelids—I will say that for him. Let me give it a try. Any last-minute tips?"

"Just keep his head above water. And take that scaredy-cat look off your face. It's not that difficult."

But bath time was no joke for a novice like me, and Sipho's vigilant presence made me even more nervous. I managed to keep a firm grip on Mandla's squirming soapy body, but the little rascal seemed to capitalize on my timidity, taking great joy in splashing me from head to toe.

When the bathroom began to resemble a flood zone, Sipho stepped in to calm his baby brother so that I could rinse the shampoo out of his hair.

"Thanks, pal," I said, and Sipho smiled shyly.

I was drenched but proud of myself for a relatively successful first bath. I lay Mandla on a fluffy white towel and patted him dry. He was an adorable baby, and I felt the urge to gently pinch his rolls of fat. Under Sipho's watchful eye, though, I didn't dare. I slathered him with baby lotion, dressed him in his dinosaur pajamas and presented him to Ella like a chef presenting a soufflé.

"Hello, my baby," she cooed. "Don't you look nice?" She put out her arms, and Mandla wriggled into them. "What have you done to poor Aunty Monica, my beautiful boy?" she said, looking me up and down.

Sipho lurked in the doorway.

"Come in, son," said Ella. "Time for your bath."

"I'm not messy like him," said Sipho.

"I know you're not, but you still have to take a bath. Come here and give me a kiss."

Sipho obliged and whispered something in his mother's ear.

Ella patted his hand. "I know you can do it yourself, 'cause you're a big boy. Monica, it's been a baptism of fire, but you'd better get home now. Your parents will be worried about you driving in the dark."

I had forgotten about that. "Are you sure you'll be okay till tomorrow morning?"

"Yes. Thanks for forcing me to eat. I feel as though I have a bit more energy now. Why is it that I find such a good friend now that I'm…"

"Don't. If I'm not allowed to cry, then that's not fair."

"Okay," she said. "You're right."

I turned to the children. "Good night, boys."

Mandla grabbed a handful of my hair and tugged.

"No, Mandla," said Ella, trying to disengage his fingers.

He spied his mother's copper bangle and let go of my hair to grab that instead. I held out my hand to Sipho. He looked at it shyly.

"Go on, Sipho," said his mother. "Shake Monica's hand."

He put his small hand in mine.

"Good night, Sipho, or should I say, Dr. Sipho?"

He gave a coy giggle. I looked at my watch—it was seven-forty-five. I dreaded driving in the dark, but I dreaded going back to my parents to discuss this move to Italy even more.

On the way home I realized that I should have phoned my parents from Ella's house. It was too late to rectify my mistake now, because I wouldn't stop at a public phone at this time of night. My poor mother and father were probably distressed, and understandably so; since my carjacking, I'd made it a rule not to drive in the dark.

My misgivings were well-founded. When I walked into the kitchen at a quarter past eight, my mother jumped up, knocking her chair over onto its side. She had the portable phone in her hand and my address book open on the table in front of her.

"Did you have a problem with the car?" asked my father, frowning.

"No, I went to visit someone and the time just flew by. I'm sorry. I should have phoned."

"Your mother was frantic. She's called all of your friends." His voice was terse.

"It's a new friend," I said quietly.

As he picked up my mother's chair, I saw that his hands were trembling.

"Sorry, Dad. Next time I'll call. I promise."

"There won't be a next time, because we'll all be in Italy soon and we won't have to worry about you there. Things will be much better. You'll see."

I closed my eyes and said a brief prayer that my father would be the one to see, but I had little hope of this happening. I had better pray instead for the courage to persevere despite his inability to understand.

Chapter Thirty-Three

Monica

Pastor Wessels might have had two hundred pairs of eyes trained on him as he paced up and down the platform, arms outstretched in an exaggerated hug to demonstrate his point, but it was as though he'd written his homily just for me. "Who is my neighbor?" he asked, his voice carrying to the far recesses of the Church of the Good Shepherd, where the teenage boys sat whispering to each other behind cupped hands.

It had been more years than I cared to remember since I'd last attended a Sunday service in this church, but for the most part everything was still the same: the dark wood pews smelling of wax polish, the formal arrangement of yellow roses and baby's breath, the red leather-bound hymnbooks, their spines now rubbed smooth. Even Pastor Wessels hadn't changed, save for the loss of some hair. Nothing had changed and yet everything had changed, because dotted among the white faces of the congregation were many brown faces, and a few black ones, too. They were families with children dressed up in suits and lace-trimmed dresses, young couples holding hands, elderly couples clutching canes, a young mother on her own holding a sleeping baby. With the sermon still in Afrikaans, I presumed that most of them were Colored, the name our classification-obsessed country gave to people of mixed race, as it was their first language, too.

Pastor Wessels finished reading the parable of the Good Samaritan and took off his glasses.

"From this wonderful story," he said, smiling, "we learn that my neighbor is the one who needs our help." He paused to let the words sink in.

That was it. Before my stay in the hospital, I would never have identified with a single black mother or an old grandmother living out in the country. I belonged to a community of white, middle-class people just like me. But I'd learned to view the world differently, and now the message was clear: Ella was my neighbor, and she needed my help.

After the service I stopped outside the church door to shake Pastor Wessels's hand.

"Welcome," he said, patting me on the shoulder.

"Thank you."

"I mean welcome back."

I was dumbstruck that he remembered me.

"How's your mother? I hope to see her with you next Sunday."

"She's…she's fine," I stammered. "I'll try to get her to come."

"Good. We've missed you both." He handed me a church bulletin. "Your father might be interested in this."

As I walked down the brick pathway to my car, I glanced at the weekly calendar in the bulletin. Sunday evenings were now reserved for a service in English.

Lunch was ready when I arrived at my parents' house. Ours was the only family I knew of that used their dining room. During the week the tablecloth was plain yellow cotton, but on Sundays my mother unpacked a beautiful white swathe of linen embroidered with pale taupe thread and edged with handmade lace. She'd bought it from a roadside vendor on the way to Sun City one summer, but always told guests it was imported from Italy.

The stinkwood table and eight chairs were made fifteen years ago in Knysna, a coastal town between Durban and Cape Town, by one of my father's clients. Last year my mother tried to order a matching server, but the man had moved back to Portugal.

There were two paintings on the wall: one a seascape my mother had bought at an arts fair at Zoo Lake, the other a sunset over the Bushveld, presented to my father by the artist after he'd tiled his bush cabin.

I'd given up my flat and moved my things into my parents' garage. It seemed strange, moving back with my parents, but nothing about my life was the same since the carjacking.

After handing my father the church bulletin and extracting a promise from him to take a look at it, I realized that both my parents were concentrating unusually hard on their customary Sunday lunch of roast chicken, potatoes and vegetables.

"Okay, out with it," I said.

My mother looked at my father, but he was examining the potatoes he'd cut into symmetrical triangles. "Tell her, Paolo."

Suddenly, I became nervous. My mother was the big mouth in matters except those that were really consequential.

He put down his knife and looked pleadingly in the direction of the living room, where the television flickered soundlessly.

"Don't even think about it, Paolo," said my mother.

"Okay, I'll tell her," he said. "Monica, I've sold the

company to Bernie du Toit. We leave for Italy in two months."

I knocked my glass of water over and made no attempt to mop it up. My mother didn't say a word, just collected our napkins, slipped them under the tablecloth and then began picking up the blocks of ice and slices of lemon. I'd spilled orange juice on the table the day it arrived, but she wasn't quick enough with the cleanup operation then. The amoebae-shaped white mark was still visible, even though Francina had polished it hundreds of times since.

"We'll make a list and work through things methodically," she said, lifting the tablecloth to inspect the table. There was no trace of the spill.

"What are you talking about?" I asked.

"All the things you'll have to do before we go," said my father.

"So I'm going with you?"

"Of course, sweetie," said my mother. "You're the reason we're going. What happened to you was a sign for us."

"Can't we put it off for a few years?"

My father shook his head. "I won't get an offer like this again."

He was going to set up a workshop in his hometown in Italy and make toy wooden boats, ornaments and Christmas decorations to sell to tourists. I was to help with the selling, or I could try my hand at making stained glass, something he knew I'd always wanted to do.

"If I knew I was going to become a salesgirl, Dad, I would have skipped my four years at university and gone straight to a department store."

He stood up. "Mirinda, see if you can talk some sense into the girl. The soccer's starting."

Ten seconds later we heard him swearing because he'd missed the first goal.

My mother didn't understand why I wasn't excited

about the prospect of starting afresh. "Now that Anton's gone, what have you got to keep you here?" she asked.

It was an opening, but my plans, at this stage, were just that—plans. And if I could not offer any specifics, how would I explain to her that my life here had new purpose?

I wanted to ask her why she'd never taken what happened to Luca as a sign to leave, but I didn't have the nerve. All I could do was promise I'd think about it. Since I was the reason they were going, it was the least I could do. I did ask her, however, why she'd changed her mind about leaving when she'd always been so patriotic, when her ancestors had been here for centuries.

"Things have changed, haven't they?" she replied, picking up my father's plate and scraping the potato triangles into a bowl to put in the refrigerator. "Come on. Help me clear the table and wash the dishes. Francina's gone to church and won't be back till five. Bless her— why their service has to last the whole day, I don't know."

Their service. It had always been *us* and *them*. And, for *us, their* lives ceased to exist the minute they walked out our back doors to go to their rooms with our leftovers and hand-me-downs. My mother knew little about this woman who had lived under her roof for years; nor did she want to. As much as it shamed me to admit it, until my stay in the hospital I had shared this attitude. Now I didn't have to go with my parents to be in a different country—I just had to open my eyes. If it weren't so sad, I might laugh.

Chapter Thirty-Four

Ella

Simple things give me pleasure, like the dappled shade of this pin oak as I sit on a bench watching two small boys in tattered T-shirts chase pigeons and pull faces at clucking, old ladies. Like the ice-cream cone I hold in my hand: Dutch chocolate—Sipho's favorite.

I wish my boys were here to enjoy this lovely afternoon in the park with me. Men and women in business suits stride purposefully in the direction of shining skyscrapers, biting furiously into hot dogs and toasted sandwiches along the way; two bearded men lie on their backs on the grass, brown paper bags clutched in the crook of their arms—guarding their liquor even as they sleep.

A large crowd surrounds the building I have just come out of. The people jostle and push, all trying to make sure they'll get a seat for the long afternoon ahead. I have no intention of going back in. I've had my fill, just like those two sleeping on the grass.

Attending a session of the Truth and Reconciliation Commission is not easy. Thankfully, I took enough tissues with me to last the morning. I listened to parents tell how their sons were picked up by the police and never heard of again; I heard the testimony of white people whose children had been blown to bits by bombs planted by an underground political movement with no legal voice; I watched the fearful eyes of ex-security policemen as they confessed horrific violations of human rights in exchange for amnesty; I listened to ex-MK soldiers confess to torturing and killing their comrades whose loyalty they'd deemed shaky.

For hour upon hour I sat on the hard wooden bench, hoping to recognize one of the men who used to come at night to our house in Soweto, hoping I'd hear the words "I'm sorry" from his lips. But I never did, and after witnessing five hours of anguished tears and mothers fainting, I picked up my pile of crumpled tissues and walked out into the bright Highveld sunshine and the lunchtime bustle of downtown Johannesburg.

And here I sit enjoying the life pulsing through the veins of the city, while inside that building the commission is preparing to hear of lives ending brutally. The ice-cream vendor chases the boys away with a stick. Once out of his reach, they laugh at him.

"Come here," I shout.

They regard me with suspicion, expecting a tongue-lashing. Then I wave a five-rand note at them, and they come immediately.

"Buy yourselves an ice cream and stop tormenting that poor old man. He's just trying to make a living."

They grin at each other. *"Ke ya leboha, Mmangwane."* Thank you, aunty, they say in unison, and scamper back to the ice-cream man, holding the money aloft like a trophy after a big game.

Monica's car is parked outside when I arrive home, so I tell the kind lady who helped me to my building that I can manage from here. She isn't convinced, but agrees to it when I tell her my husband will be down in a minute to help me up the stairs. I don't want Monica to know I collapsed on the sidewalk after getting out of the bus. She worries enough as it is.

I don't know what Monica tells her parents, but she comes here after work every day. Often, she stops at the store on the way for necessities such as milk, bread, tea and fruit. I insist on reimbursing her, but she hides the money—in the bread box, behind the teacups, in the refrigerator.

Mandla thinks Monica's better than chocolate milk. Whenever he hears her at the front door, he abandons his cartoons and charges at her legs like a little bull. Then she lifts him onto her shoulders, and he becomes a human periscope as they scan the room for Sipho. Sometimes they'll catch sight of an eye peeping out from behind the sofa, or a shoelace sticking out from under the table. Sometimes the search will spread to the rest of the flat. "Where's Sipho?" Monica will say, lowering Mandla to the floor so he can do the hunting. Then he'll totter around on his important mission and roar with laughter when he finds his big brother.

Sipho is a patient participant, but games and rough-and-tumble play do not interest him. Monica caught on quickly, though, and won huge points when she brought him her old children's encyclopedia. I wonder if she regrets it, because each evening she receives a simplified refresher course on the first moon landing, how tides work, the invention of the telephone, the rise and fall of the Tyrannosaurus Rex or whatever it was that Sipho found interesting that day.

I usually collapse on the sofa when I come home from work, but today I head straight for my bed. Monica brings me a glass of apple juice and feels my forehead.

"You're burning up," she says. "You have to see your doctor again."

"I can't afford to miss any more work. Bob will fire me." I turn around and smack my pillows. "These things are like wedges of cardboard."

She jumps up as my elbow knocks over the glass of apple juice.

"I'm sorry," I say. "I'm in a foul mood."

"No kidding." She blots up the juice with tissues.

"I can't believe my luck. A lifetime spent in exile waging the almighty Struggle, only to return home to be sentenced to death by my husband's vanity. I can't believe this is how it's going to end. And my little ones…"

I cannot bring myself to tell her that, after my glorious time in the park, I went to a public phone and called the welfare department. I wanted to ask them, in private, what would happen to Sipho and Mandla when I died. The lady's first question was, "Have the children contracted HIV, too?" I came close to pulling that blasted phone out of its cubicle. Her voice wasn't unkind, but she could have pretended that this wasn't routine for her. She said they'd be put in an orphanage in downtown Johannesburg until foster parents could be found. The worst of it was that she couldn't guarantee they'd be kept together, because the baby would be snapped up—her very words—but not many people wanted to adopt a boy of eight.

Chapter Thirty-Five

Monica

I had expected my mother to break down and cry, but her voice was like dry ice. "I don't believe you, Monica. After everything you've gone through, you want to stay here? I'm going to get your father."

The color had drained from his face when he walked into the kitchen. "Is this true?"

"I'm sorry, Dad," I said, sounding more confident than I felt. "It's been a difficult decision to make, but I've made up my mind."

He clenched and unclenched his fists at his sides.

"I'm sorry, Dad," I whispered, "but my home is here."

He pulled out a kitchen chair and sat down heavily.

I sat down across from him. "I belong *here* now, Daddy.

He cupped his chin in the palm of his hand and stared at the sugar bowl.

"I'm not saying it's forever. I'm not saying I'm never going to make those stained-glass windows with you. Maybe in a year or two I'll join you. I don't know. But, for now, this feels right."

My mother put her hand over her mouth, as though preventing a scream from escaping.

I leaned over to take her other hand. "Mom, don't. Please."

"I'm never going to see my grandchildren." Sobbing, she collapsed onto the chair next to my father.

"Oh, Mom. Let me get a husband first," I said, my voice teasing.

She fell against my father's shoulder. "Tell her she can't do it, Paolo. Tell her."

He put his arm around her. And I felt like a traitor.

Our household went into a state of mourning. My father spent his days and nights at his office explaining the tile business to Bernie du Toit and his sons, and my mother wafted from room to room with a whipped expression on her face, randomly sorting through a lifetime of accumulation while Francina trailed behind, accepting hand-me-downs with a broad smile. She'd already found another job with a neighbor, who was about to give birth to twins.

"I can't wait any longer for you to bring babies into the house," she told me.

I had failed everyone. But something told me that I would not fail to fulfill my true purpose in life.

It was a Friday afternoon and I was at my desk trying to figure out a news angle for a nonstory Le Roux had given me, when Ella phoned.

"Are you all right?" I asked. She never contacted me at work.

"Relax. I only wanted to let you know that Mrs. Dube just called. Her son's trial date has been set. She sounds awful. I think we should go and see her after the trial, just in case…"

"What else did she say?"

"Not much. Someone in the background kept shouting at her to hurry up. I also wanted to tell you not to come after work today."

"But who'll—?"

"I seem to have a bit of energy this afternoon. Go and spend time with your family."

Had she guessed my plan? Impossible. She didn't even know I'd told my parents I wasn't going with them to Italy.

"You're early," said my mother. "I presume there wasn't much work today?"

They had assumed I was working late when I was at Ella's, and while I hadn't outright lied to them, I had let them continue in their mistaken assumption. I didn't want them panicking about my driving in that part of town—I did enough of that myself. And if my mother knew that Ella had AIDS, she'd give me a list of instructions: Don't drink from Ella's cups, don't use her bathroom, don't let her children touch you in case they have it, too.

I poured myself a glass of cream soda and flopped onto the sofa. "My editor said he'd do the tapes."

"Your father has something to tell you. Go on, Paolo." She gave him a look of encouragement.

He cleared his throat. "You know we're not happy about your decision to stay here, but how about we give it a try for a year? If you find it too hard, too lonely, too frightening, then you'll join us in Italy at the end of the year." He looked up at the ceiling, his eyes narrowing as though he were trying to remember the next point on a list.

"Dad, I—"

"Shh, I'm not finished. I know, financially, things are going to be difficult for you. I'm not saying you can't look after yourself, but that place you work for doesn't pay much. So we want you to keep this house and your mother's car."

I couldn't believe what I was hearing—a part of me felt suddenly abandoned. But it did make my plan that much easier to carry out.

"There is one condition. You must get a roommate." His voice was resolute. "This place is too big to live in all alone. I'll have more burglar bars installed before we leave, and you know the armed response car will be here within three minutes if the alarm goes off. But I mustn't think about that now, or I'll change my mind."

"Dad…"

He put up his hand. "Because of exchange control, we won't be allowed to take all our money out the country, so I'm leaving you half my shares. They're doing quite well now, so I advise you to leave them alone, but you can sell them if you ever need money. Okay, I've finished what I had to say, and now I must go and meet Bernie." He rose, eager to escape the rush of emotions he knew was coming.

I grabbed his hand. "Oh, Daddy!" Tears streamed down my cheeks.

He looked at me, not with the glazed look of the past when it had seemed he was thinking of other things, of another child, but with a look of loving tenderness, just for me.

I threw my arms around him. "I love you, Daddy."

"I love you, too."

The words felt hot on my scalp.

Chapter Thirty-Six

Ella

Kindness is always overanalyzed by the ill. Where a healthy person would be touched, sick people turn paranoid, second-guessing method, motive, even character. Because we know the time is approaching when all we'll have is our dignity, we guard it jealously, suspiciously, lashing out at those who bustle around us, accusing them of being patronizing, of treating us like children, of using us for their own philanthropic ends in order to rack up points with the Almighty.

"I thought you'd be happy," says Monica in a small voice. When she arrived, her eyes were shining, her face so flushed she looked like a pomegranate about to burst. Now she looks as though she might cry. "You can sell your flat and then you won't have to drag yourself off to work anymore to make the mortgage payments. Wouldn't you like to stay home all day with Mandla, spend the afternoons with Sipho, and—"

"Hang around waiting to die?" I roll up a pair of Sipho's black school socks and add them to the pile of clean laundry on the bed.

"You know that's not what I meant. Here I thought I was giving you great news...."

"And you were thinking what a good person you were."

"Look, I don't need this." She picks up her bag. "I'm going home to spend time with my parents."

"Monica, wait!" I grab her hand. "I'm sorry. It's just that I feel so useless because I can't look after my family anymore."

How strange life is—Monica's mother is leaving, and mine died waiting to come back. She was sewing a little gold Going South label into a slinky wedding dress for a local nightclub singer when it happened. Sometimes I dream of it: her song ending midverse as she slumped forward, her chin hitting her chest, her arms unfurling as though in surrender, her thread tin crashing onto the concrete floor. I ran to call the doctor from the clinic up the road, but it was too late. It had been a massive stroke.

In one of those cruel curve balls life is apt to throw, word was sent four days later for the exiles in Lusaka to return to South Africa. Nelson Mandela had been released after twenty-seven years in prison, and plans were underway for negotiations that would hammer out a new democratic constitution. My mother, the woman who'd left her country a second-class citizen, never got the chance to make her cross on the ballot paper, something she'd dreamed about for fifteen long years in exile. Our little neighborhood of exiles shed their mourning clothes to dance in the streets. The men cooked three whole pigs over roaring fires and the women stirred pap, cabbage, and thick tomato-and-onion sauce in oversize cauldrons while the children listened wide-eyed to stories of the beloved homeland they'd never seen.

"I can't live in that big house all alone," says Monica. "You'd be doing me a favor."

"What do your parents think about it?"

"Well...um..."

"You haven't told them, have you?"

"I'll get around to it."

"I'm not stupid. I won't let my pride get in the way of accepting your offer. Thank you, Monica."

"Good," she says, smiling again. "Now's the fun part. Go into your boss's office and touch every pen, pencil, eraser and file you can find. Then tell him you quit."

I give her a high five. "Now you're talking, sister. Sipho! Mandla! Come in here!"

Mandla waddles in ahead with Sipho in tow.

"Mom, it's *National Geographic* on TV." Sipho's face shows the torture it is to be dragged away from his favorite program. "Tonight they're showing how baby kangaroos are born."

"Boys, how would you like to move to a place where there's a garden?"

Mandla jumps up and down on his chubby legs. He doesn't know what a garden is, but it's been a long time since he's seen me this happy.

Sipho's not so sure. "Will I still be able to go to the same school?"

Monica screws up her face at the question in my eyes.

"I'm afraid not," I tell him.

He bows his head and puts his finger in his mouth.

Monica kneels in front of him. "But the new school you'll go to has lots of wonderful things. Like computers. Do you know what a computer is?"

He nods his head and frowns. "Of course. I am eight." His eyes brighten. "Even for children in standard one?"

"Oh, the younger, the better. And they've got soccer fields, tennis courts, a swimming pool."

She needn't bother. The computers have already bought his vote.

Mandla reaches up for me to hoist him onto the bed. Once he's got his wish, he bounces up and down, toppling my neat piles of laundry. But I don't care.

"Will there be any other black kids in Sipho's school?" I whisper to Monica. "I don't want him to feel like the odd one out."

She places a hand on my arm. "All taken care of. I phoned the principal, and he said that thirty percent of the pupils are black."

"Really? Where do they all come from?"

She laughs. "Allow me to tell you about the new South Africa, my friend. A lot of black families have moved into the neighborhood."

"What am I doing wrong if all I can afford is this little flat?"

"Excuse me, but you're going to be living there, too, now—as a lady of leisure."

"Goodness, you're right. Maybe I'll take up bridge."

Hearing me laugh, Mandla bounces over, squealing with delight, and sticks his fingers in my mouth.

When I first heard my diagnosis, I felt as though God had closed the door on me and my children. But now, in sending Monica to help us, He has thrown a window open wide. I should have heeded my mother's wisdom. How could I have lost faith?

Chapter Thirty-Seven

Monica

My parents' hand luggage felt as though it were filled with bricks. They'd gone on a mad buying spree, stocking up with seven bottles of South African wine, five bottles of chutney, ten jars of anchovy paste, four extra-value packs of Rooibos tea and three boxes of curry powder. My urge to chicken out was almost overwhelming. Why had I been so foolish, so filled with juvenile camaraderie, even craziness? This was the most difficult thing I'd ever have to do.

"The security firm gets paid on the second of each month," said my mother, "the water and lights on the fifth, the—"

"It's okay, Mom. You've written it all down for me."

Deprived of something to say to delay the goodbye, she opened up her purse for about the fourth time since arriving at the airport to check the tickets and passports.

"This is nonsense," said my father in a stern voice. "I know I've promised to let you give it a try for a year, but let's make it six months. It's not right for you to stay here.

The family in Italy are going to think we're terrible parents."

"Dad, you were younger than I am now when you came here. And you didn't speak the language or have any money. This is my home. I have a job. And there's a fortune in the bank I'm going to blow on CDs this afternoon."

He ignored my feeble joke. "That was different."

I knew he meant it was because he was a man, but I let it slide.

"Sweetie, your father's right. Please reconsider in six months."

Sensing that it would be impossible for them to get through this without the prospect of a reunion in the near future, I agreed.

My mother grabbed my hand. "Thanks, sweetie. I feel much better now."

"I've given you the name of my bank manager," said my father. "Phone him if you have any problems."

"I will, Dad."

In half an hour they'd be thirty thousand feet in the air, and I'd be completely alone down here on the forlorn tip of the great African continent.

"Take care of yourself." My mother put her arms around me. "I don't know if I can do this," she sobbed, tightening her hold.

"Of course you can, Mom," I sobbed back, angry with myself because it was my fault we had to go through this. But it was too late to back out, even if I wanted to.

I saw my father concentrating on the light flashing next to their flight number and broke away from my mother to hug him.

"Goodbye, Dad."

His arms enveloped me in a python's grip.

"This is the final call for all passengers on flight 286 to Rome," said a nasal voice over a crackling public address system.

"Monica," said my father, pulling away so he could look at my face. "I know I should have told you this before, but I've always been very proud of you." Then he hugged me again so I wouldn't see the tears coursing down his cheeks.

"Would passengers Brunetti, traveling on flight 286, please board immediately. You are delaying the flight." The nasal voice was one octave higher.

He picked up their hand luggage. "Come on, Mirinda. It's time."

"Oh, sweetie, I'm going to miss you so much." She hugged me one last frantic time until my father pulled her away.

As he steered her through the metal detector into the passengers-only departure hall, she looked back and waved wildly in my direction. I watched my father hand their passports to the official and then put his arm around her heaving shoulders while the man checked their foreign exchange stamps. Once their passports had been returned to them, they broke into a trot to get to the gate in time, and I lost sight of them.

Through a blur of tears I managed to find my mother's car—my car now—in the parking lot. They'd left something on the front seat: a parcel wrapped in brown paper and an envelope, which was not sealed. "Dear Monica," said the card inside. "We miss you already. Just something to keep you company. Love Mom and Dad."

I tore off the brown paper. It was a Paddington Bear. I'd loved him since I was a child, and only last week had asked my mother why I'd never had one. She said we couldn't afford expensive toys back then.

I leaned my forehead against the steering wheel and abandoned myself to loud, ugly sobs of self-pity. If the alarm in the next car hadn't gone off for no reason at all, I might have stayed like that for hours.

* * *

Francina was exultant when I arrived home and asked her to stay on to help with two little boys.

"I'm happy I'm not leaving you," she said, "but I'm even happier that we're going to have some children in the house at long last."

Her joy was contagious, and I felt a sudden sense of peace— as if all the house needed was Ella's children in residence to fill the emptiness left by my parents' departure.

Chapter Thirty-Eight

Ella

With his nose pressed to the car window, Sipho surveys the landscaped sidewalks, high walls, and elaborate wrought-iron gates of Monica's neighborhood. We pass an elderly black man cutting the edges around a driveway with a pair of garden shears. As we pass the man straightens, rubs his back and waves at Sipho. Sipho lifts his hand once we have already gone by. Berea is never this quiet in the dead of night, let alone on a Saturday morning. An American sport utility vehicle waits in a driveway for Monica to pass before entering the road. The woman at the wheel sounds the horn, and Monica waves at her.

"My mother's bridge partner," she explains. "Could be yours, too."

"*Ja,* sure," I tell her.

I cannot believe that this Greek-island-postcard house with the magnificent bougainvillea is going to be my home. And to top it all, when the sale of my flat goes through, I'll have a nice little trust fund for Sipho and

Mandla, thanks to a surge in prices as a result of a housing shortage in the city. Because I don't want Themba getting his hands on the money, I've asked the sweet family who want my flat to wait until my divorce comes through before coming to sign the papers. I know I shouldn't be feeling so vindictive toward Themba. The Bible tells us to forgive our enemies, yet I cannot find it in my heart to forgive the man who has so injured me and our sons.

Mandla claps as the garage door opens in front of us.

"How did she do that?" Sipho whispers in my ear from the back seat.

"Ask Monica," I tell him, but he is suddenly shy.

As the garage door closes on us, Mandla begins to whimper and Sipho clutches the back of my neck.

"Don't worry. I'll turn on a light," says Monica.

We unload three suitcases from the trunk and decide to leave the bags of shoes for later. Mandla bangs on the kitchen door until Monica opens it, then charges ahead making growling noises. Sipho refuses to get out of the car.

In the kitchen, Mandla spies the cat, lying peacefully in a patch of sunlight on shiny ceramic tiles. He grabs its tail, and it hisses at him, teeth bared. He falls backward onto his rear, screeching as though his face has been scratched.

Monica bends down to stroke both of them. "You mustn't pull the kitty's tail, Mandla. She's old. She's a grandma."

He looks at Monica, takes a giant gulp of air and nods.

"What about Sipho?" she asks me.

"He'll come in his own time."

"Okay. I'll leave the door unlocked." Beckoning me to follow, she picks Mandla up and carries him into the living room. "Make yourself comfortable," she says. "This is your home now."

The front door opens. It's the woman I saw peeking at us the day I came for coffee. She's carrying a bunch of daisies.

"Good afternoon," she says, then turns to Monica.

"I've made up the beds, but the towels are still on the line. They're almost dry, so tell me when your friends arrive."

"They're here," says Monica.

"I mean the house guests."

"These are them."

She looks me up and down. Mandla creeps behind my legs.

"No," she says emphatically.

"Yes, Francina," says Monica.

I shift from one foot to the other.

"You could have told me, Monica," she says. Then she clicks her tongue and stalks out.

Monica gives me a wry grin. "I'm sorry. I won't be a minute."

In the kitchen, Francina is slamming cupboard doors and drawers.

I hear Monica's voice first. "What's the matter?"

"You could have told me it was *that* woman who was coming to stay. I'd rather work for the lady next door than *her*."

"What do you mean, *that* woman?"

Francina does not answer.

"I'm trying to understand, Francina, but you have to explain it to me."

"She's just so…"

"So what?"

"So *black*." Francina draws out the vowel in a long, flat sound.

She's right. I'm very dark compared to her.

"And she's one of those ANC people. You told me so."

"Is that going to be a problem?" asks Monica. "Because if it helps any, she's not active in politics anymore, so you don't have to worry about her bringing people over for meetings or anything."

"I just think you should tell me things *before* they happen, not afterward." Francina's voice is sulky.

"You're right. You live here, too. I'm sorry, Francina. She's really very nice. You'll see."

I notice Monica doesn't mention my illness, but Francina has had her fair share of surprises for one day.

I sit down quickly.

"For goodness' sake, Ella, you're balancing on the edge of that sofa like a gymnast," says Monica, coming back into the living room. "I told you to make yourself at home."

Mandla tries to take the lid off one of the antique snuff boxes.

"No, Mandla," I say, clapping my hands.

He jumps with fright. This child of mine is a risk taker; he tries another box and gets the same response. Over and over we go through this, until he tires of my scolding and disappears into the kitchen. Monica motions for me to stay seated. We wait a couple of seconds. Silence.

Then Francina's voice. "Hello, my baby. What's your name? Oooh, you're heavy. Do you want a biscuit?"

We look at each other and smile.

"See what I see?" Monica motions with her head in the direction of the kitchen.

An eye peeps at us from behind the door.

"Come in, Sipho," I say.

Slowly he edges around the door, head bowed, finger in his mouth.

"Come, Sipho," says Monica, taking his hand. "I'll show you your room. Ella, you'll have my old room. I've moved into my parents' room because I thought you might feel a bit uncomfortable there."

She leads me into a room fit for a fairy princess, a six-year-old one, not one pushing thirty like Monica.

I stroke a fluffy elephant lying next to its safari friends in a military row on the bed. "It's beautiful," I tell her. "It's very...umm...pink."

"I know, I know. Okay, Sipho. Now it's your turn."

We follow her into the room next door, and Sipho gasps at the huge collection of trophies lining the bookshelves. I don't think his school owns a quarter as many, and definitely nothing as large. Springbok rugby heroes from the early eighties grin broadly at us from posters on the walls, their faces confident, full of expectation. A squadron of model airplanes hangs from the ceiling on fishing gut, their colors mute like the bush, little SADF emblems peeling from their tails. Most of the floor space is taken up by a large pine double bed.

Monica opens the closet. Men's clothes are stacked so neatly on the shelves it could easily be a department store display.

"I'll clear this out," she says.

"It's not necessary," I tell her. "They don't need much space."

Her voice is firm. "No, I have to. It's way overdue."

Chapter Thirty-Nine

Monica

Luca's room was a shrine even though he had never lived in it. I'd tried to stop my mother from tidying out his closet every spring, but she said she needed it for her sanity. Like a blind woman rediscovering a long-forgotten text through touch, she'd feel the fabric of those T-shirts, once soaked in her son's sweat, those socks worn thin at the heel, those gray school trousers still stained with stubborn ink, and a smile of recognition would appear on her face. If I had to, I'd guess that she'd taken at least one item of Luca's clothing with her to Italy.

When I once mentioned turning the room into a sewing room, it was as though I'd suggested we set fire to the house. My only hope now was that she would see the beauty in two real live boys sharing the space.

Those rugby trophies, which I'd hated for so many reasons, had to go. One day my mother found me drawing all over the largest in the collection with a felt-tip pen. I was about thirteen and knew better, but all she did was take me into the bathroom, close the door, and tell me that it wasn't important that I didn't have any trophies of my own.

"Men need them more than women, because they have fragile egos," she said. "They need constant proof of how strong and wonderful they are."

I didn't feel any better; I just wished I'd been born a boy.

Those trophies were supposed to keep Luca safe in the South African Defense Force. He told my father not to worry about him, he'd get into the Defense Force rugby team and wouldn't be posted anywhere. There were boys from all over the country at the trials. Luca didn't even make the final forty-five.

As a child, I tried out for all the school's sports teams. I'd lie awake the night before tryouts visualizing my backstroke tumble-turn, my follow-through on my backhand, my quick baton handover, my lightning dribble to the goal, and the next morning I'd arrive at school with black rings under my eyes and a queasy stomach. All I ever managed was a spot as a reserve left wing for the field hockey team, and I only once played a full match when some of the regular players were away at the provincial trials. Luca had a rugby match against the school's biggest rival that day, so my father didn't even see me help set up the winning goal.

In my parents' room there was an open moisturizer bottle on my mother's blond-wood dressing table, an empty aspirin box on the matching nightstand on her side, a paperback and a glass of water on my father's. I pulled Paddington out of his wrapping and placed him in the middle of the king-size bed. He looked almost regal on the teal jacquard comforter. I read the card again— twice—and stood it on the dressing table next to the black-and-white photo of my parents on their wedding day.

Chapter Forty

Ella

I do not feel any different, although as of today I am no longer a married woman. The nice girl at Legal Aid called this morning to tell me that the divorce had gone through without a hitch. "Good luck," she said, "and if he gives you any trouble don't hesitate to contact the police." I assured her he would not be able to find me, even if he wanted to—and I have my doubts about that. Now that family whose offer on the flat I've accepted can sign the papers and move in.

Sipho hasn't mentioned his father since the morning he woke up and saw all his stuff gone. Even then I didn't give Sipho the standard fare: your father still loves you, nothing's going to change between you, etcetera, etcetera, etcetera. My son does not deserve to bc lied to. The truth is revealed over time, and so far it seems I was not wrong. By not telling him about the divorce, I'm not lying to him. It's just a delay. I'll tell him as soon as he asks about his father.

It's Themba's fault that I am ill, but to wish that I'd

never met him would be to regret the birth of my sons, and I can never do that. Trials come our way in life, but so do blessings, and with these boys I've received more than my fair share.

We are all sitting in front of the TV, eating our dinner off trays. Francina sits next to Mandla, spooning *farfalle* into his mouth. The evening news is on, and twice already he's grabbed a handful of pasta and flung it at her while her head was turned toward the screen.

"How was your first day at school, Sipho?" asks Monica.

He finishes chewing before speaking. "Good, thank you."

"Are there any children like you in the class?" I ask.

"You mean boys who like reading and watching *National Geographic* on TV?"

I notice Monica hide a smile.

"No, I mean boys who look like you."

Sipho thinks for a while. "I don't know, Mom. I am much shorter than the rest of the class."

"I mean, are there any black kids in your class?"

He lays down his knife and fork. "Yes, but our teacher said she doesn't want to hear us say that *white* boy or that *black* girl."

Monica winks at me.

"Oh, I'm sorry, son," I say. "I won't do it again."

Taking advantage of Francina's distraction for a third time, Mandla flings a handful of *farfalle* onto the carpet.

"That's enough," she says, hoisting him onto her hip. "Naughty boys have to eat in the kitchen."

He begins to cry. Monica looks at me, but Francina is right. Although she never addresses me directly and dusts around me as though I'm part of the furniture, she is wonderful with my sons. I have no choice but to learn to trust other people with them.

Months have gone by since I wrote to my cousin, and still she has not replied. Could she have moved? Why, then, has the letter not been returned to me? Could the new residents have thoughtlessly thrown it away? These pointless questions are a waste of my precious energy; God has a plan for my children's future, and He will reveal it to me in good time.

Chapter Forty-One

Monica

Ella's room smelled sour like old milk, but when she apologized for it, I pretended I didn't know what she was talking about. With the plum-red blood she was coughing up, boxes of tissue didn't last more than two hours, and we'd moved on to paper towels.

I'd promised myself I'd tell Francina the truth the first week after Ella moved in, but I'd never mustered the courage to do it. Now it couldn't wait, and I felt relieved that the omission would not be weighing on my conscience any longer.

"What do you mean, she's not going to get better? Why doesn't she go to the hospital?" asked Francina, slamming the lid of the washing machine and twisting the dial around four times before finding the right setting.

I was late for work, but I'd wanted to wait until Sipho was at school before doing this.

"I took her to the hospital yesterday, but there's no point in her staying there. There's nothing they can do for her."

"Which hospital did you take her to—the white or the black one?"

"Francina, there's no such thing anymore as a white or a black hospital."

"I'll only go to a white doctor," she said matter-of-factly, as though expressing a preference for butter over margarine. "What did he say?"

"It was a she."

I still found it unnerving when Francina's right eye rolled back and her left one stayed in place. She lifted the lid of the washing machine and dumped another cup of detergent into the already foaming wash. I had often wondered why we ran out of detergent so quickly.

"She gave Ella some more pills," I continued, "but she didn't tell us anything new. Ella's known for a while that…Francina, Ella has…"

"She's got TB, hasn't she? I can hear it in her coughing. My uncle had TB. He caught it when he worked on the mines. We'll all catch it now." She covered her nose and mouth with her apron.

"No, Francina, Ella doesn't have TB. She has AIDS."

"Ahhh, no, no, no!" She shrugged off the hand I placed on her shoulder.

"It's true."

She dropped the apron and folded her arms. "Then she can't stay here."

"This is her home now."

"But we have to be around her all day. Well, I do. You go to work."

I started to laugh, but then I realized that there was real terror behind her aggression. "You can't catch it from being in the same room."

"I know. I saw a program about it on TV."

"Then there's no problem."

"*Kuyaxaka ngalababaleki. Bahamba iminyaka, bephila kamnandi, manje kuyamangaza ukuthi kungani begula.*"

"What's that? You know I don't understand Zulu."

She pulled a face.

"Tell me what you said, Francina. You're free to voice your opinion."

"I said it's typical of these exiles. They go away for years, live the good life and then wonder why they get sick." She spat the words out as though they would contaminate her if she didn't rid herself of them quickly enough.

"Francina! She did not get AIDS living the good life. She got it through no fault of her own. But that doesn't matter anyway. What matters is that she's sick and needs our help."

Her top lip curled. "They all come back with their fancy degrees and their photos of places around the world, and they expect everyone to welcome them like heroes. They get all the best jobs and make friends with the rich and important people. Puh! They make *me* sick."

"I'm not rich or important, and Ella isn't throwing her weight around at all."

She scowled at me. "What do your mother and father say about this?"

My father didn't even know that Ella was staying here. My mother had written to say that she was too afraid to show my father my letter, but would have to get around to it soon because he kept asking if I'd found a roommate. Her exact words had been, "Don't you have any nice friends at work who want to move in with you—not that Ella's not nice, she's very pleasant, but wouldn't one of your old friends be better?" If those were *her* words, I dreaded my father's. And what would both of them say if they knew Ella had AIDS? I hated to be enmeshed in deception like this, but protecting Ella and her sons was my paramount concern.

I put my hands on Francina's shoulders, and this time she did not shrug them off. "I asked Ella to move in because I can't live in this big house alone. She's doing me a favor, too."

She shook her head. "I don't know...."

"Don't you like the boys? Do you want her to move out and take them with her?"

She squealed as though she'd been slapped. "No, no, I love those two."

"Then you're going to have to come to terms with Ella being here—and with her illness."

She thought for a moment, and then in a slow, deliberate voice said, "Okay, but I won't wash her sheets, and she must use only *one* plate, *one* cup, *one* knife and *one* fork—and she must wash those herself." Her lips puckered into a tight little grimace, and I sensed I'd be wise to take the deal. She gave the washing machine a violent shove with her hip. "What's wrong with this thing? Why's it stopped?"

I pointed to the dial. "You've got it on—"

"I know how it works. I've been washing your clothes for more than half your life."

I put up my hands. "You're upset. I understand." I decided not to point out that she'd set the machine on the hand-wash cycle, which meant that there'd be long periods of just plain soaking.

The phone rang in the entrance hall.

"Feel free to come to me if you have any questions about Ella's disease," I said, making a mental note to pick up some AIDS literature the next time I went to the hospital with Ella.

"Monica!" yelled Ella from the bedroom. "Should I get that?"

"It's okay. I've got it." I picked up the receiver. "Hello."

There was silence on the other end. Then a click. I slammed down the receiver.

"Who was that?" called Ella.

"Nobody." I walked into her room and flopped into the armchair.

"Nobody?" She was lying on top of the comforter with a half-done crossword puzzle.

"I can't understand people. All they have to say is, sorry, wrong number."

"Monica, I have to talk to you." Slowly, she pulled herself up until she was almost sitting.

My stomach did a flip-flop. Did she want to discuss the children, and what would happen to them once she'd gone? I didn't know if I had the strength to talk about her death.

"When you were at work yesterday, I phoned Mrs. Dube," she said.

Thank goodness. It wasn't about the children. Another day, but not now.

"Monica, her son's trial has started. They should know the verdict tomorrow morning, and I think we should be there for her."

"Tomorrow?"

"Could you get the day off work?"

"Yes, I suppose so. But, Ella, how will you manage?"

"I'll have you to help me."

"Yes, but…"

"You're afraid because there might not be another white person around for miles. But I'll be with you."

"What if people don't want me there?"

"Don't be silly. You do want to see her, don't you?"

"Of course."

She had a sly little smile on her face. "Believe me, it'll do more good than you can imagine." She picked up the crossword. "What's an eleven-letter word for *petrified*?"

I slung my leg over the arm of the chair. "Very funny. I told you I'd come."

She grinned. "No, I'm serious. If I can get nine across, it'll open up the whole top right corner."

"Let's get the thesaurus."

"That'll take all the fun out of it," she said.

I stood up. "I'll leave you, then, with the fun of figuring it out while I go to work."

"Call yourself a journalist, hey?" She picked up a pillow to fling at me, but barely managed to toss it farther than her own knees.

Although Ella's physical strength had begun to deteriorate since moving into my home, her spirits had improved immensely and the boys responded with delight. I was thankful that the only vacant bed in that crowded hospital ward had been the one next to mine.

Chapter Forty-Two

Ella

A blanket of smog hovers over the township, a noxious hangover from the thousands of fires lit to cook breakfast. There are no skyscrapers, no buildings of any height to form a skyline, just a sprawl that starts on the verge of the highway and continues back across the flat Highveld land.

The traffic coming out of the township is heavy. Minibus taxis, carrying more than their legal capacity, weave between cars and trucks, racing each other to the next taxi rank. As the highway forks, Monica veers to the right, avoiding the route that will pierce the very heart of Soweto. The houses we pass are made of corrugated iron, cardboard and planks, with stones to hold down the patchwork roofs. There is no grass, just dirt the color of ox blood. Chickens perch on the hail-dented roofs of rusted, old cars. In one garden, a woman hangs out bright white sheets on a line stretched between two thorn trees, while a little girl of about four sweeps the dirt with a grass broom.

As the road hugs the western edge of the township, the houses grow in size. Here they are made of brick and have roof tiles; some even have garages. We see a bright yellow bulldozer smoothing out a wide tract of red earth, his machine spitting out puffs of black smoke into the dusty haze. Two Bedroom, One Bath, Eat-In Kitchen. You Pick the Finishes, reads the sign. The wire fence alongside the highway is pasted with old newspapers, fast-food wrappers, cigarette packs, even a broken umbrella.

"Where now?" says Monica, as what looks like the end of the highway looms ahead.

I study my notes. My handwriting has deteriorated; the words all seem to run into one another. And Mrs. Dube wasn't clear on too many of the details, either. "Left, then about twenty minutes later we take a right—I think." I cough into a square of paper towel and sneak a peak at its contents. Not too bad. Just a little mucus. No blood.

"Okay?" asks Monica.

"Fine."

Twenty-five minutes later I tell her to watch out for Azania Fresh Produce. Our final turn is just after that.

"Is that it?" she asks.

I thought it would be a store, but it is nothing more than a wooden lean-to with a tin sign planted in the ground.

The single-lane road leads us into a blond sea of veld, stretching as far as the pointed *koppies,* or hills, in the distance. Shadows from spindly thorn trees fall like cobwebs across the hood of the car. We pass the broad black scar of a recent veld fire, the acrid smell of singed grass still sharp in the air. There are huge *dongas* in the road—no doubt from alternating periods of drought and violent rain—and Monica sometimes has to drive into the veld to avoid them.

It is fifteen minutes before we see signs of human inhabitation: a small tin building that looks like it may be a church or school. A bell sounds as we drive by, and children in black skirts or trousers and white shirts pour out the double doors, shouting and laughing, ecstatic to be finished with lessons for the day. The littlest ones wave; some of the older boys run behind us with their hands out.

Monica asks me if I will answer a question with absolute honesty. I tell her that there is no other way.

"Do you think my invitation to come and live with me was patronizing—inspired, maybe, by feelings of guilt over some deep-seated racist sentiments?"

The words are so solemn, so well rehearsed, I feel the urge to reach over and hug her. "I thought so in the beginning. They say that if you're allergic to cats, you should get yourself one and nuzzle your face in its fur until your allergy goes away."

There are a few small cement brick houses dotted around the veld like dice, but no sign of the lime-green one Mrs. Dube has told us to look out for.

"You were trying to prove something, weren't you, Monica?"

She sighs. "Even if I was, is that so bad?"

"Token sincerity never lasts, and I think you're way past that."

"It was more than trying to prove something," she explains. "It just felt right. Like I was doing what I was meant to."

"You mean what God was leading you to do?"

She nods.

"I felt His hand in it, but I didn't realize you did, too. Look, Monica, there it is. Wow! I don't think my old company even makes a green paint that bright."

The house sits back from the road, surrounded on three sides by wavy rows of *mielies,* papery leaves bleached by the white-hot sun and cobs as thick as a child's forearm.

"Where should I park?" she asks.

"As close as you can. Don't be shy."

She shoots me a look and stops the car at a brown metal gate on which a sentinel in a crisp white shirt, red tie and black trousers swings back and forth. He peers at us through the bars, then sprints up to the house, shouting in a shrill voice.

Mrs. Dube appears in the doorway, wearing the burgundy dress with the lace-edged collar. I've never seen her out of bed, and she's much shorter than I expected. She's only a few feet taller than the boy, who now cowers behind her.

Monica helps me out of the car, and I notice she pushes the button down before nudging the door closed with her hip. My legs feel unsteady, as though I'm on the rolling deck of a boat, but she keeps a tight hold of my arm.

I kiss Mrs. Dube on both cheeks. The old lady grins, lowers her eyes. Monica puts out her hand and Mrs. Dube takes the tips of her fingers in a featherweight grip.

"Look at you, Monica," she says, whispering as though in church. "You're walking. Thanks be to God. It's a miracle."

Monica looks at her legs shyly, as though she, too, is surprised.

"I'm so happy to see you both," says Mrs. Dube. "This is my grandson, Nelson. My son named him after Mr. Mandela. I told him it was a bit saucy, but you know what you young people are like nowadays."

"What's the news, Mme?" I ask.

She clasps her hands together. "Not guilty. My son is free."

From inside the house, we hear the sound of clinking glasses and laughter that comes straight from the belly.

"Congratulations, Mme." I hug her tiny frame.

"I knew it all along," she says. "A child doesn't change so much."

But that's not true. Monica has undergone a transformation over the past few months.

Chapter Forty-Three

Monica

A man with graying temples appeared out of the shadowy gloom of the doorway and put his arm around Mrs. Dube. It appeared that his shiny, ostrich-skin belt not only held up his pinstriped trousers, but also pulled in his paunch. There were rows of tiny gold anchors on his navy tie, and I could not help but wonder if his wife or mother had pressed his dazzling white shirt so neatly.

"Welcome to our home," he said. "I'm Edward Dube. Please come inside. My wife is busy in the kitchen. Lunch will be ready soon."

It was dim inside, the only light coming from a square window next to the front door. The two gold-and-beige brocade sofas with plastic covers took up most of the space in the living room, and I noticed that there was no television, just a large old-fashioned turntable on which a Hugh Masekela record played softly, the horn tooting as if he were giving it his last living breath.

"Sit down, please," said Edward.

I helped Ella lower herself onto the sofa, and then I perched on the edge next to her, as she had done the day she came to live in my home. Mrs. Dube pulled up a wooden chair from a corner and sat down on the other side of Ella.

A vase of silk flowers stood on top of a dark wood coffee table. The magazine rack underneath was empty.

"I made the cloth," said Mrs. Dube, noticing me studying the beige crocheted runner with scalloped edges.

"It's beautiful."

"Something smells good," said Ella.

Mrs. Dube nodded. "Beef stew. I made it last night. My daughter-in-law is just heating it up and cooking the rice."

"I'll go and see how much longer," said Edward. He disappeared through a doorway at the corner of the living room with his son trailing behind him.

"How is it going with her, Mme?" asked Ella.

Mrs. Dube shook her head, as though she could not believe what she was about to say. "I think Edward's arrest gave her the shock of her life. She hasn't been to the shebeen in months. She's like a new person now she's not drinking."

"And your pension?" said Ella. "You need that money so you can go to the clinic for your tablets."

Mrs. Dube pressed her hands together, as though in prayer. "I'm thankful for so many things, my child. I spoke to my son about it when we went to visit him in the prison. He had no idea she was taking my money. He was very angry." She leaned forward. "But even better than the money, they asked me to come and live with them again."

"Oh, I'm so happy for you," I said.

Ella grunted. "It's only right."

"I have two more visits to the clinic left," said Mrs. Dube. "I'm not even coughing anymore. Now that my dear son has been set free, everything is perfect. The Lord has truly blessed me."

Me, too, I added silently.

Edward came in, rubbing his hands together. "Okay. It's ready. Let's all go to the kitchen. As you can see, there's no dining room."

Was that for my benefit? Did my presence make him ill at ease? He wasn't showing it if it did.

Ella leaned heavily on me as we walked to the kitchen. She'd only coughed into a paper towel once since we'd arrived.

"This is my wife, Lena," said Edward.

The woman stirring the stew turned around and smiled. I'd imagined a big woman, her face coarsened by years of alcohol, but Lena was as tiny as a sparrow, with delicate features and hair braided close to her scalp in the pattern of a snail's shell.

"Please sit down," she said, waving a hand at a table set with six places. "Nelson, don't forget what I asked you to do."

The boy scampered out and came back puffing under the weight of his grandmother's wooden chair. Edward took it from his son, placed it at the head of the table, and offered it to Ella. I sat down on the kitchen stool on her right. Then Lena took Ella's plate and served up a huge portion of rice and stew. I was relieved; I thought they'd make an embarrassing fuss of seating and serving me first.

"Because we're celebrating today," said Edward, "we'll have a toast with our dinner."

"Toast at night?" said Nelson, and his mother put her hand on his head and laughed.

Edward poured lemonade from a pitcher into six glasses. He handed the first to Ella.

"A toast to God—" Edward raised his glass, and the rest of us did the same "—for allowing justice to be served."

"Amen," said Lena.

"And thanks be to God for my mother's health," continued Edward, smiling at her. "And thanks be to God for these good friends who have come a long way to celebrate this day with us."

"Amen," said Nelson loudly.

"This is lovely, Mrs. Dube...and Lena," I said. It was the first time I'd opened my mouth since sitting down at the table.

Mrs. Dube beamed. "Thank you, my child. Later I'll tell you how to make it—if you want to know."

Without asking, Lena heaped our plates with a second helping, and then took a baked custard out of the oven. I told her that Sipho and Mandla loved sweet, milky desserts, and she stood up immediately and began making another one for us to take home.

Ella looked at me with one eyebrow raised as if to say, "Is this so bad after all?"

Maybe it was the change of scenery; maybe it was the company, but Ella seemed to gain strength as the afternoon wore on. She only coughed into her paper napkin twice, and each time Lena gave her a new one without a word.

Everybody was enjoying her tale about Mandla's recent meal of earthworms. Francina takes him outside each afternoon while she has her tea, and he wobbles around like a drunkard in the sunshine, pulling the petals off my mother's lovingly tended border flowers and digging up all her newly planted seedlings. My mother wouldn't be impressed with the boy wonder's love for gardening, but Ella did have a way of making things sound funny.

Hoping to make her realize that I was nervous about being caught in the rush-hour traffic around Soweto, I caught her eye as she was starting a new story.

"We'd better be on our way," she said, understanding me perfectly.

Edward and Lena stood up to help her, but it was my arm she grabbed. Childish as it was, I felt proud.

Lena held up a Pyrex dish with the dessert. "You can bring it back next time you come," she said.

Outside at the car, I noticed that Ella and Mrs. Dube both had tears in their eyes when they hugged.

"God be with you, my child," said Mrs. Dube.

Ella blinked furiously before pulling away. "Thank you for a wonderful day—all of you," she said. She glanced at me. "You don't know how much this means to both of us."

"Anytime," said Edward, putting an arm around Lena's narrow shoulders.

Nelson climbed on the gate and pushed against the ground with his foot. The gate swung out, then crashed into the fence. He laughed and put out a hand to push himself back again. Mandla would love this game; Sipho would think it pointless.

"Thank you," I said, shaking hands first with Edward and then with Lena.

I hesitated in front of Mrs. Dube. Then I took a step forward and put my arms around her. Just as I'd feared, she stiffened, but I held on and soon her body relaxed.

I whispered in her ear, "Come and visit us when your son has business in Johannesburg. I'm sure the three little ones will play together nicely."

"Thank you. I'd like that," she said.

It would never happen; I was almost sure of it. Mrs. Dube was home to stay and would probably never leave her son's house again.

As I pulled off down the dusty road, I looked in the rearview mirror at the four of them waving.

"Nice family, huh?" said Ella.

"Yes, very nice." I hoped she wouldn't belabor her point. "But there's just one thing I don't understand."

"What's that?"

"Why didn't Mrs. Dube ask after your health? She could see that you're much sicker."

Ella fastened her seat belt. "She knows. I told her when we were in the hospital together."

I took my eyes off the road. "You told her and not me. Why?"

"Simple. You were having a hard time just being around us black people. If I'd told you I had AIDS, too, you wouldn't have been able to handle it." She said it firmly, as though there was no room for discussion.

I switched on the radio. The crackle of two stations fighting for the same frequency filled the car like a snowstorm. A quick search through the other channels turned up nothing; they were all faint and full of static.

There was a three-car pile-up on the highway, and by the time we got home, Francina had put Sipho and Mandla to bed. She picked up the remote and switched off a Zulu game show as I walked in.

"Carry on watching," I told her.

"Agh, it's boring," she said. "The skinny *meerkat* man is winning everything." She covered a yawn. "The boys were tired, so I put them to bed early. Now I've got to go and finish sewing a dress for one of my friends. She's going home tomorrow."

I watched until she was safely in her room, then locked the back door and armed the alarm. Ella's bedroom light was still on, and I found her asleep and fully clothed on top of the comforter. She woke up while I was undressing her.

"I can't keep my eyes open," she said.

"One more second and I'll have this nightie over your head."

She fell asleep again before I'd even tucked her in.

I went to my bedroom with the newspaper, but it felt as though the sentences ran on and on without punctuation. Eventually I gave up trying to concentrate and turned off the light. Far away on the other side of Soweto, Mrs. Dube, Edward, Lena and Nelson were asleep in their beds. They'd never had a white person in their home before—Mrs. Dube had told me this—yet they'd acted as though it were nothing more unusual than doing the laundry on a Tuesday instead of a Monday.

I threw back the comforter and padded barefoot to the kitchen, hoping a cup of Rooibos tea would help me sleep. There were no cars on the road outside and not a lick of wind in the air. Even the pool filter was quiet. It was as still as a glacier in the Antarctic.

Taking my cup with me, I tiptoed into the boys' room. It was only their second night in the new bunk beds. Luca's old bed was already on its way to Francina's family in KwaZulu-Natal. Mandla had kicked off his new comforter and lay sprawled out, as though sunning himself on the beach. I'd taken him with me to buy the comforters. He'd made a beeline for the racing-car ones and had refused to even look at any of the others I'd waved in his face.

As I pulled the comforter up to his chin, his hand flopped out to the side and touched my leg. Sipho was curled up in a ball on the top bunk with just the top of his head showing. How could he possibly get enough air, snuggled way down like that? I put a hand on him to feel for his breathing.

He opened his eyes. "Is it time for school now?" he asked, yawning.

"No, not yet. Go back to sleep, Sipho."

He ducked his head back under the comforter, and in a couple of seconds I felt the steady rise and fall of his breathing again. He was wild about his new school, especially the computer class. Poor little thing; he was going to be disappointed when he woke up and realized that it was Saturday.

The security light outside shone through a chink in the curtains, falling on Luca's biggest trophy like a laser beam. I ran my finger along the engraved plaque for the Best New Player of the Year. There was no dust on it at all. These trophies were extra work for Francina and would be better off going to a charity shop, or a school that could use them again. But a move to the garage would do for now.

The shrill ring of the phone pierced the silence, and Sipho sat bolt upright in bed. I ran to answer it before it woke the rest of the household.

"Hello," I said softly, then held my breath as all the dark possibilities of a late-night call scuttled through my mind.

There was breathing on the other side. Then a click.

"Who is it?" said a wheezy voice behind me, and I turned to see Ella pulling on her dressing gown.

"Nobody."

"What do you mean nobody?"

"They didn't speak. Very weird at this time of the night, don't you think?"

The next day I had to go to the airport to interview an aging American tennis star who was on his way to Sun City for an exhibition match. Since it was a Saturday, Le Roux said I'd be paid overtime, but I had little faith in his assurances. I still hadn't been reimbursed for my unpaid leave while I was in the hospital.

The tennis star rattled off a few inane sentences while dashing to catch his connecting flight; it was plain that he was a man accustomed to speaking in sound bites. My tape wouldn't require much editing to become a perfectly usable filler, so I decided not to go back to the office to package it, but to go in earlier on Monday instead.

As I turned into my street, I saw a hatchback parked on the grass outside my house. There were men inside it.

I changed gear down to second and drove past slowly. A cheer from a large crowd floated through the car's open windows. I turned right, did a U-turn, and came back again, embarrassed that I'd almost set armed guards on three men whose only crime was pulling over to listen to the final minutes of a soccer match.

A letter from my father lay in wait for me on the living-room coffee table. I stared at it for a few minutes, willing his words not to be cruel. Then I grabbed it and ripped it open.

Ella staggered into the living room and slumped into my father's recliner.

"What are you reading?" she asked, panting from the effort of getting out of bed.

"A letter from my father."

"And? He wants you to evict me?"

"He thinks you're part of a syndicate that's going to clear out the house while I'm asleep."

"Agh, I've checked it all out and we're not interested in your Swatch," said Ella, laughing as though it were the best joke she'd heard in years.

Chapter Forty-Four

Ella

The air is crackling dry and hazy with winter dust. Swirling pirouettes of grass, as yellow as old newspapers, whip across the lawn, minitornadoes in a land with no such thing. I haven't been out of bed for days, but I know that it is cold and dry outside, because my skin is taut, my lips chapped and I feel every draft that slides through the house whenever someone opens a door or window. Monica has put her brother's old comforter on top of the sweet-pea one, but still, I feel the cold. I snuggle with Mandla whenever I can; however, something's always calling him to come and investigate it, stick his fingers in it, prod it, lick it. Being a toddler is hard work.

Since Sipho woke me this morning, I've had an uneasy feeling, like something is about to happen, or not happen. Could the mailman be bringing a letter from my cousin today?

It's Thursday—Francina's day off. Mandla plays in the corner of my room, building a castle with his blocks.

Outside, the wind has picked up. It slaps at the shutters, rattles the doors, howls through the eaves.

Mandla stops jabbering, and I look up from my crossword to find him staring at the window, eyes wide.

"What wrong, Mandla?" I ask, but he's transfixed.

Suddenly, there is a loud knocking on the glass.

"Mandla!" I scream. "Come here!"

He is at my bedside, crying, clutching my arm. Where's that panic button Monica gave me?

"Ella!" shouts a voice outside, and I know immediately who it is.

Mandla tries to haul himself onto the bed and howls even more when he can't. Somehow, I manage to help him up.

"Ella, let me in!"

"Go away before I call the police."

Themba knocks again, furiously. It sounds like bricks raining on a tin roof. "Don't be like that, Ella. Let me in. You're alone. Francina's out. Monica's at work."

He knows their names! Those anonymous telephone calls. He's been watching us for months.

"If you don't let me in, I'll go to Sipho's school."

He knows where Sipho goes to school, too! How could I have been so naive as to think I could escape him by moving to the suburbs? The suburbs were supposed to be my haven—it's what I've been aiming at for so long. But everything follows you. There's no escape, no matter how high the walls. I cannot have this man frightening my son at school, father or no father, and so, instructing Mandla to stay put, I drag myself out of bed and let Themba in at the front door.

He inspects me from head to toe like I'm a whore on display. "You're skinny," he says, frowning.

"Thanks to you giving me the virus."

He looks me straight in the eye and says, "How do you know it was me?"

I don't know why that upsets me when there are greater issues at hand, yet I feel like running my fingernails down his cheeks. But I will end up the loser if I try. No, the only weapons I have are words.

"It'll take you down sooner or later," I tell him.

"Oh, no," he says, with the smile of someone about to take the last remaining spot in the lifeboat, "I took care of it."

"Agh, there's nothing you can do."

"For men there is. Two months ago I cured myself by sleeping with a virgin."

"Did you tell her?" I ask, tears stinging my eyes.

He looks at me as though I am a stupid child, or worse, a dumb animal. "Of course not, or she wouldn't have done it. She thinks I'm going to marry her." He shakes his head, then wanders off down the passage toward Sipho and Mandla's room.

"What's all this?" he shouts.

I find him tugging at the model airplanes.

"Why do my sons have our oppressors' war machines in their room?"

"Give it a rest, Themba."

"No, I mean it. What's all this junk?" One by one he plucks the tiny airplanes from the ceiling and throws them to the ground.

"Don't, Themba. That's not your stuff."

"And these," he says, starting to rip the rugby posters from the walls. "Rugby is a Boer game." The posters are old and tear like tissue paper.

"Stop this, Themba."

He moves toward the trophies. "For rugby, too, I suppose?"

I put myself between him and the trophies. "Don't you dare lay a finger on these." My voice is no longer breathy, but venomous—the hiss of a wildcat defending her young.

He looks at me, amused. "A few months in a fancy house and you've turned against your own people."

"You're pathetic, Themba."

"Where's my son?" He walks out the boys' room and opens my closed door.

I hurry after him. Mandla has burrowed his head under the comforter. He screams as Themba picks him up.

"It's me, your father," says Themba.

Mandla screams even louder and shakes his head violently while kicking his father's stomach.

"She's turned my son against me, too."

What's the use of arguing with a man who lacks basic insight into his own failures? The main thing is to get him out of here.

"What did you come for?" I ask, taking Mandla from him.

Immediately, my child stops screaming. I can feel his little body shivering as I cradle him in my arms.

Themba gives him the look he normally reserves for barmen who refuse to sell him another drink. Mandla turns his head away and buries it in my chest.

"My money," says Themba.

Of course he hasn't come to see his sons. He's here for the money.

"We went over that the day you left."

"I didn't leave. You kicked me out."

"The flat was in my name because you didn't contribute a thing—not even ten cents."

"I was going to. You didn't give me a chance."

"When? You joined the new National Defense Force for two months, then left. And you certainly didn't make an effort to get another job."

"I cannot serve in an army with the—"

"Enemy of the people. So you've said, over and over. You're living in the past, Themba."

"That's what you think. A new revolution is coming."

"Oh, Themba, I'm so tired. Please go now."

"I came for my money, and I'm not leaving without it."

"What I made on the sale of the flat is in a trust fund for the boys. Do you think growing children live on air? Schools cost money. Their clothes cost money. I have to make sure they've got something for the future. The account is in their names."

"Ella, I need that money."

"Would you take money from your sons to pay for liquor and women?"

I expect him to slap my face, but he doesn't—probably because I have Mandla in my arms. I need to get him out of the house before Sipho comes home from school. Even though it's Francina's day off, she still walks him home, and I know she'll tell Monica that Themba was here. I have brought more than my fair share of problems into Monica's life. Themba must not be another one.

"I have five hundred here that I was going to give to Monica for groceries. Will you go away if I give you that?"

His face lights up so much, I realize now that he's desperate. But I have no sympathy to give. Desperation comes in varying degrees.

I get the money out of my shoe in the closet and press it into his hand. He begins counting it out loud.

"It's all there. Just go now."

From the front door, I watch him saunter down the path and climb over the gate.

"Next time I'll set off the alarm," I shout after him.

I hope he heard me, because I really do mean it.

Chapter Forty-Five

Monica

I woke with a jolt and immediately reached for the panic button on my bedside table. The strange, far-off rasping noise grew louder. It sounded like someone was being strangled. Taking the panic button with me, I slid out of bed and hurried down the passage, pulling my weak right leg along with my hands to make it go faster.

Ella's palms were pressed against her chest, her eyes were wide, and she was fighting for air.

I touched her cheek and said in a voice as steady as I could manage, "I'm taking you to the hospital."

"What about—?"

"Shh. Don't talk. Francina will look after them."

I deactivated the alarm and went outside to call Francina. She took Ella's shoulders, I took her legs, and between the two of us we managed to get her into the car. As I reversed out of the garage, Francina waved to me as my mother had done on my first day back at work, bending lower and lower while the door closed, until, finally, disappearing from sight. Thankfully, the boys had slept through it all.

The sky was filled with the milky light that appears out of nowhere just before dawn. There were no cars on the roads, only a few bakery and newspaper delivery trucks. Little boys in raggedy coats stood at major intersections guarding their piles of the morning paper and stamping their feet to keep warm. Every time there was a lull between gasps from the back seat, I'd look over my shoulder, terrified that she'd lost consciousness. But she never did. She soldiered on, grabbing the air into her lungs, keeping it there as long as she could.

The doctor in the Emergency Room of the Johannesburg Regional fastened an oxygen mask on her face and rushed samples of her blood to the laboratory. Half an hour later he told me that her T4 cell count was forty-five and that the X ray showed a bilateral pneumonia.

When I asked him what that meant, he shrugged and said, "There's not much we can do now."

I walked alongside the gurney, holding Ella's hand all the way to the ICU. She wasn't battling for breath anymore; she looked peaceful, as though she were dreaming of chubby babies and birthday cake.

At eight o'clock I called my editor and told him I needed leave for a family emergency.

"But your family is in Italy," he said.

I muttered something about explaining it all later and slammed down the phone without saying goodbye.

I sat at Ella's bedside the whole day as she slept, only getting up three times: once to go to the bathroom and twice to phone Francina to let her know what was happening. She'd heard Sipho telling Mandla not to worry, that Mommy would come home from the hospital. But he'd refused to go to school, and I knew it was because he didn't believe it himself.

At four o'clock another doctor came to check on Ella. His coat was buttoned up over a huge belly, making him look like a pregnant woman in a white maternity smock. He leafed through the notes on the clipboard at the end of the bed. Then he stopped, looked at Ella, looked at me, and shook his head slowly.

I got to my feet. "Doctor, what is it?"

He replaced the clipboard. "Can I have a word with you in the corridor?"

I looked at Ella. She was still asleep.

"Fine."

Outside in the corridor, we flattened ourselves against the wall as a gurney came trundling past, but the nurse went out of her way to brush up against the doctor. He smiled and stared after her.

"Doctor?" I said.

He turned back to me. "My girlfriend. Lovely, isn't she?"

"What did you want to tell me?" I wasn't interested in complimenting him on his taste in women.

"Ah, yes. You are her employer, aren't you?"

"No, of course not. What's going on here?"

He put up his hands. "My mistake. Sorry. Well then, what, may I ask, is your relationship with the patient?" When I stared at him without answering, he added, "No disrespect, but I can't discuss a patient with a complete stranger."

I massaged my temples with the tips of my fingers. "We live together, if that's any help."

"Ah, I see." He gave me a strange look. "In that case, I *can* tell you."

Suddenly, it dawned on me what he was thinking, but I let it slide because I wanted to hear what he had to say.

"I just read Ella's notes."

"Yes, and…?"

"The lymphoma in her lung is…"

"No, no, no." I shook my head. "Ella has AIDS, not cancer."

"It's one of the possible complications of AIDS, but your, er, *friend* refused chemotherapy, so we…"

"She what?"

"It wouldn't have helped much. They caught it too late."

"She didn't even try?"

He shook his head.

"She should have. For her little ones."

"She probably *was* thinking of her kids. The chemo would have made her extremely sick, and with her low T-cell count it could've been dangerous. Anyway, at best it would only have bought her another month. Would her kids have coped, seeing her like that? Imagine the memories they'd have of her last days."

I slumped against the wall. "You think you know someone and then…"

"Maybe she didn't want to worry you any more than she had to."

"There are so many things I don't know about her, that I'll never know," I said, more to myself than to him. "How long? How long does…does she have?" I felt like putting my hands over my ears before he answered.

"It could be anytime now," he said, in a gentle but firm voice.

Anytime now. Anytime now Ella would close her eyes, never to open them again. Anytime now the orderlies would whip her away to the hospital morgue, the nurses would strip the bed, and I would be handed a plastic bag with her silver earrings, wallet, maybe her shoes. Anytime now those two boys would be left without a mother. Out of sheer frustration at my utter helplessness I pounded my fists against the wall—and the doctor made a hasty retreat. Then, when my hands began to ache, it dawned on me; there *was* still something I could do for Ella.

Chapter Forty-Six

Ella

Voices rumble outside the ward like a far-off storm. Monica's is the shearing wind, the doctor's the ominous thunder. My sheet is so full of starch it drapes over me like a tent. Sipho has never made houses out of sofa cushions, sheets and bedspreads. Come to think of it, neither did I, nor any of my friends when we were children. Maybe it was because we saw our parents and relatives making their homes out of sheets of corrugated iron.

The voices stop, and Monica comes back into the ward, a fake smile on her face. She has been told.

I push the oxygen mask aside. "How long do I have to stay here?"

"The doctor said indefinitely—until you're better."

"The truth, Monica."

She sighs.

"Please."

"He doesn't think you'll ever go home."

I put my oxygen mask back on, and she takes my

hand. After a minute of silence, I push the mask aside again. "I want to go now."

She presses the call button and tells the nurse who arrives a short while later that I'm leaving.

The nurse's eyebrows swoop upward. "I'll have to speak to the doctor about that." She picks up my chart and stalks off.

"Are you sure about this?" asks Monica.

"Yes. I want to be at home with my kids, and with you."

She lays her head on my arm, not bothering to hide her tears now.

"Oh, excuse me," says the nurse, returning with a stack of papers in her hand. *"O lehlohonolo ha wena le monga hao le utlwana. O mohau."*

I have to laugh, even though it feels like acid swishing around in my lungs. The nurse dumps the papers on my bed and stalks off again.

"What did she say?" asks Monica.

"She said... Oh, I can't stop myself... She said I'm lucky you and I get on so well."

"What does that mean?"

"She thinks you're a kind madam."

"She didn't say that?"

"Oh, yes, she did. She thinks I clean your house."

A few minutes later the nurse comes back with a portly doctor.

"See what I mean, Doctor?" she says.

He looks at us holding hands and crying with laughter, and gives a strange smile, as though he knows a secret. "It's okay," he tells the nurse. "Give me the discharge papers to sign."

As Monica helps me into a wheelchair, he hands her two prescriptions. They are for morphine: one short-acting, the other extended release.

It is the extended release of heaven that I now go home to await, the reunion with my sweet mother and father, my chance to meet my Savior. And so I no longer fear for myself, only for the future of my boys. But, in this instance, I will not allow my faith to waiver.

Chapter Forty-Seven

Monica

Ordinary chores can take up a lot of time while someone we love is dying. The iron needed to be descaled so it wouldn't leave ugly brown marks on Sipho's school uniform; the lightbulb in the dining room had to be replaced; the left burner on the stove had to be cleaned because I'd let a pot of milk boil over; laundry had to be folded; sandwiches made; CDs alphabetized. Francina and I, partners in the bustle of death, were trying our best to give Sipho and Mandla time alone with their mother.

"My mommy's going to die, isn't she?" said a voice behind me, and I turned from the kitchen sink where I was polishing the faucets to see Sipho, his little face bright with sweat as though he'd been running. "You can tell me. I'm going to be a doctor."

"Come here, Sipho," I said, drying my hands and sitting down at the kitchen table. I tried to lift him onto my lap.

"No," he said. "I'm a big boy."

I let him go, but he remained pressed against my knees.

"The truth is, Sipho, your Mommy *is* going to die."

He swallowed hard and looked directly into my eyes. "Why isn't she in the hospital where the doctors can look after her?"

I cupped his face in my hands and wiped away his tears with my thumbs. "Your mommy wants to be at home. She wants to be here with you and Mandla."

He brushed my hands away. "But in the hospital they could give her pills and injections and maybe a *lummy puncha* to make her better again."

I wanted to nestle my face in his sweet warmth and let the tears come, but instead I smiled weakly and said, "Wouldn't it be nice if we could heal each and every sick person? Sipho, there's no cure for the disease your mother has. The doctors wouldn't be able to do much except make her comfortable."

"But I heard them talking on the news about new medicines for AIDS."

My stomach lurched. I wasn't aware that he knew why his mother was dying. "Patients in Africa can't get all the new drugs they have in Europe and America, Sipho. They're too expensive."

"But, Monica, I have some money in my sock drawer. You can use it for my mommy."

A sob caught in my throat, and I gave a little cough to disguise it. "That's very kind of you," I said. "I know she would appreciate it."

"Well then, take it." He pouted, for once acting his age.

"You're a sweet boy, Sipho." I stroked his head.

"It's not fair." His bottom lip trembled as he began to cry.

"I know, I know, Sipho. Maybe by the time you're a doctor, we'll have a cure for this dreadful disease."

"I want to help her now," he said, swiping at his wet cheeks with the sleeve of his sweater.

"You'll make a fine doctor one day, Sipho, but right now, what your mother needs is your love. And you know where she's going, don't you?"

He nodded solemnly.

His Sunday school teacher had been talking to the class about heaven ever since I'd told her of his family situation. Both boys had been shown nothing but kindness since I'd enrolled them in the church, and not once had anyone asked why they were there with a white woman.

A while later I took a peek at the three of them in the bedroom. Hospice had lent Ella a tank of oxygen, and she had the mask on. Sipho lay next to her, holding her hand; Mandla was on his haunches next to her head, tugging on her braids.

Ella pushed the mask away and said, "Come in, Monica."

For more than a month I'd been expecting her to broach the subject of the children's guardianship. Now, against my will, I felt I must do it. But not in front of Sipho.

"Why don't you go and brush your teeth, little man?" I said.

He looked at his mother. She nodded and he trudged off slowly, looking over his shoulder until he was out the door.

"I know what you want to discuss," said Ella. "I think it's time, too."

I sighed. "We have to."

She kissed Mandla's cheek, and he stuck his tongue out at her. "I have a cousin in Durban," she said. "We used to be close when we were children. I've written to her and asked her to look after the boys when I'm gone."

"What?" Her words felt like a stinging slap. "You never told me this. Why didn't you say something?"

"I haven't received a reply from her yet, but—" she struggled for the breath to complete her sentence "—you know what the postal service is like."

I slumped back in the wing chair next to her bed. It was still green. "And this is what you want? For them to go to this woman?"

"She *is* family."

"So's their father, but you don't want *him* to look after them, do you?"

"I don't want them within a hundred miles of him. Anyway, who knows how long he'll last?"

"Do you know this woman's circumstances? Have you seen her lately?"

"Not since we left South Africa, but she sent us a card when my mother died. She has a good job as a lecturer at the University of Natal." She coughed and I quickly tore off another square of paper towel for her to spit into.

"Maybe this is too much for you now," I said.

She crumpled up the paper towel. It was full of blood. "We might not get another chance."

"How can you ask her to do this when you hardly even know her?"

"She's family."

"Are you sure this is what you want?"

Her eyes looked dull, defeated. "I don't have any choice. Family is better than a foster home."

I took a deep breath. This was the moment to share with her the sudden, staggering insight I'd had in the hospital corridor.

"Why do they have to go anywhere when they can stay here?"

"Oh, Monica." She tried to lift her head off the pillow. "I can't ask that of you. You have your whole life ahead of you. How many men are going to want to marry you if you have two adopted black sons?"

"One will be sufficient," I said, squeezing her hand.

She smiled. "You know what I mean."

"Yes, and for the right man, it won't be a problem."

"And what about your six-month trial separation from your parents? It's nearly up."

"I don't think I could bear it if the boys went away," I said quietly.

She opened her mouth to speak, but no sound came out. When I got up to put the oxygen mask on her again, she grabbed my hand.

"I've been hoping—" her voice was barely a whisper "—hoping you'd want to take care of my little ones, but I didn't dare…say anything because…I wanted it…I wanted it to come from you. They love you, too. I can tell." She closed her eyes.

"Ella!" I prodded her arm.

Her eyes flickered open. "I'm still here."

I got down on my knees next to her and pulled the oxygen mask back into place. Mandla grabbed hold of one of her fingers and put it in his mouth.

"I even flossed, Mom," said Sipho, coming back into the bedroom. Then he saw my tears and ran over to his mother.

"She's okay, Sipho," I said, but he patted his mother's arm insistently.

"Yes, Sipho?" Her voice was muffled by the oxygen mask.

His chest fell, as though he'd been holding his breath. Then, without a word, he squeezed himself onto the bed between us and lay down.

Ella pushed the oxygen mask aside again. "There's something I want to say…."

"Shh, don't talk," I said. "Save your energy."

"For what?" She stretched her arm across Sipho and took hold of my hand. "Thank you," she said. "Thank you so much. I can go in peace now."

Mandla began bouncing on the bed.

"One more thing," she said. "Don't let Mandla tire you out. He's a firebrand…a bit like…I used to be. And Sipho…sometimes he's too serious. Get him to laugh."

"I will, Ella."

My tears dropped onto Sipho lying between us. I could feel his little body shuddering. Mandla stopped bouncing and stuck a finger in his mother's ear. Sipho batted his baby brother's hand away, but Mandla did it again, this time giggling. Sipho put his arm around his mother and sobbed silently into the warm hollow of her neck. His tears ran down her emaciated chest, soaking the front of her nightie.

After a while I realized that her tight, painful breaths had stopped. Silence filled my old pink room again.

I was waiting for Francina when she knocked on the back door early the next morning. Words were not necessary; she took one look at my face and broke out into a high-pitched ululation, the traditional Zulu cry of mourning. As she rocked back and forth, covering her forehead with the heels of her hands, I tried putting my arms around her, but her wailing only grew louder.

"Shh, Francina. Remember we have children in the house. They need us now more than ever."

She stopped and said in a perfectly calm voice, "Does that mean they're staying?"

"Yes, Francina, they're staying."

"Oh, thanks be to God. I thought we were going to lose them, as well."

"No," I told her, "things are going to continue much as before."

I had no experience raising children, let alone juggling parenthood with the demands of a career, yet I felt filled with a strange calm. The Lord would help me work it all out. I believed that with all my heart.

Chapter Forty-Eight

Nothing ever turns out the way you want it to. This went through my mind when Francina told me there were three men ringing the buzzer at the gate.

"Must I call the security people?" she asked. "They look like township gangsters."

I felt a dead weight in the center of my stomach, like severe indigestion. I knew who it was, and what they wanted.

"I'll deal with them," I told her.

"Fine, but then *you* open the gate. I'm locking myself in my room."

"Take the children with you."

She scooped up Mandla and pulled Sipho along by the hand. The look on her face told me she thought I'd lost my senses.

I walked down the path and stopped fifteen feet short of the gate.

"Can I help you?"

The tallest of the three stepped forward. The resemblance was unmistakable.

"I've come for what's mine," he said, his thick gold chain catching the sunlight and sending a flash across my face.

"They're not here."

He grabbed hold of the bars on the gate and peered through them with eyes the size of the old fifty-cent coin.

"Come on, Monica." His voice was flirtatious.

How did he know my name? It was an unusually warm spring day, but I suddenly felt cold.

"I want my money."

I was only right about the who, not the what. "What money?"

"The money Ella got when she sold the flat. It's mine."

"Ella put that in a trust fund for the boys' education."

His top lip twitched. "You better get it for me."

"I can't touch it. Talk to a lawyer."

He shook the gate. "Where are my boys?"

"They're not in my house." Technically, I was not lying; they were in Francina's room in the backyard. I felt sure God would forgive the deception, which was for the children's sake.

"Monica." He smiled and nodded his head. "A lovely name."

I froze, and his smile widened but didn't spread to his eyes. I put my hand in my pocket and felt the smooth plastic of the security firm's panic button. His two companions made a move toward the gate, but Themba put out an arm to stop them.

"I don't know what you think you're playing at, pretty little white madam," he said, winking at me.

He was not threatening me, but should I press the button anyway? My brain said yes, press it now. What if he was armed? Only God knew what would happen when the security guards arrived with their guns drawn. But this man was not a stranger; he was the boys' father. I owed it to them to hear him out.

He looked me up and down, the smile still on his lips. "I don't know what that wife of mine told you. She always was a crazy one."

"She's dead."

"I know. I saw the ambulance leave."

Themba didn't look sick, a bit thin maybe, but not sick. He took a key out of his pocket and ran it along one of the horizontal bars of the gate, shaving off a thin spiral of black paint with a horrible squealing noise. He rolled it into a little ball between his thumb and forefinger.

"I want my children, Monica."

"And I told you they're not here." Somehow I managed to keep my voice steady. It went against my nature to be untruthful, but the well-being of the boys was at stake.

"I'm going to get them back—them *and* the money."

"How will you take care of them? You know you're dying."

The dead weight in my stomach heaved. The creep was a murderer. He'd killed Ella and seemed to have no remorse about it. But his turn was coming. A vindictive joy coursed through me at the thought of that certainty.

"It's none of your business," he said, not a flicker of emotion on his face. "But if you must know, I'm sending them to my mother in the Eastern Cape. They belong with *family*, not some bleeding-heart liberal who thinks she can make up for her people's cruelty by playing house with some cute kids."

I knew that the boys had never met Themba's family because Ella had never liked them. She'd called them drunkards and ruffians.

"But Ella wanted me to have them," I told him.

"She was dying and demented. She didn't know what she was saying. I'm their father, and I *will* get my children back."

I wanted to rush over and pull that gold chain toward me so that his head slammed into the bars; instead I started walking back to the house.

I was shocked at the viciousness of my thoughts, but I could not stop them. If taking care of these children was what God wanted me to do, why was He making it so difficult?

"Don't think you can get away with this," he said.

I stopped, but didn't turn around.

"I'm following your every move."

My steps were slow, forcefully slow. I would not run and fumble frantically with the locks. That's what he wanted. I imagined his laugh: a low-rolling poisonous snicker, full of contempt and superiority. No, I refused to be his entertainment. Even though I was light-headed with fear, I would not let him pull the strings to make me dance.

Once inside, I watched them through the peephole. The other two stepped up to the gate and peered in at the house. Themba said something to them, and they both nodded. Then all three walked away. A minute later their car screeched off in the direction of the highway.

I picked up the phone, then put it down. Did I want my parents on the next flight to Johannesburg? I couldn't sit still, I couldn't pace up and down because my legs shook and I certainly couldn't go and get the children from Francina's room in the state I was in. So I lay down on the sofa, put my arms over my eyes and cried until my throat hurt.

"Wake up, Monica."

Someone tapped my arm.

"Monica, what's happened? Are you okay?"

I sat bolt upright. "Where are the boys, Francina?"

"In the kitchen eating hot dogs. We waited for hours in my room for you to come and tell us it was okay to come out."

"I'm sorry. I didn't mean to fall asleep."

"What did those men want?"

"Promise you won't make a scene. I don't want the boys upset."

She nodded.

"It was Themba, their father. He wants them back."

"Nooo!" she cried, holding her head.

"Shh, Francina. You promised."

She glared at me. "I told you to call the security company."

"We'd have to deal with him sometime."

"We'll hide them."

"He is their father, Francina."

"But Ella asked *you* to look after them."

"I know. I should probably get legal advice."

I'd met Nick Stavos while covering the "hammer trial." He'd represented a woman who'd calmly bludgeoned her husband to death as he slept. He'd lost the case, but she only got two years because the judge said twenty years of physical abuse was more than anyone should have to endure. I remembered being impressed with Nick's complete lack of showmanship; he was sincere, to the point, and nobody would have known that he'd torn up the woman's legal bill if she hadn't made a statement to the media.

I didn't expect him to remember me when I phoned, but he did. There were only two options, he said. If Ella had been granted sole custody of the children in the divorce and her will stated that I was to be the legal guardian of her children, Themba didn't have a chance. Without both of these, the law was on the father's side.

Francina and I hunted among Ella's things for the papers and found the divorce decree. It said exactly what I knew it would: She had been granted sole, uncontested custody. There was no sign, however, of a last will and testament.

"Isn't your word enough?" asked Francina. "You can swear on the Bible."

I told her I'd speak to Nick again in the morning, and in the meantime would ask the security firm to keep a closer watch on the house. I'd also take a few days off work in order to drive Sipho to and from school. We couldn't take any chances.

"Okay," she said. "And you better get me a panic button and a phone for my room." She was gone before I could answer.

In the kitchen, Sipho had finished eating his hot dog— with a knife and fork—and was watching his brother lick sweet mustard off his plate.

"Look at him," he said, disgust plain on his face.

Mandla's nose and chin were freckled with yellow. He glowered at me as I took the plate away from him.

"Want some apple juice boys?"

"Juice," shouted Mandla, banging his fists on the table.

"Monica, why did we have to hide in Francina's room?" asked Sipho.

I paused. "I had some business to take care of and needed some quiet in the house."

He thought about this for a while. "Babies are a lot of trouble, aren't they?"

Outside the kitchen window, a bird tried to thread a length of red wool into the nest he was building under the eaves. All the silent phone calls, the men sitting in the parked car. If only I had been more suspicious.

"No, Sipho," I said, "they're no trouble at all."

After tucking the boys under their racing-car comforters, Francina went to her room in tears. I wandered into Ella's room and sat on the bed. Her tin of beads was still on the bedside table, as was the bracelet watch she'd bought at a secondhand store in Toronto. I held it to my cheek and felt its soft tick-tick-tick on my skin.

Chapter Forty-Nine

Monica

The dull light of an overcast sky struggled to penetrate the gloom of Nick's tenth-floor office, its windows smoky-gray from years of exhaust fumes wafting up from the frenetic streets of downtown Johannesburg. I wondered why he didn't turn on his desk lamp instead of holding the divorce decree two inches from his face.

He had grayed considerably since I'd last seem him, but he'd cut his hair short so that he no longer looked like a disheveled graduate student. He still had that earnest way of looking deep into your eyes as you spoke, as though every word was of personal importance to him. There was no sign of a wedding ring.

The building where his office was located was occupied mostly by clothing wholesalers, and his space was so cramped it made me think that the murder trial I'd covered wasn't the first or last he'd done pro bono. I sat ramrod straight on a lopsided typist's chair, waiting for words of hope, a loophole, anything.

Le Roux had been unsympathetic when I called this morning to tell him I needed a few days off work.

"Of course they should go to their family in the Eastern Cape," he'd said. "What do you want with them anyway? You'll have your own one day."

Nick put down the certificate and folded his hands in front of him as though he were about to say a benediction. He was such a gentle man, so unassuming, so quick to help others while requiring nothing in return. If, one day, I were to marry, I'd like it to be to someone like Nick.

"So she asked you to look after the children just before she died?" he said.

"Yes."

"And you're sure she didn't put it in writing?"

"She could barely breathe, never mind write."

I should have discussed it with Ella the night she came home from the hospital, but I was so afraid of upsetting her.

"I know you mean well, Monica, but the law always favors a biological parent in these cases."

The room seemed suddenly darker. Raindrops streaked down the dirty windowpanes in spindly paths, collecting in a pool of grime on the window ledge. It was a good thing I was picking Sipho up from school.

"Monica, are you okay?" His face was creased with concern.

"I suppose so. I'd better get going." A loud clap of thunder punctuated the end of my sentence.

"I'm sorry I couldn't give you better news. If there's anything else I can help you with, please ask." He rose out of his chair and extended his hand to me.

"Thanks for your help," I said.

In the car on the way home, I searched through the stations for something classical and settled on Beethoven's *Coriolan Overture*. Turning up the volume, I let the crashing crescendos pound my brain until it felt numb. There was no need to think. I knew what had to be done. Like wet rags the windshield wipers struggled vainly against the torrent. *Flip-flop-flip-flop*. Their pathetic effort was useless, and eventually I had to slow down to a crawl because I couldn't see more than a few feet ahead.

There was a car waiting on the grass outside when I arrived home.

"Vulture!" I screamed, my hot breath forming a circle of condensation on the closed window. "Can't you wait a day or two?"

As the automatic door closed behind me, Francina threw open the kitchen door. It was the first time I'd seen her without her head scarf. Her minute black curls glistened with gel. She looked ten years younger.

"What's happened?" I asked, lowering my window.

She came toward the car. "I'm so glad you're back."

"What's the matter?" I switched off the ignition.

"The buzzer at the gate rang, and when I looked through the dining room window to see who it was, he screamed at me to tell you he's coming to get them on Monday at ten o'clock."

"If he's giving us a week, what's he doing sitting out there in the rain?"

"Trying to scare us. He's ex-MK. This is nothing for him."

I began to cry, and Francina slipped an arm around my waist. Anton had left, my parents had left, Ella was gone. Francina's solid warmth felt familiar, comforting.

"What did the lawyer say?"

I averted my eyes.

"Nooo…" she cried.

I laid my head on her fleshy shoulder and she patted it, as she did Mandla's after he'd taken a tumble.

"Why should we let them go?" she asked. "You told me he never cared about them."

"That's what Ella said. But people change." I nodded, willing Francina to tell me that it was a possibility

Themba had. Then I thought of the way he'd asked about the money before anything else.

"You said he was going to die," said Francina, "so when he does, the boys can come back to us."

I shook my head. "We'll never get them back from his family after that."

It was a while before Francina spoke. "How are you going to tell them?" Her voice was not much more than a whisper.

"I don't know. We have to be careful. Their father has to be the hero coming to get them because he loves and misses them."

"Hero!" Francina pretended to spit on the garage floor. "He's a gangster."

"Shh."

"The poor little things. Mandla doesn't know his father at all, and Sipho thinks he's dead. He told me."

"We have no choice." I wiped my eyes on my sleeve. "Thanks for—"

"Agh," said Francina, flapping her hand just like Ella.

Sipho looked up from his encyclopedia when I walked into the living room, but Mandla was too busy tearing pages out of the TV guide to notice my return.

"Monica, did you know that the world's first heart transplant was done in South Africa?"

"Yes, we're a clever nation, aren't we?"

He thought about this for a while. Then he said, "It's funny, they can put a new heart in someone, yet they couldn't help my mommy."

How could I tell him? But it had to be done; springing it on him the day before his father arrived would be cruel. He needed time to prepare himself.

"Sipho, I have something to tell you." My voice sounded far too somber, so I tried injecting some gaiety into it. "It's good news, sweetie. Guess who came to see me?" I didn't give him a chance to try. "Your father. He misses you and would love for you and Mandla to go and live with him." It seemed best to portray the reunion with his father in a hopeful light, since it was inevitable. And perhaps if I prayed hard enough, Themba would undergo a change, at least as far as his children were concerned.

Sipho pursed his lips and frowned. "But he's dead. He went away and never came back. If he wasn't dead, he would have phoned or written."

"Oh, sweetie, he's not dead. He's so excited about seeing you again. He told me he can't wait."

"I don't want to go away. I want to stay here with you and Francina."

"He's your father. And he wants to take you to meet your grandmother." I tried to pull him toward me, but he slipped away.

"I don't want to."

"You'll meet your cousins. Won't that be fun? Lots of children to play with."

"I don't want to play with children. I want to be here with you." His chin trembled.

"Mandla wants to go, don't you, Mandla?" I picked Mandla up and he gurgled.

"He's a baby. He doesn't know what you're talking about," said Sipho.

I put Mandla down and placed an arm around Sipho, but again he wouldn't let me get close.

"You don't want us here," he said.

"Sipho, that's not true." My voice was stern. "More than anything, I want you to stay here."

"Then why do we have to go?"

"Because he's your father." I looked at Francina, but she was sniffling into a tissue and couldn't help at all. I swallowed hard. "Because he loves you."

"Mommy didn't like him. I heard her call him an ugly word."

"Sipho, sometimes adults don't get along and they stop loving each other. But they don't ever stop loving their children."

Once again I felt as though I'd turned traitor on those I loved, and prayed for Themba to change.

While Sipho was at school, I wandered around the house with Mandla in my arms, holding him even tighter when he squirmed to get free. In my parents' room, the red numbers on their old clock radio formed their digital shapes with horrifying speed; in the boys' room, the alarm clock ticked so loudly I wondered how they ever managed to sleep; and in the living room, I had to stop myself from pulling the cuckoo from its hideaway and decapitating it. Each tick of every confounded clock in the house taunted me. *Give up,* they seemed to be saying. *You can't stop us. We're massing on your borders. Out in the dark, we're adding to our ranks. Forget about it. You're fighting a losing cause.* Monday loomed larger and larger.

At night I'd creep into the boys' room to watch them sleep, and Francina would come in just before midnight to drag me off to bed, where I'd lie staring at the clock radio, my face outlined by its vindictive red glow.

During the day Francina and I communicated with each other through silent nods or shakes of our heads. We didn't trust ourselves.

On Friday morning Sipho refused to go to school. He was afraid his father would come and take him from there, robbing him of the chance to say goodbye. I assured him that this wouldn't happen, but relented anyway, and we sat in the living room the whole day doing a four-hundred-piece jigsaw puzzle. On Saturday, with rain falling steadily, we began another one. In the evening I tried telling him that he was going to his family.

"Only talk to me about my father if he changes his mind," he said.

There was no hope of that. We hadn't heard from Themba and his car hadn't been parked outside the house again, but I knew he'd be back on Monday at ten sharp.

I never knew that following God's will would be so difficult. My faith had been shaken, yet I couldn't believe that He would lead me all this way only to let Themba snatch the children away. Suddenly, I had the sickening feeling that I might have misconstrued what I was supposed to do with my life. What if my purpose in life *wasn't* to adopt the boys? I didn't think I could accept that.

Please Lord, I prayed, *help me to surrender to Your will.*

On Sunday morning Sipho said goodbye to his Sunday school class, Mandla to the nursery volunteers he'd grown to love. It was a shame they had to leave the church when they'd both been made to feel so welcome.

In the evening I bought pizzas and asked Francina to join us for dinner. It would be our last together.

"Why aren't you eating, little one?" she asked Sipho, watching him play with his slice.

He didn't answer.

"Anchovy's your favorite," I said.

"I'm not hungry."

"You'd better eat up before your brother wants yours, too," said Francina.

Mandla had devoured a huge slice of the Napolitana and was eyeing Sipho's plate.

"He can have it."

Francina stifled a sob. "Thanks for the pizza, Monica, but I think I'd better go now."

She ran out, and we heard muffled sobs as she locked the back door. I looked at Sipho. He'd taken another bite of his pizza, but had stopped chewing.

"Chew it, Sipho, or you'll choke. Right, who wants to watch a video?"

Mandla jumped up and down. He knew what a video was.

Sipho swallowed his food and said, "Can I phone you to come and fetch me if I don't like it?"

I wanted to say, "Yes, Sipho, and I'll come immediately," but I forced myself to say, "You will like it, Sipho."

"But if I don't?" His eyes pleaded with mine.

"Yes, Sipho, then phone me and I'll come and get you." It was a rash reply, because I didn't have the legal right to do that. But I meant every word.

Sipho seemed a bit easier with the whole idea after that. I didn't even know if his grandmother had a phone, but I was not going to let Themba take them away without at least giving me the address of where they'd be living.

I awoke the next morning with a crick in my neck from sleeping propped up against the bookcase in the boys' room. Instead of leading me to bed just before midnight, Francina had lain down on the carpet next to me and fallen asleep.

After breakfast she packed their clothes. They didn't have many, but she completed the task with such care she might well have been a young girl preparing her hope chest. I smiled at her, and she managed a weak, trembling smile back. I had never felt this close to her before.

At nine o'clock the boys were dressed in their Sunday best: Mandla in navy pants and a navy-and-green checked shirt, Sipho in khaki pants and a white cotton shirt. He refused to let Francina put a tie on him. We sat in the living room, not saying a word, looking at each other and then looking away.

Mandla toddled up to the TV, put out a chubby finger, and pressed the power switch. The old Telefunken hissed with static. Then a thin, straight line appeared in the middle of the screen and grew into a picture of two men running up and down a strip of worn grass with bats in their hands and helmets on their heads. Mandla giggled and turned around to check if we were watching him. When nobody said a word, he pressed the color button. The men's clothing went from sparking white to murky gray. Still nobody spoke. Next he set his sights on Ebony, who was asleep on the recliner. As he patted her back, she lifted her head and peered at him through one slitted eye. Then she went straight back to sleep.

The doors on the clock opened. *Cuckoo! Cuckoo!* said the bird with his smug, little, painted smile.

"Francina, please do something about that clock. I can't stand it."

"It's your mother's. I can't take it away."

"He's late," said Sipho.

"He'll be here." This time I could not hide the bitter tone in my voice.

The minutes ticked by. Mandla grew tired of the inactivity in the living room and wandered into the kitchen.

Francina got up to follow him. "Where are you going, my baby?"

"Swim, swim."

It was the second word Mandla had learned after "Mama." He loved the water, which worried me, because he was too young to realize the danger of jumping in without his water wings. Francina spent hours holding on to his hands and pulling him around like a motorboat. She couldn't swim, either, so I was nervous in the beginning, but she held him as though he were her most precious possession, and they never ventured off the top step.

"No, my baby, you can't swim now. Your father's coming." Francina was also struggling to keep the derision from her voice. "Don't cry. Come here."

The minutes flew by. I heard Francina filling the kettle. She needed something to occupy her hands.

Ten minutes later she arrived with a tray of tea and lemon cream cookies. Mandla made straight for the plate like a bee to a picnic. Francina picked up the little cushion I'd embroidered for Mother's Day when I was fourteen and sat down in my mother's usual place on the sofa. My stitches were so tiny they were almost indiscernible. Up in the corner was a bright yellow sun with fluffy blue clouds scattered around it; in the middle, in looping pink letters, were the words World's Best Mom. My mother had written to say that she'd forgotten the cushion, but would collect it when she came to visit—if I didn't join them in Italy first.

Slipping the cushion into the hollow of her lower back, Francina began pouring the tea from high up, English butler style, so that it made a lovely cascading sound in the china cups. Then she handed each of us a cup and sat back to sip hers, baby finger crooked in a little salute.

"Are you sure he said today?" asked Sipho, holding his saucer with both hands.

"Yes. He's only an hour late. He'll come," I said. But I was beginning to doubt it myself.

By lunchtime Mandla had licked the lemon cream from all the centers and left soggy piles of cookies on the Navajo rug. Ebony got up, stretched, and with a disdainful look in Mandla's direction, left the room to follow the sun's best rays to the kitchen. Mandla's shirt looked as though it had seen rough seas. I pulled him toward me and lifted it over his head. Knowing what was coming, he squealed in delight.

"Let's go outside to the pool," I told Francina and Sipho. "We may as well wait in the fresh air."

By five o'clock I had almost convinced myself that it had all been a nightmare and that Themba was nothing more than a name Ella had mentioned in one of her stories.

"What shall we have for dinner?" I asked, as though it were a normal day. Francina looked at me with a frown, but I shrugged and said, "Fish and chips or lasagna?"

"Zanya, zanya!" said Mandla.

Sipho nodded in agreement. He hadn't mentioned his father the whole afternoon, and I suspected he was also hoping it had just been a bad dream.

The phone rang during dinner, and my whole body stiffened. Sipho and I let out a unified sigh of relief when Francina announced that it was a wrong number.

At nine o'clock Francina put Mandla to bed and went to her room.

"Am I going to school tomorrow?" asked Sipho, once we were alone in the living room.

"No. He may come tomorrow."

"I'm missing lots of stuff in computer class."

"You're a bright boy, you'll catch up." I didn't want to tell him that there wouldn't be a computer class at the school in his grandmother's village.

During the night I woke up about ten times thinking I'd heard a car pull up, but it was just the security firm doing their rounds. The dreaded buzzer at the gate remained silent.

On Tuesday evening I decided that Sipho should go to school the following morning.

"What will I tell them?" he asked. "I've already said goodbye to everybody."

"I'll talk to your teacher, and you can tell your friends there's been a delay in your plans."

He skipped to the entrance hall to retrieve his suitcase, and a short while later I found Francina humming to herself as she ironed his school uniform.

A whole week went by and everybody relaxed, everybody, that is, except me.

"We have to find out what's happened to him," I told Francina.

She emptied a packet of veal strips onto a chopping board.

"Maybe he's changed his mind—" she grinned wickedly "—or maybe wild dogs have eaten him alive."

I did not smile. "Francina, you know it's the right thing to do."

"Are you crazy? You want us to go looking for the man who's going to take the boys away?"

Although I didn't understand it myself, I knew that God wanted me to seek out Themba. Was He testing my faith? Maybe so. I would trust Him and try to find Themba, but I still wasn't sure I could accept it if the children were not to stay with me.

"He might be in trouble," I said.

Francina snorted. "In trouble? Have you forgotten that your friend, Ella, died because of him? And now you want to go running out into the night to help him."

"What if he's in the hospital?"

"Good. Hopefully he'll die and leave us alone."

"Come on, Francina, you don't mean that. I'll phone around."

She picked up the kitchen mallet and began pounding the veal.

I took the portable phone into the dining room and sat down at the table next to Sipho's open school reader. He'd finished it two weeks before the rest of his class and was now trying to teach Mandla to recognize letters on the page. So far he hadn't had much success. After only two calls, I did.

"Found him," I shouted.

Francina slouched into the dining room.

"He *is* in a hospital—the Johannesburg Regional."

She bent down to pick up a toy fire engine on the floor. "He didn't look sick to me."

"He *was* thin."

"Now what happens?"

"You know what we have to do."

She cocked an eyebrow and said, "Wait for him to die and then carry on as usual?"

I shook my head. "If he dies, his mother and family in the Eastern Cape will come for the boys when they collect his body." My eyes drifted to the door. There were two columns of tiny black marks on the white wooden frame. Even though the inscribed dates were the same, the spaces between the marks in the *M* column were much larger than those in the *S* column.

Francina's eyes followed mine. "You're right about that," she said, nodding slowly. "So, we have to… What do we have to do, Monica?"

"Go and see him before he dies."

"And tell him that…?" She spun the wheels of the toy fire engine in her hand.

"Francina! I have to ask him to make me their guardian."

"Okay, okay. But I'm not coming. No way, not me, not to see an MK soldier." Her voice was firm.

I didn't want to face him alone, this man who liked whites so much he was disappointed South Africa hadn't been torn apart by a civil war. But I knew I had little chance of persuading Francina to change her mind.

"He's not going to give me any trouble now," I said, though I didn't really believe it.

Francina shook her head and clicked her tongue. Neither did she.

I thought of Ella, the young girl, hiding under the kitchen table with her parents while broken bricks rained down on their tin roof and the frenzied barks of police dogs grew louder and louder. "Faith is all we'll ever need in this life," Mrs. Nkhoma had told her daughter. As I prepared to go out and seek my adversary, I struggled to hang on to mine.

Chapter Fifty

Monica

The reviewer had an acerbic, almost brutal wit, and he was laying into the actor as though he were guilty of crimes against humanity. Normally, I would have enjoyed this manic display that fell just short of libel, but now I was concentrating too hard on not retching. I hadn't slept the whole night, and it was only the pot of coffee Francina had made just after dawn that was keeping my hands on the steering wheel and my foot on the accelerator.

What I was about to do was presumptuous, yet it was what Ella would have wanted, and I believed it was what God wanted, too. The strange thing was that this certainty did not come from a reasonable process of deduction. I just felt it in my heart, or, as Ella always had, in my bones.

Without looking up from her paperback, a young receptionist with frizzy red hair gave me directions to Themba's ward. I took the elevator to the fifth floor, where a middle-aged nurse with dreadlocks informed me that his condition had deteriorated.

"You're not going to do anything crazy, are you?" she asked, shooting me a warning look.

"Crazy? No, why?"

"Yesterday one of his visitors tried to slit his throat with a dinner knife. She was hysterical. Poor woman—I think she just found out she was positive."

"No, I'm not going to do anything like that."

"Okay, first room on your left, first bed on the right."

There were five other beds in the room, all occupied by men. Except for the emaciated frame in the first bed on the right, the patients were all watching a television, bolted high up on the pale yellow wall.

I barely recognized Themba. There were bony hollows and sagging skin where once he'd had cheeks, and his teeth seemed enormous, protruding through thin, cracked lips. His eyes, which had always been big, now bulged like giant milky marbles in his sunken flesh, making him look quite ghoulish. He wore a faded green cotton hospital gown with the words Property of Johannesburg Regional printed in red over his left breast. An oxygen mask hung from a vertical metal stand on his right.

I touched his arm. "Themba. Can you hear me?" He opened his eyes, but they did not focus on me.

"Huh, who's that?" he growled.

With a shock, I realized that he was blind. "Monica," I said in a soft voice.

"What do you want?" he snapped.

"To see how you're doing. When you didn't turn up, we—"

"Satisfied?" His voice was more breathy this time.

"No, I'm not. I'm sorry to see you're ill. You looked so healthy before." I stopped and waited for him to ask after his children. When he didn't, I said, "The boys are doing fine."

Themba made a sound that could have been a grunt.

"Sipho has gone back to school. He gets anxious when he misses his computer class."

Themba's eyes closed, his lips parted. I wondered if he'd just died in front of me. Then I noticed his eyelids flutter and forced myself to go on.

"I want to talk to you about them, about their future."

"They…don't…belong…with…you," he said in staccato blasts of breath. Then he inhaled deeply and said without pause, "They belong with their own people."

"Ella didn't agree."

Instantly, I regretted mentioning her name. I wouldn't be able to tolerate it if he insulted her again.

"She always had softer views than mine," he said, seeming to gain strength from his remembrances. "The fool. She believed in the Rainbow Nation and all the hip-hip-hooray propaganda the West churned out. You know it was just so they'd have an excuse to pull out after the election and leave us with the mess they started. They should have taken all you whites with them. We don't need you, any of you."

I restrained myself by focusing on why I was there.

"It's Sipho and Mandla I want to talk about, Themba. Remember your sons?"

"I never forgot them. Who do you think paid for the food in their bellies and the clothing on their backs?"

If he could lie to me on his deathbed in order to preserve his inflated ego, there was little chance he'd agree to make me the guardian of his children.

I suddenly became aware of loud voices around me. One of the patients wanted to watch a game show where the set resembled a shebeen; another wanted to watch Formula One motorcar racing, live from Monza, Italy. The insults grew more personal, the swearwords more colorful, and, fearing it might turn physical, I left Themba's side to call a nurse. As I was about to walk out the door, a third patient went over to the television and pulled its plug out the socket. The arguers looked at each other with raised eyebrows.

"Dog," said the black man.

"You're right about that," muttered the white man.

They turned their glares to the killjoy, but he hopped back into bed, picked up a book, and pretended not to notice.

I went back to Themba.

"The boys are happy where they are now," I told him. "I wish you could see them with us."

"You wouldn't let me in the gate, if you remember."

I didn't reply.

"I'm the father," said Themba, tapping his chest. His finger landed between the words *Property* and *of* on his hospital gown. "You can't deny that."

"Nobody's trying to, Themba. But don't you think they'd have a good life with me?"

"Just because you have money, it doesn't mean you'll give them a better life."

Though he was weak and emaciated, I still wanted to reach out and shake him. Who was he to pontificate on who would give his children a better life? Even before he'd dropped out of their lives, he'd left it to their mother to earn the money to feed them. But there was much more at stake than proving a point, so I let the temptation slide.

Lord, I prayed, *let me say the right thing here. Give me the words to soften this man's heart.* And, as if of their own volition, the words came.

"I agree with you, Themba, but I love them as though they were my own."

"You'd give them new English names and they'd forget how to speak their language."

I'd made a breakthrough. My prayer had been heard.

"Out of the question. I couldn't call them anything else. And we would make sure that they kept up their language. I'm prepared to learn it myself, and Francina will always help them. She's Zulu, but speaks Sotho. She's our—"

"Domestic servant," he said with a smirk.

"Well, she's like one of the family," I said, aware of how patronizing it sounded.

With a trembling hand, he pulled his threadbare cotton blanket up to his chin. It was identical to the one I'd had on my hospital bed, with the words Hospital Property printed vertically up the middle. He gave a wet cough.

"If Ella thought it was the right thing to do." He stopped and seemed to lose his train of thought for a while. "Things didn't work out between us, but I always knew I was onto a good thing with her. Life was just too crazy back then."

We were both silent, each thinking about the Ella we'd known.

"All right then," he said quietly. "I've always believed that Ella was a good mother. She knew best."

It didn't feel like a glorious victory. In the next twelve hours or so this man was going to die, and he knew it. I almost regretted having asked Nick to draw up the legal papers; it should have been an agreement of honor, a covenant. But I didn't want to worry about future claims on the children's custody by their grandmother or aunts and uncles.

"Let me read the document to you, Themba."

His voice was so soft I could barely hear him. "It's not necessary," he said.

After calling two nurses to act as witnesses, I put the pen between his fingers and guided his trembling hand to the place for his signature. His skin felt rough and thin, like fine sandpaper. As soon as I let go, his hand dropped back to his side. I tried again, but this time I didn't let go. After two false starts, he made a shaky cross on the dotted line.

Gently, I laid his hand back on top of the blanket. It was a while before I let go again.

Chapter Fifty-One

Monica

Two months had passed since Themba's death and we had settled into the rhythm of a regular family.

"Come, come, come." Mandla tugged at my free hand.

"Mom, I'd better go," I said. "Sipho's dispatched Mandla to fetch me. I'll phone you tomorrow and tell you all about it."

Doing his best to carry out the difficult task his big brother had set him, Mandla now tried tugging with both hands.

I said goodbye to my mother and hung up. "Okay, I'm ready," I told Mandla. "Let's go."

Sipho was sitting two feet away from the TV on a chair he'd brought from the kitchen. Francina was on the sofa with my point-and-shoot camera in her lap.

"What are you going to do with that, Francina? Sipho, pull your chair farther away from the TV. You'll strain your eyes."

Francina beamed at me. "I'm going to take a photo to send to your mother."

"It's starting. Let's be quiet," said Sipho in a school-teacher voice.

Urgent electronic music ushered in an aerial shot of the Johannesburg skyline at night, while an imaginary type-writer clattered out the words *In-depth* in block letters at the bottom of the screen.

Sipho sat ramrod straight, but Mandla bounced up and down, clapping his hands.

"Shh, Mandla," said Sipho. "We can't hear."

An exquisite girl with long braids announced the first story of the night in a clipped BBC-English accent.

Francina muttered something about never seeing Zulus on TV, only ANC people.

"Shh," said Sipho.

A string version of the theme tune filtered in as the camera panned across a Bushveld scene, the sun barely skimming the umbrella tops of the scattered acacia trees, twitching birds of prey in the highest branches etched black against the lightening morning sky. Both the camera and the music stopped as two rhinoceroses lying next to a giant boulder came into view. At first glance they appeared to be resting, but as the camera zoomed in, you could see that their horns had been severed and the flattened blond veld grass around them was stained plum red. The camera focused on the back of a woman bending to look at the animals. Then she straightened and turned around.

"It's you, Monica," shouted Francina, flinging her hands into the air.

Ebony yowled and flashed out of the room as the camera landed two inches from her nose. Francina grabbed it and began clicking away at the TV in a paparazzi-like frenzy.

Sipho turned around in his chair, eyes gleaming. "You're really on TV."

Thankfully, I'd prepared him for the gruesome nature of the story because he was acutely sensitive to the suffering of animals.

Mandla squeezed past Francina and put his finger on the close-up of my face. He looked at the screen and then at me on the sofa.

"Monca, Monca," he squealed. Then he rushed at me and jumped into my lap, laughing hard.

It was strange to see myself talking. "These two white rhinos were shot in the middle of the night, in the southwestern part of the Kruger National Park, by poachers who will earn thousands of rands from the sale of the rhinos' horns to buyers in the Far East."

I'd often heard myself on the radio, but this was my first time on television. Next time I'd pack on the face powder; my nose was so shiny it was probably helping to keep the circling vultures away from the decomposing carcasses.

Landing this job had been an absolute fluke, and I owed it all to a terrible case of morning sickness; the show's regular reporter was pregnant with twins and had taken unpaid leave until her official six-month maternity leave began. Since it only entailed one day a week, Le Roux said I could do it, provided I also produced a radio version of each story.

The weekly show followed a newsmagazine format and included four twelve-minute segments on subjects with an eco-tourism or environmental slant. It had been on the air for eighteen months, and, after a somewhat shaky start because of its 11:00 p.m. time slot, had been moved to eight-thirty and was now the most watched program on Wednesday nights.

I knew it was just a temporary assignment, but I was going to work so hard they'd find a place for me somehow, even if it was on another show. At last I was in.

The music started to come up under my voice. "I'm Monica Brunetti reporting for *In-depth* from the Kruger National Park." The report ended with a shot of me limping alongside the tracker as he pointed out the poachers' tire marks in the sand.

"You're famous, Monica," said Francina, scooping Mandla into her arms.

He laid his head against her shoulder and closed his eyes.

"It's way past your bedtime, boys," I said.

Sipho groaned.

"It's a school night, Sipho. Let's hop to it."

"Can I stay up next week to watch you?" he asked, dragging his chair back to the kitchen.

"Absolutely."

I lingered at their door before going in to say good-night.

Sipho was saying his prayers. "God bless Francina and God bless my brother and God bless Monica and God bless Mommy." He paused. "And God, please tell her we miss her, but she shouldn't worry about us. We're doing okay."

Instead of kissing him, I patted his head because I didn't want him to feel the hot tears on my cheeks. Mandla was asleep and had already kicked off the comforter. I pulled it up around his chin and kissed him on the forehead.

Back in the living room, I switched off the lights, turned down the volume on the television, and sprawled out on the sofa. Just the other day, a booming laugh from the boys' room had startled me—it was her, I was sure of it. I peeped in and saw Mandla with my old fairy-tale book open at a picture of Jack shimmying down the beanstalk to get away from the thundering giant. I always gave the characters different voices when I read to Mandla, and he was immersed in his own reenactment. His giant's laugh was Ella's exactly.

I'd never stop missing her. Every day I saw her in her children, and every day I renewed my promise to her to look after them. I didn't kid myself; it wasn't going to be easy. Like all South Africans, we lived with the constant threat of random danger. But some nights, for a brief, magical time while we were sitting around the table for dinner, watching a cartoon or playing board games, I'd forget about it and relax.

A magazine article I'd written about Ella before her death had been published, but I couldn't face reading it yet to see if the editor had made any changes. The special savings account I'd opened in Sipho's and Mandla's names for my earnings from my writing was growing rapidly.

My mother had taken the news of her instant grandchildren surprisingly well and phoned regularly to check up on us. My father refused to speak to me, but he'd come around; he always did. My mother was arriving soon for a three-week visit and had already bought the boys matching soccer shirts. Sipho would have to pretend he liked the sport. Things would be awkward at first, but I wouldn't be surprised if she extended her visit.

In the flickering blue glow of the soundless television, Sipho stared down at me from a school photo next to the ones of myself and Luca. Mandla had put one of his building blocks on the coffee table among my mother's antique snuff boxes, allowing it to escape Francina's nightly cleanup operation. My mother's magazines had been replaced by a pile of *National Geographics*. Although Sipho didn't understand all the scientific terms, he did a good job of sounding them out and spent hours gazing at the maps and fold-outs.

The curtains rippled, and I felt a cool breeze on my bare arms. We'd had our customary brief summer thunderstorm late this afternoon, and the garden still smelled wet and lush.

My parents had not given up on me joining them in Italy. Who knew what the future would bring? Maybe the boys would be the ones to leave South Africa when they grew up. Sipho might become a Rhodes scholar and decide he liked it in England; Mandla might pack his bags to go and see the world. Maybe they'd be big brothers to my own children one day. Anything could happen. I'd learned that the hard way. All I could think of now was the present, and Sipho was right; we were doing okay. With God's help, we'd found the road to home.

* * * * *

DISCUSSION QUESTIONS

1. Why did the author choose to tell the story from two perspectives instead of sticking to Monica's? Why do you think the author uses first-person narrative instead of third? And what is the effect of her use of the past tense in Monica's narrative and the present in Ella's?

2. The main theme of the book is the search for purpose in life. Of her life's journey before the reawakening of her faith, Monica said, "There was no map, no route markers, merely a meandering road and a number of stops along the way that served as pleasant distractions from a horizon with no destination in sight." Mrs. Dube tells her that the Lord saved her life for a purpose, but how does Monica discover just what that purpose is? Does anyone help her in the process of this discovery? Do you have purpose in your life?

3. What motivated Monica's growth in, redemption in and reawakening of her faith? What role did Ella and Mrs. Dube play? Is a radical change in a person's worldview possible without the impetus of a dramatic event?

4. One of the book's themes concerns the bonds that women share despite the differences in their cultures. What are the bonds that Monica, Ella, Mrs. Dube and Faith share? What are the bonds that Monica and Francina share? Do you think that women will always be able to find common ground, even if their cultures are radically different? Can the same be said of men?

5. How are the men in this book portrayed? Do any of them evoke sympathy?

6. Do you think that there is a strong evocation of place in this novel? What is the relationship between its setting and themes? Do you think that a story like this could take place in any country?

7. When Themba lay dying in hospital he told Monica that the boys "don't belong with you. They belong with their own people." Monica promised him that they would keep up their own language, but does she have a responsibility to do more than that? Should she help them preserve other aspects of their culture? If so, how would she do this? Does this apply to all cross-cultural adoptions?

8. Which events in the novel can be seen as a consequence of apartheid? How does the novel deal with the themes of retribution, forgiveness and the shift of power in the new South Africa?

9. Ella's mother died while waiting to return to her country a free woman. Monica's mother chooses to leave. What does that imply about the nature of home and belonging?

10. How would you describe Ella's faith, and Mrs. Dube's? How does it help them deal with the problems they face?

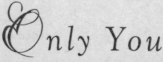

REQUEST YOUR FREE BOOKS!

2 FREE INSPIRATIONAL NOVELS
PLUS 2
FREE
MYSTERY GIFTS

YES! Please send me 2 FREE Love Inspired® novels and my 2 FREE mystery gifts. After receiving them, if I don't wish to receive any more books, I can return the shipping statement marked "cancel." If I don't cancel, I will receive 4 brand-new novels every month and be billed just $3.99 per book in the U.S., or $4.74 per book in Canada, plus 25¢ shipping and handling per book and applicable taxes, if any*. That's a savings of 20% off the cover price! I understand that accepting the 2 free books and gifts places me under no obligation to buy anything. I can always return a shipment and cancel at any time. Even if I never buy another book from Steeple Hill, the two free books and gifts are mine to keep forever.

113 IDN EF26   313 IDN EF27

Name	(PLEASE PRINT)	
Address		Apt. #
City	State/Prov.	Zip/Postal Code

Signature (if under 18, a parent or guardian must sign)

Order online at www.LoveInspiredBooks.com

Or mail to Steeple Hill Reader Service™:

IN U.S.A.: P.O. Box 1867, Buffalo, NY 14240-1867
IN CANADA: P.O. Box 609, Fort Erie, Ontario L2A 5X3

Not valid to current Love Inspired subscribers.

Want to try two free books from another series?
Call 1-800-873-8635 or visit www.morefreebooks.com

* Terms and prices subject to change without notice. NY residents add applicable sales tax. Canadian residents will be charged applicable provincial taxes and GST. This offer is limited to one order per household. All orders subject to approval. Credit or debit balances in a customer's account(s) may be offset by any other outstanding balance owed by or to the customer. Please allow 4 to 6 weeks for delivery.

Your Privacy: Steeple Hill is committed to protecting your privacy. Our Privacy Policy is available online at www.eHarlequin.com or upon request from the Reader Service. From time to time we make our lists of customers available to reputable firms who may have a product or service of interest to you. If you would prefer we not share your name and address, please check here. ☐

LIREG07